# SHIFTERS OF BLACK FOREST RIDGE: RHETT

## SEDONA VENEZ

# WANT FREE SEDONA VENEZ BOOKS?

Sign up for Sedona Venez's Newsletter and receive FREE BOOKS. In addition to the free stories, you will also get special pricing, exclusive previews and news of new releases.

**GET A FREE SEDONA VENEZ BOOK!**

Join Sedona's mailing list to be the first to know of new releases, free books, special prices and other author giveaways.

https://sedonavenez.com/free-book

# CHAPTER 1
## RHETT

"Sheriff Ward, can't you do something about Sam?" Dean—a skunk-shifter—demanded as he sat in the chair across my desk from me. "Ever since I kicked Sam out of the Sleepy Skunk Motel, he keeps showing up at my place at random times of the week, making threats against me and my mate, Agnes."

I rubbed the bridge of my nose, trying to ignore the loud snoring sounds in my head coming from my inner jaguar.

"Dean, we've staked out your place several times, but he's not going to show up if he smells us there. He's not that stupid. He's an elusive motherfucker who can't be found until he pops his head out of whatever hidey-hole he's taking refuge in now."

Sam was always causing trouble. His last attempt had been last year when he'd riled up the townsfolk after Imani, our town and pack alpha female, arrived inside the Ridge.

"Well, something's got to give," Dean complained. "Last time he showed up, he threatened to kill my mate if I didn't give him a room." He rubbed his eyes. "I think something's wrong with him. He's acting pretty crazy."

I scoffed. "Sam was born crazy."

Dean shook his head. "No. This is different. I've seen this

kind of thing before. You know, when a shifter has the feral sickness."

I leaned forward in my chair, eyeing Dean. "Feral sickness?"

It wasn't unusual for unmated male shifters to turn violent and lose touch with their human side, slowly going feral because they couldn't find their fated mate.

"Yes, Protector. I've seen the signs—glossy, wild eyes, talking gibberish—of going feral in some of my kin." Dean gave me a bleak look. "Before they ran deep into the forest, never to be seen again."

Dean's new perspective on the Sam situation gave me food for thought. *Is Sam's erratic behavior escalating because he's going feral?*

"Sam will show up in Main Square sooner rather than later," I promised. My extensive military training taught me that patience was a virtue. "He loves attention and stirring the pot."

*And when he shows his ass in town, I'm going to lock him up and throw away the key.*

"I know that you're stretched thin with just you and Mack, but can you continue checking on my place?" His mouth worked. "I'm terrified Sam's going to do something to hurt Agnes and me."

"When I took this job as the Protector of the Ridge, I swore to serve and protect all the residents of this town regardless of who they are and what they've done. And I'm going to continue doing just that."

"Thanks, Protector. I'll let Agnes know not to worry."

I rose to my feet, and so did Dean.

"Good. You do that," I finished as we shook hands.

Dean turned, shuffling out of my office.

Plopping down in my chair, I propped my booted feet on the edge of my desk, running a hand through my hair.

Even over six years after relocating here, I still felt like an outsider, and getting the residents to trust and confide in me was a work in progress. But I loved my job as the sheriff—aka

Protector—even if it was a major change in lifestyle after spending years traveling all over the world while serving in an elite military unit with my band of brothers—Quinn, Mack, Emmett, Jasper, and Brody.

Taking a swig of my now-cold coffee, I nearly choked when my beast snored even louder in my head.

*Get the hell up.* I verbally nudged him. *We're on duty.*

*I'm bored,* he complained. *Nothing ever happens here.*

*As it should be,* I snapped.

Except for the clusterfuck Sam had started when Imani had arrived, things in Black Forest had been calm and quiet, and that was how I liked it.

*Wake me up when it's time for dinner,* my inner animal demanded, then went silent.

I sighed heavily. The relationship between my inner beast and me was tense. He was pissed off because—his words, not mine—*You're a lazy ass for giving up the search for our fated mate.*

His accusation couldn't be further from the truth.

Laziness wasn't my problem. It was fear.

I'd already failed as the protector of my sister, Maggie; there was no way I wanted to add a fated mate to my list of failures.

# CHAPTER 2
## NOVA

I drove into a tunnel cut through the mountain, slowing inside the dark passageway with the beams of my headlights guiding me.

Several times during my long drive to Black Forest Ridge, Alaska, I'd contemplated turning around and heading back in the opposite direction. But I couldn't, not after I'd found the letter from my estranged father with detailed directions on how to reach his mother.

After forty years of letting my imagination connect the dots about my absent father, I needed answers about why he'd abandoned me. And if traveling to a place that was on no known map was the answer, so be it.

So distracted by my thoughts, when I exited the tunnel, I didn't see the crisscross lines made of white lights shimmering in front of my SUV until it was too late.

"Oh shit!" I pushed my foot down on the brake pedal firmly, but my vehicle sped up instead of stopping, barreling me right through the light show.

Loud popping sounds echoed around me, and a weird pulse of energy skittered along my skin. My heart raced. I slammed on my brakes, but my SUV kept sailing down the road.

Abruptly, the bright white lights vanished, and my vehicle screeched to a stop.

"Holy hell. What the fuck just happened?" With trembling fingers, I put my vehicle in park. My SUV had no power. Gripping the steering wheel, I screamed, "Why!"

Blowing out a breath, I glanced around the deserted, heavily forested area. "Okay, Nova, get your shit together." I grabbed my cell off the passenger's seat. "No signal. Great." I scanned the massive clearing surrounded by a thick forest. I had two choices—wait here for help or find help.

It was getting late.

There was no way in hell I wanted to sit in my SUV at night with no cell phone signal.

"Time to go." I grabbed my handbag and hopped out of my vehicle. Glancing inside my vehicle, I saw my backpack tucked on the floor of the passenger's side. I contemplated taking it with me, but I didn't need the extra weight, not when I had no idea how long I'd have to walk to find assistance. "Aren't small towns supposed to have low crime?" I murmured. It was a deserted road, so I decided to take my chances by leaving my backpack behind.

I locked the doors out of habit despite the fact that my front windows were down and couldn't be rolled up due to the lack of power.

I took off, walking along the rutted stretch of dirt road, admiring the surrounding lush green landscape. Something about the scenery called to me.

Glancing at my cell again, I saw I still had no bars even after over thirty minutes of walking. There were no cars on the road and no people in sight. The stillness of the Ridge was unnerving. If I didn't find civilization soon, I'd be stuck outside at night without shelter, surrounded by a forest full of God knows what kind of dangerous predatory animals, which was never a good situation.

Stopping in my tracks, I was contemplating going back to my

SUV for shelter when a rustle in the bushes caught my attention. I inhaled sharply and prepared to run when I saw a tiny flash of black fur in the underbrush.

I squinted at the object. *Is that a feral cat?*

A head popped out with dark eyes, pink nose, brown mask, and white chin.

It was a ferret.

I grinned when it wiggled out of the bush. The furry creature with a cone-shaped nose, thin tail, and long, pear-shaped body with short legs and long claws stared up at me.

"Oh my God, aren't you the cutest?" I gushed even though it was unusually big. "What the hell have you been eating? I hope not humans."

The ferret stuck its nose in the air, sniffed, then its eyes widened. It backed away from me.

"I won't hurt you," I promised, stepping away from it.

The ferret made a *dook-dook-dook* sound.

"Adorable." I took its photo, and it blinked at me while making an odd little clucking noise, then squiggled its way down to the stream to drink.

The ferret popped its head up to look at me now and again.

Following it, I stood a good distance away in the grass, taking more photos.

The ferret glared at me before the little bugger bounded toward me.

Yelping, I backpedaled, then ran while it made angry sounds as it chased after me. I glanced over my shoulder and saw its back hunching between bounds like a furry slinky.

*What the hell did I do to make it want to attack?*

The ferret launched itself at me, chattering.

"Eek!" I screamed with arms flailing. Falling on my chest, I landed on the lush grass. Wasting no time, I rolled onto my back. I batted at the crazy ferret when its forepaws bounced off my belly, and then its teeth closed on the edge of my phone. With one hard yank, it had my cell and was scrambling away with my phone in its teeth.

"Oh no, you don't, little shit." Clumsily getting to my feet, I sprinted after it.

The little beast bounded ahead of me, too fast to catch but apparently enjoying the chase from the way it kept slowing a little and looking back at me.

"You're teasing me." I made a flying grab, catching the end of its fuzzy tail just before my body slammed onto the grass. The wind was knocked out of me, but I managed not to let go.

The ferret squeaked in outrage, dropping my phone, circling back to snap at me. Letting go at the last second, I scrambled forward, grabbing my phone, quickly pulling it under my belly.

The ferret bounded around me, chattering and squeaking until it caught one of my sneaker's shoelaces in its teeth, untying it with a hard tug.

"Knock it off, you little shit." I was laughing too hard to be really angry.

Holding the phone firmly against my chest, I sat up, and the ferret bounded off in the direction it had been fleeing.

"Don't be mad!" I yelled after it. "I won our battle fair and square, my furry friend."

Gingerly getting to my feet, I stuffed my phone in my front pocket, retied my shoelace, and stood up, shaking out my now-sore body. The ferret was gone.

"Playtime is over, Nova," I mumbled.

Scanning the area, I noticed the ferret had led me into a clearing that had a break in the tree line ahead. My heart leaped with excitement at the possibility of finally finding help.

Walking through the gap in the trees, I found myself standing in another mossy green field with no one around except for a light gray horse that was galloping through the grass with wild abandon.

"Well, ain't you a pretty horse," I whispered, mesmerized by its beauty.

I traipsed across the field, making it halfway toward the horse before it stopped midprance, flicking its head to glare at me. One minute, the horse was there. The next, a tall nude old man with long gray hair and a handlebar mustache stood in the same spot.

I stumbled back. "What the fuck!"

I blinked, then blinked again. I wasn't hallucinating. He'd just transformed from a horse into a man.

"You're trespassing, female!" the man yelled while picking up a pile of clothes before striding toward me.

"What?" I squeaked, still trying to process what I'd just seen.

Placing his cowboy hat on his head, he responded, "You shouldn't be here, hybrid."

My heart pounded in my ears. "Hybrid?" I echoed.

*Why is he calling me hybrid?*

"You got cotton in your ears?" He stood before me, wearing nothing but his cowboy hat.

"What's happening?" I asked.

Ignoring me, he pulled out a cell from the pile of clothes in his hands, then dropped the garments onto the grass.

Flicking his finger over his phone, he pressed it to his ear. "Sheriff Ward, this is Henry. You better get your ass over here, pronto. I found a hybrid trespassing on my land."

# CHAPTER 3
## RHETT

I glanced up from my laptop when I heard several rapid knocks on my door.

"Yes?" I demanded.

The door opened, and Josie from Yonder Biscuits stood in the doorway with a basket clutched in her hands.

"Can I come in?" Her full lips curled up in a seductive smile.

*Send her away,* my inner jaguar demanded. *We don't want her.*

I couldn't agree more. Nothing about Josie appealed to me. Yet here she was—again—at the station, trying to flirt with me.

I stood up, striding over to the front of my desk. "How can I help you, Josie?" I crossed my arms.

I smelled the lust rolling off her body as she licked her pouty pink lips while she gazed at me like I was a steak on the menu.

She walked inside my office with an exaggerated sway to her curvy hips. "I brought you some freshly made biscuits." She held out the basket.

My jaguar laughed. *Why is this owl-shifter trying so hard? Not interested.*

Ignoring him, I said, "Thank you. But as I've told you several times, I don't take gifts from residents."

Her pink lips pouted. "I don't see why." She hooked the basket handle over her arm.

"Because I said that I don't," I said, eyeing her coolly. "Anything else?"

She batted her eyelashes. "I'd like to invite you over to my place for dinner tonight. I have a nice pot roast with your name on it." She pushed out her ample breasts.

*I don't care if she has a whole cow. The answer is no,* my animal protested. *She's not our fated mate.*

"Josie, I'll have to decline… again."

Josie had been inviting me to her place for dinner for over five years, but I wasn't interested in having dinner or anything else with her. I'd made it clear to her—and all the other single females in town who'd invited me over for dinner—that I was not interested in fucking around and that I was waiting for my fated mate.

She stepped closer. "Look, Sheriff, I don't know how much blunter I have to be." She flicked her blond hair with one hand. "But I'm offering myself to you. You and I can go far together. You have the power, and I'm the best-looking female in this town."

My animal scoffed. *Please, she's far from the best-looking female in town.*

"Protector…" She inched closer. My nostrils flared when I smelled her unpleasant scent of burned toast. "We're a perfect match."

"You're not my fated mate."

"How many times do I have to tell you that doesn't matter?" She cupped my jaw.

"Hands off, Josie." Her touch made my skin crawl.

Reluctantly, she removed it. "I don't see the problem," she whined in a high-pitched tone. "You're in your forties, for Pete's sake. If your mate hasn't shown up yet, she never will."

"You're not my female and never will be."

"But we can have lots of fun together." She licked her lips. "Until your mate comes along."

My days of casual hookups were done when I retired from the military and moved here. If I couldn't have my fated mate, I didn't want any female at all.

"Not interested," I barked. "Bye, Josie."

"But…"

I pointed to the door.

"Fine," she huffed, turning on her heel and stomping out.

I heard the sounds of squeaking sneakers pounding against the floor outside my office.

"Watch it, Jacob," Josie snarled.

"Sorry, Miss Josie!" Jacob yelled. "Protector!" Jacob screamed. "Sheriff!"

I bolted out of my office.

Jacob, a skinny, stripey-haired kid in gray jeans, skidded to a stop in front of me, almost falling over on his ass. For a ferret-shifter, he could be pretty clumsy sometimes.

"Sheriff Ward!" he squeaked with sheer panic on his face.

"Jacob? What's going on? Are the otters and penguins fighting again over who gets to swim first in the water fountain?"

"No." Jacob propped his hands on his knees while panting. "Another hybrid like Imani has crossed the veil."

"Are you sure?"

*Did Freya's mating spell bring another hybrid into town?*

"Yup. I saw her for myself. She was up by Old Man Henry's place, taking photos of me." Jacob heaved a few huge breaths; he'd probably run the entire way from Old Man Henry's place to get here. "I tried to get her phone away from her, but she chased me down and grabbed it back. But before I ran off to come get you, I sniffed her real good to confirm that she's hybrid like Imani. My grandma says that busybody witch Freya had no business casting that mating spell." With wide eyes, he asked,

"Is it true them hybrids are going to be the downfall of this town?"

I sighed heavily. "No. Freya saved the Ridge by casting that mating spell. Without it, unmated males would never have a chance of finding their fated mates."

Truth of the matter, without Freya's spell, eventually all unmated men—including me—would go feral.

It bothered me that prejudiced, ignorant elders who despised hybrids were tainting young pups like Jacob. The hatred full-blood shifters had for hybrids was ridiculous.

"Why are we still talking about this? We've got to go!" Jacob screamed, his lanky arms flying about in agitation. "The hybrid has photos of me."

I frowned. "Shifting?"

"No, as a ferret."

"Jacob, it's just a photo of a big ferret."

I had no concern about her posting photos or videos of anything she saw in Black Forest. Jasper, our pack technology expert, had created a security grid that blocked all non-Ridge cell phones from getting signals.

"I don't care. We need to do something about her."

"We?" I arched a brow.

"Yes." He shook his head up and down like a bobblehead. "You and me. When we find her, I'll interrogate her. It'll give me plenty of practice for when I become your deputy."

I rolled my eyes. "I already have a deputy."

"Well, you'll have two. Me and Deputy Mack." He rocked back and forth on his heels.

I ruffled his hair. "You're only ten."

"I'll be eighteen in no time," he boasted, puffing out his skinny chest.

"Until then, I'll make do with Deputy Mack." Walking into my office with Jacob on my heels, I grabbed my tablet. "Give me the female's description."

"She's maybe five foot six, with dark skin and curly brown

hair about to her shoulders. Her eyes are hazel and almond-shaped. She had on jeans, sneakers, one of those Supergirl T-shirts with a big *S* across her"—he cupped his hands in front of his chest dramatically—"big boobs. Like, you know, big enough that the edges of the *S* kind of disappeared around the sides." He waggled his eyebrows.

"Okay, I get it, she's stacked," I cut in. I had to fight down a laugh. *Boys.*

"Yes. And she's beautiful." He grinned boyishly before continuing, "And she didn't even freak out when she saw me either."

"Well, obviously not, if she was taking your photo." I smiled a little. "Did she say anything?"

He turned a little red, grinning awkwardly. "Yeah, she said I was cute."

I snorted. "Well, she probably didn't mean it that way. You were a fur ball all the time." I fought the urge to snicker at his crestfallen look. *Poor kid.* At his age, all I had thought about besides having fun had been girls too.

"You don't know that." He scowled.

Ignoring his statement, I asked, "Is she on foot?"

"Yes. Like I said, she's on Old Man Henry's land, and you know how ornery he can get about people on his property."

Shoving my tablet under my arm, I eyed him. "Then why were you there?"

He shrugged, his face turning redder.

My cell rang, and I pointed a finger at him. "Don't you move," I ordered before answering my cell with, "Sheriff Ward."

"Sheriff Ward, this is Henry. You better get your ass over here, pronto. I found a hybrid trespassing on my land." He ended the call abruptly.

"Shit," I grumbled, grabbing my cowboy hat before tugging Jacob with me as I exited my office.

"You taking me with you?" Jacob asked as I ushered him along the hallway.

"Nope." I released him when we reached Heidi, my administrative assistant. "You go home."

Jacob frowned. "But I can help."

"Go home, Jacob."

Shoving his hands in his jeans pockets, he sulked. "Not fair."

"Life often isn't."

"Ain't that the truth," Heidi chimed in while patting her protruding belly. "I haven't seen my feet in years."

"That's because you're pregnant," countered Sally, the department analyst at the station. "Again."

"Oh hush." Heidi gave her the evil eye while taking a big bite from the donut in her hand. "I can't help it that I'm fertile."

Sally laughed. "I have a solution for your problem. You and your mate need to stop going at it like rabbits."

"But we are rabbits," Heidi whined.

Sally rolled her eyes. "As your best friend and loving godmother to all six of your children, I beg you to slow down the baby-making machine. Their birthdays alone are costing me a fortune."

"Hush your mouth, Sally," Heidi said. "You love children."

"I love *your* children," Sally said pointedly.

"Exactly." Heidi grinned.

"I give up." Sally threw her hands in the air, then turned to Jacob. "You want some donuts as a consolation prize for not getting to ride along with the sheriff?" She pointed to several fresh boxes of donuts from Bessie's Coffee Shop cluttering her desk.

"I guess so," Jacob said.

When I spotted the basket Josie left at the front desk, I clenched my fists. "And will you toss that basket out?"

"My pleasure," Sally answered. "I can't stand that hussy." She picked up the basket.

"Wait," Heidi pleaded, snatching a biscuit from the basket and biting into it.

Sally dropped the basket into the trash with a loud thud.

"Yuck," Heidi proclaimed, tossing the half-eaten biscuit into the garbage. "That tasted like sawdust. How the hell is that owl-shifter still in business?"

The door to the station slammed open, and Mack stepped in, announcing, "The otters and penguins are at it again. I just broke up another fight at the fountain."

"That's the least of our troubles," I countered.

My heart raced with excitement. Some lucky unmated male might finally find his fated mate.

"What's going on?" Mack asked.

"We have another hybrid in town," I replied. "I'm heading over to Old Man Henry's to check it out."

"I'll call Quinn to let him know what's going on," Mack said.

"Make sure Jacob gets home," I told Sally and Heidi.

I didn't need Jacob following me over to Old Man Henry's place. I had enough trouble on my hands with trying to calm down a cranky old man and a hybrid that probably didn't know that the residents of this town were all Others.

# CHAPTER 4
## NOVA

My mind continued to retrace what I'd just seen. A horse transforming into a man. *How is that shit possible?*

Propping my hands on my hips, I asked again, "What are you?"

"Single," he replied, twirling both sides of his handlebar mustache. "In case you're interested."

"Does it look like I'm interested?" I retorted.

"Nope, but you can't blame an old man for trying." He winked at me, then started to whistle a country song.

"Are you going to put on your clothes?" I asked, keeping my eyes on his face. I'd already caught an eyeful of his cock, and the man was literally hung like a horse.

"No. I love the freedom of my pecker flapping in the wind."

I scrunched up my nose. "Well, I don't."

"Why? The body is nothing to be ashamed of. In fact, my people believe it's a beautiful thing."

"Your people? Do you mean alien beings?"

I'd watched enough television shows about aliens to know that, according to conspiracy theorists, Alaska was a hotbed for alleged alien spacecraft sightings.

He barked out a laugh. "Do I look like an alien?"

"How do I know? I've never seen one in person."

"Well, I'm not some damn alien."

"Then what are you?" I asked.

"That's none of your business, young lady."

I scowled. "Are you on medication?"

He frowned. "Why you asking?"

"Because you're acting insane."

"Back in my day, we used to call this polite conversation," he grouched.

Ignoring him, I stared at my cell, but it still had no signal. "What's taking your sheriff so long to get here?" Right then I needed two things—a ride into town and a strong drink.

"What's your rush, female?"

"My name is Nova, not female."

"Whatever." He shrugged. "All I know is you have no right pitching a hissy fit when I found you trespassing on my land."

I tapped my foot. "Where are the markers telling me that it's your property?"

He snorted. "I don't need a stinking marker. It's my land, missy."

"Fine. Then I'm out of here." I started to storm away.

"Hold your horses." He stepped in my path. "I haven't decided whether I'm pressing charges against you. I'm waiting for the sheriff to get over here to sort this shit out."

"Are you kidding me?" I shouted. "Are you really going to press charges?" The last thing I needed was to call my estranged grandmother to bail me out.

"Depends."

"Depends on what?" I sassed back.

Ignoring my question, he scratched his chin. "You know, you look mighty familiar, but I can't place the face. You can't have kin here since you're a—"

I cut him off. "Hybrid. You said that already."

"Wowee, you're one sassy filly." He adjusted his cowboy hat. A hat that looked ridiculous because he was still buck naked. "I got it." He snapped his fingers. "You look like a younger version of…" His words trailed off at the sound of a vehicle approaching. "Oh hey, that's Sheriff Ward."

"Thank God." I turned around, waving my arms wildly, flagging him down. "I'd rather be locked up than spend another minute with your crazy ass."

"I guess that's the thanks I get for keeping you company."

"Company?" My eyes widened. "You're detaining me."

He shrugged. "Tomato. Tomahto."

"Is everyone in town as crazy as you?" I snapped.

"I'm sane compared to those uppity yahoos."

"Shit. I'm in trouble," I grumbled.

A black cruiser pulled up and parked. The driver's door flung open, and a tall muscular man with a crew cut got out. Slapping a white cowboy hat on his head, he shot me the same challenging look a cat gives you before batting the fuck out of you.

Not intimidated, I scowled at him.

"What took you so long?" I started walking toward him. The closer I got, the more aware I was of the strange way my skin prickled with awareness and my heart raced with excitement.

"Lady, don't move," Sheriff Cowboy barked. "Stay right there."

His cool tone was like a bucket of icy water had been thrown over my head. Glaring at him, I stilled my feet.

"What are you going to do? Arrest me?" I taunted with my hands on my hips, watching him stride over to Naked Cowboy and me.

He whipped off his dark sunglasses, revealing sky-blue eyes. "Don't tempt me, female." My skin tingled while his eyes roamed over me from head to toe. It was as if his gaze was stroking me in all the hot, sensual ways I loved.

*Jesus*, he was the most beautiful man I'd ever laid eyes on. He wasn't carrying a weapon, and instead of a uniform, he dressed in jeans with a gold shield buckle hooked on his leather belt and a gray shirt that barely contained his biceps.

Everything about this man—except his asshole attitude—made me want to climb him like a jungle gym for kids.

His nostrils flared, and a low growl sounded deep in his throat. The slightly animalistic sound made my nipples throb.

*Did he just growl at me?*

*And what in the hell is going on with my body?*

Henry sniffed the air loudly. "You two cut that foreplay shit out. This ain't no dating show." He glared at both of us. "This female is trespassing on my land. Aren't you supposed to be interrogating her?"

The sheriff's eyes narrowed on me before staring over at Naked Cowboy. "Don't tell me how to do my job, Henry." He frowned at him. "And why the fuck are you wearing your hat and not your clothes?"

He scratched his chin. "I was fixin' to get dressed, but I didn't have time."

"All lies." I rolled my eyes. "I repeatedly asked—no, begged —you to cover your bare ass."

He snickered. "That you did." He eyed the sheriff. "She's one of those uptight nudist haters."

I slammed my hands on my hips. "I am not an uptight nudist hater."

"Sure you are. Not once have you checked out my magnificent body." He waggled his eyebrows.

"That's it." I held out my hands to the sheriff. "Handcuff me. Arrest me. Just take me away from this crazy man."

Naked Cowboy grinned. "Apparently, I'm too much cowboy for her."

"Henry, get dressed," the sheriff ordered. "No one wants to see your dingle-dangle bits."

"That's not what all the ladies in town say," he said.

The sheriff crossed his beefy arms. "Don't make me arrest you, Henry."

"You ain't here for me, Protector."

*Protector? Is that some weird nickname for sheriff?*

Naked Cowboy pointed at me. "You're here for beautiful over there." He winked at me. "In case you're wondering, I'm single and ready to mingle."

"I'm done!" I yelled, marching over to the cruiser, opening the back door, and getting inside. "Take me to jail, Protector," I ordered before slamming the door. I'd rather spend the night in lockup than put up with any more of Naked Cowboy's crazy talk.

I watched the sheriff step closer to Henry, but I couldn't hear their conversation.

My eyes drifted down to his ass, encased in well-fitted jeans that left little to the imagination. I whispered, "Damn. Sheriff Stick-Up-His-Ass has a smoking-hot body."

Suddenly, the sheriff's head whipped around to stare at me. His mouth was moving, but I couldn't hear what he was saying, so I opened the door.

"Huh?" I asked.

"Sheriff Stick-Up-His-Ass?"

*How in the hell did he hear my nickname for him?*

He arched a brow.

I slammed the door, scooting across the seat.

A few minutes later, Sheriff Ward took off his hat before sliding behind the wheel. Pulling out his cell, he tapped out a text before taking off.

"I assume your alien kind has superhearing," I said.

"Alien kind?"

"Yes. Alien. Like Henry."

"He's not an alien, and neither am I."

"I call bullshit on what you just said. Henry transformed from a horse to a man. And the cruiser's door was closed, so the only way you could have heard what I was whispering about you is with superhearing."

He snorted. "I think you've been watching way too many science fiction television shows."

"Whatever," I said, refusing to acknowledge that I was a science fiction movie geek.

"Can we start over?" he asked. "What's your name?"

"Nova King."

"King?" He eyed me in the mirror. "And who are you here to visit?"

"Why?"

"Because I'm the law, and you're here in my town."

"I'd rather not say," I quipped, staring out the window at the weird but beautiful scenery. "It's personal."

"Did you just say that it's personal?"

"Yes, I did." I pursed my lips.

"How about a night in jail? Will that loosen your tongue?"

"Nope."

"Let me get this straight. You believe you're in a town with aliens, and you're not afraid to spend the night in our jail? Aren't you afraid of being probed?"

"No. If you all were going to probe me, you would have done it by now."

"How do you know I'm not taking you to get probed right now?"

My lips curled up into a smile. "Is that what you'd like to do? Probe me in private, Sheriff?" I wasn't normally flirtatious, but something about Sheriff Ward revved up my flirt-o-meter.

He chuckled. A sound that made my toes curl with pleasure. "I don't do probing while on duty."

"So you say, Sheriff." My pussy pulsed, just imagining all the freaky, sensual ways he could probe me with his cock and tongue.

*Nova. Take your mind off sex.*

Peering out of the window, I gawked at what looked like a lush rain forest. "How is there a rain forest in Alaska?"

"Black Forest Ridge is unique."

I snorted. "It sure is. Uniquely alien. Did your kind bring your planetary habitat to earth?"

"For the last time, we're not aliens," he barked.

"Uh-huh. So you admit that you're like Henry."

"What are you, a lawyer?"

"No," I said. "Just a midwife on vacation."

"That's a lie," he snapped. "No one comes to the Ridge for vacation."

"Fine," I snapped. "I'm here to see someone."

His eyes flicked to the rearview mirror before going back to the road.

When we reached the crest of the long, winding road, I could see buildings sprawling across the middle of the valley, with a body of water surrounding it. We descended onto a flat road and drove a few more minutes before reaching the section of Black Forest that seemed to be the center of activity.

"Is this Main Square?" I asked. According to my sperm donor's letter, once I got into town, I was supposed to go to Main Square and find my grandmother at a place called Panthera Onca Fine Art Gallery.

"Yes."

There were no streetlights, and the tree-lined street had a host of shops with rustic brick exteriors. My heart raced with excitement when we passed the shop that allegedly belonged to my grandmother. I was so close yet so far from meeting the woman who gave birth to the man who walked away from me.

My palms started to sweat.

*What will I say to her when we finally meet?*

*Hi, I'm Nova King, the daughter of your son who dumped me.*

*Hi, I'm Nova King, and I think your son is a piece of shit.*

*Hi, I'm Nova King. Why didn't your son want me?*

"Something wrong?" the sheriff asked.

"No." I rubbed my palms against my jeans. "Why?"

"You look nervous about something."

My eyes narrowed. "I'm not nervous."

"That's strike two," he argued.

"What are you talking about?"

"It's the second time you've lied to me. First, about being here on vacation. Second, about not being nervous. Don't let there be a third time, Ms. Nova."

I normally didn't lie, but my whole equilibrium had been thrown off from the moment I drove into this alien town.

He pulled up in front of a police station.

"Are you kidding me?" My eyes widened. "You're going to arrest me?"

He turned off the cruiser, got out, and opened my door. "I'm not officially arresting you… yet."

"Yet?"

"Yes."

He gestured for me to step out. Reluctantly, I obliged.

"But if you don't come clean with me about your true intentions in this town"—he slammed the passenger's door—"I won't hesitate to throw your ass in jail."

I squared off with him. "You have no right."

"Make up your mind, woman. First, you begged me to arrest you. Now you're pitching a fit. What do you want?"

"For you to let me go." I batted my eyelashes at him.

He scowled. "To go where?"

"None of your business."

"Two can play this game." He pointed to the front door of the station. "Straight ahead, Ms. Nova."

"Fine." I stomped away, but he beat me to the door, opening it for me.

Stepping over the threshold, I froze when everyone inside sniffed loudly, then stared at me as if I had two heads.

"What's with the sniffing?" I mumbled. *Do I stink?*

A man with hair the color of a penny strode up to me with a huge grin. "Well, hello," he said. "Ain't this my lucky day. My name is Logan," he finished with an outstretched hand.

Logan was stunningly handsome and built like a tank, with muscles bulging everywhere.

*Are all the aliens genetically modified?*

*Or maybe they're just cyborgs.*

"Hello," I returned, moving forward to shake his hand. Sheriff Stick-Up-His-Ass pushed my hand down.

"Get out of my station, Logan," the sheriff ordered, pointing to the door.

Logan didn't move an inch. "No need to be so snappy. I'm just being polite to the beautiful lady."

"That's a lie," said a very pregnant woman. "You were flirting… badly." The female turned to the sheriff. "We got a call from Dean. He said he saw Sam running across his property. Mack went to investigate."

"Thanks, Heidi," the sheriff replied, then glared at Logan. "What are you doing here anyway?"

Logan crossed his beefy arms. "Reporting a robbery at my butcher shop. Last night Clancy broke in and stole all my short loin—that's my money cut. I smelled him all over my shop."

*Smelled him?* This Clancy person must have very distinct body odor.

The sheriff frowned. "Well, get to reporting," he said before grabbing my elbow, ushering me away.

My stomach growled when I spotted boxes of donuts on a desk. Not breaking his stride, Sheriff Cowboy grabbed a box before ushering me away.

I fought to keep pace. "Where's the fire?"

"Less talking, more walking," he ordered.

I glared over at him. "I don't like to be alien-handled."

"And I don't like being lied to, so I guess we're even."

When we reached an office, he motioned for me to go inside. Plopping down onto the chair in front of the massive desk, I gave him the death stare.

Unfazed, he slid the box of donuts in front of me. "Help yourself," he ordered, standing over me like a jailer.

My stomach growled again. I was hungry, and donuts were my kryptonite. But I wasn't going to eat the offered sugary goodness, just to show Sheriff Cowboy that I couldn't be bribed with donuts.

"I'm not hun—"

"Do you really want to finish that statement?" He held up three fingers. "Because three strikes and you're out, Ms. Nova."

"Fine," I grumbled, digging into the box, snatching a huge donut covered with white glaze. I almost danced with joy when I bit into the pillowy goodness. The harmony of flour, sugar, plus the filling of guava and cream cheese gave me a foodgasm.

"Yummy," I groaned.

"You enjoying yourself?"

"Immensely," I answered.

"I see." He stared down at me. "You have something on your face."

"Where?" I mumbled around a mouthful of donut.

"There." He pointed to my face.

I brushed my lips. "Is it gone?"

"No." He paused. "Do you mind?"

"Mind what?"

"Me touching you."

"Sure, you can touch me." I grinned. "Just do it nice and slow, Sheriff Stick-Up-Your-Ass."

"You really have to stop calling me that," he complained.

"Why? It fits."

He sighed heavily before leaning down, wiping a callused thumb across my chin.

"Slower," I demanded huskily.

His thumb traced across my lips. "Is that slow enough?"

"Uh-huh."

With eyes locked on mine, he brought his thumb to his lips, and his tongue flicked across the pad.

*Jesus. Sheriff Stick-Up-His-Ass is hot with a side of dirty sex.*

I bit my bottom lip, watching him swirl his tongue against his finger and imagining all the hot, filthy things his tongue could do to my body.

"Donut filling," he declared before clearing his throat and striding over to his chair to sit down.

An awkward silence fell over us as he leaned back into his chair and scrutinized me.

"It's not polite to stare," I told him while taking another bite of donut.

Ignoring my comment, he said, "Henry decided not to press charges against you."

I stopped midchew. "Then why am I here?"

"I told you. I can't have you running around town when I don't know why you're here."

Swallowing my mouthful of donut, I placed my elbows on his desk. I was done wasting time with the sheriff. I needed to find my estranged grandmother, ask her all the questions I'd waited years for answers to, then hightail it out of Alien Town.

"I'm here to see Bonnie King. I've been told that she can be found at Panthera Onca Fine Art Gallery."

He drummed his fingers against his desk. "Do you mind my asking why she's so important to you?"

"Bonnie is my grandmother. I found a letter from my estranged father with directions on how to get here to meet her. I'm here for answers. Nothing more. Nothing less."

"I see." His eyes scanned my face. "Hold on a second. I know someone who can straighten this out." He pulled out his cell, swiping his finger across it. "Hi, it's Rhett. You need to come down to the station. There's a Nova King here to see you." He paused. "Yes. I'm sure. Okay. We'll be here."

When he ended the call, he said, "I guess it's time to get your answers."

# CHAPTER 5
# RHETT

My world spun out of control when I inhaled deeply. Her scent was unmistakable.

*Nova is my fated mate.*

I almost felt dizzy with the need to leap over my desk, clutching her against me.

*Her scent. It's the most wonderful thing I've ever experienced,* my jaguar asserted.

I couldn't dispute his assessment. Nova's scent reached out to me, pulling me toward her like nothing else had in my lifetime.

Her scent was a delicious combination of a sweet apple, creamy vanilla, and oranges that conjured up thoughts of a sunny day.

I watched Nova sitting in the chair, staring at nothing in particular. "You're nervous," I noted. The sounds of her heartbeat thumping rapidly strummed in my ears.

"How did you know?"

"Your adrenaline rose, and so has your heart rate."

Her eyes widened. "You can smell my adrenaline?"

"Yes," I replied. It made no sense evading the truth, given the fact that she was mine—and a hybrid, from her scent of human and shifter blood.

"And you can hear my heart too?" she asked.

I nodded.

"If you aren't an alien"—she leaned forward, pressing her palms against my desk—"then what are you?"

"Other." I rose, coming over to her.

She stared up at me. "And what does that mean?"

"I'll let your grandmother explain that." I extended my hand to her.

She hesitated.

"I don't bite... much," I joked, hoping she'd appreciate my attempt to lighten the mood. I held my breath, waiting for her to place her hand into mine. When she did, a static shock pulsed against my skin.

She yanked her hand away. "Did you feel that?"

"I did." I glanced at my fingers as if they were foreign. "That's never happened to me before."

*More proof that she's ours...* my inner beast crowed.

"Ditto, Sheriff."

"You can call me Rhett."

"So we're on a first-name basis now?" Her lips curled up into a seductive smile.

Nova was more than beautiful.

She was intelligent, brave, and alpha to the core. Thick, curly chestnut hair framed her face. Her mahogany skin was accented with high cheekbones, and her full, pouty lips begged me to nibble and taste them.

I shrugged. "I don't see why not, since I'm clearly not going to lock you up... today."

She laughed huskily. "So you're leaving that door of opportunity wide open, I see."

"Yup." I winked.

She eyed me. "Well, I have no aversion to handcuffs, given the right situation."

Her words made my cock twitch, and a wild need to possess her raced through me. "Is that so?"

There was a loud commotion outside my office that made us jerk our heads in that direction. But even without the noise, I scented the person about to enter my office.

"You have a visitor," I said.

*This is the moment of truth… to confirm my suspicions.*

Nova was so nervous that she swayed a little when she stood.

"You okay?" I asked, placing a hand against her lower back to steady her.

"No. I'm not," she answered roughly, leaning into my touch for a moment longer.

The door banged open. Bonnie strode inside, racing across the office with such speed that her long kimono billowed around her tight leather dress like curtains. Quinn and Imani were on her heels.

"Quinn? Imani? Why are you here?" I asked. "I told you that I'd debrief you after I figured out what's going on."

"Bo asked us to hightail our asses over here," Quinn replied. "She said she needed to tell us something really important."

Without a word, Bonnie wrapped her arms around Nova, hugging her tightly. Nova hugged her back awkwardly.

After a beat of silence, Bonnie pulled back, cupping Nova's face. "What took you so long to find me?"

"I didn't know you existed until I found his letter."

Bonnie frowned. "What letter?"

"The letter my father wrote, giving me directions how to get here."

Tears glistened in Bonnie's eyes. "God, you look so much like your father."

"Where is he?" Nova asked.

"I'll explain everything in a minute," Bonnie answered, touching Nova's hair. "But time is of the essence. Gossip travels fast in this town, and I'm worried about what will happen when the townsfolk find out about your Hunter bloodline."

My stomach plummeted. "Nova's a Hunter?" I felt light-headed from the disappointment. There was no way my fated mate could be a Hunter.

Quinn wrapped a protective arm around Imani. "She's a Hunter, and you brought Imani here? Endangering my mate's life?"

"Let's all take a deep breath," Bonnie demanded. "You didn't let me finish explaining."

"Well, get to clarifying before I lose my shit," Quinn demanded.

Bonnie squared off with him. "Look here, Quinn Bane. I'm an elder in this town. So you will watch your fucking mouth."

Someone knocked at the door.

"This better be important," I barked. "Come in."

The door swung open. Heidi strolled in, pushing a cart filled with bottles of water, cups of coffee, and plates with slices of pie.

"Not the time for refreshments, Heidi," I declared.

"Make time," she sassed back, stopping the cart in the middle of the office.

"Oh pie," Imani exclaimed, excitedly grabbing a plate. "Thank you."

"My pleasure," Heidi said, then eyed Quinn and me. "The festival events planning committee just arrived at the station for their scheduled meeting, so I figured I'd share some of the food and refreshments they brought tonight."

"That's tonight?" Quinn exploded.

Heidi nodded. "Yup. Rhett gave them permission to have the meeting here because their usual meeting location at the town hall is being used by the beaver-shifters tonight."

I rubbed my chin. "I forgot that meeting was happening at the station tonight."

"I figured that, so I told them tonight's meeting is canceled,"

Heidi replied. "But they're still inside the station, lingering and listening to everything you all are saying inside this office. I'd give it an hour before the station's phones start ringing off the hook from nosy-ass townsfolk asking about the Hunter in town." She turned to Nova and grinned. "Damn, you're the spitting image of your grandma." She winked at her. "Welcome to Black Forest," she finished before hustling out and closing the door firmly behind her.

"Shit, she's right," Quinn affirmed. "Let's speed this up, Bonnie. My pack and I need to strategize a plan for damage control."

"I vote for kicking her ass out of the Ridge," I grumbled even when everything in my head rebelled against that idea.

*And I vote that we don't,* my jaguar interjected.

Nova rounded on me. "Kick my ass out?" Her scent had changed and was now mixed with a light note of hot peppers. She was pissed off. "Are you always such an asshole? Or is this a special occasion, Sheriff Stick-Up-Your-Ass?"

"I told you to stop calling me that."

Quinn, Imani, and Bonnie looked back and forth between us like it was a tennis match.

Nova glared at me. "Does it bother you?"

"Yes," I said.

"Good," she retorted.

"I like Rhett's new nickname," Imani commented around a mouthful of pie.

"Imani, don't add," Quinn replied.

Imani shrugged. "I'm just saying the truth." She held out a forkful of pie to Quinn, who opened his mouth to eat it.

I shot her a dirty glare. "Whose side are you on?"

She pointed her fork at Nova. "Hers."

"Traitor," I grumbled.

Imani grinned, then winked at Nova.

Nova smirked. "Imani, I give you full permission to put that nickname on a T-shirt and give it to him for Christmas."

"Can we get back to the business of Nova?" Quinn demanded.

"I already voted," I grunted. "She goes."

Both Nova and Imani rolled their eyes.

"Well, your vote don't count, Sheriff," Bonnie rebutted. "Only votes from the council and Quinn matter."

"I'm the Protector of this town, so I have a say," I asserted.

"You're not the only Protector, Rhett," Bonnie argued. "Quinn's whole pack is Protectors too. But like I said, your vote don't count."

I widened my stance. "My job is to protect the residents of this town from harm and to keep this place safe."

"Well, do your job and protect my granddaughter," Bonnie said.

"She's not a resident," I rebutted. "She's not one of us."

"Yet," Bonnie said with a hard stare.

"Quit it, you two," Quinn interjected. "No disrespect, Bonnie, but you can't just throw out the word Hunter and not expect hackles to rise."

"Hello?" Nova waved her hand. "Why is everyone talking about me like I'm not here?"

Bonnie glared at Quinn and me. "Do you really think I would have brought you all here if Nova was a danger to any of you?"

"She's your kin," I replied. "So we have no damn clue what you'd do for her." And I knew from experience that family could make you do the most despicable things, crossing many ethical lines.

"She's my blood." Bonnie peered at each of us before locking eyes with Nova. "I'd lay down my life for her. But I wouldn't endanger the town. Now if all of you would just put your biases aside for a second, I'll explain everything."

"I agree with Bonnie," Imani said as she started to move closer to Nova and Bonnie. Quinn gently tugged her to his side. Imani frowned at him. "Nova is not a secret assassin. Baby, please release your death grip on me." He did so reluctantly. She rewarded him with a quick kiss before moving to stand by Nova.

"You're playing with fire, Bonnie." Quinn crossed his arms, glaring at her. "Once all the residents get wind of Nova being a Hunter, they'll tear her and anyone associated with her to pieces. I won't have that chaos in this town. Not when I have my mate to protect." He nodded toward me. "Rhett, get her out of town."

Bonnie stepped in front of Nova. "You touch her, and it will be me, you, and Rhett tussling in here." Her fingers rippled, and long black claws grew from the tips.

Nova stepped back with eyes glued to Bonnie's deadly claws. "Holy shit! My grandmother's an alien too?"

I slapped my forehead. "For the last fucking time, we are not aliens."

Bonnie frowned. "I'm not an alien. I'm Other. All of us in this town are."

Nova's eyebrows rose. "Other?"

"Others are mythical beings you've probably read about in human folklore and fairy tales," Bonnie explained. "In essence, we're a society of witches, vampires, shifters, and other supernatural beings."

"Vampires? Witches?" Nova's eyes widened. "Monsters from fantasy books and movies are real?"

"We aren't the monsters," I hissed. "Hunters are."

Nova shot me an annoyed stare. "Sheriff, will you get that stick out of your ass? I'm trying to sort shit out in my head. So stop snapping at me like a pit bull."

"I'm a jaguar-shifter," Bonnie interjected. "That makes you a hybrid jaguar-shifter."

I edged closer toward Nova. If I could get her out of my office, then I might have a chance of escorting her out of the Ridge quickly, before the shit hit the fan.

"Don't make me tear you a new asshole, Sheriff," Bonnie threatened. "Back away from my granddaughter."

Easing away, I said, "Simmer down, Bonnie." The last thing I needed was Bonnie shifting into her jaguar form.

Bonnie sheathed her claws, placing her hands on her leather-encased hips. "Well, don't threaten my kin."

"Let's all take a deep breath," Imani said. "Quinn and Rhett, stand down."

"I'm the Protector," I said. "That means I'm responsible for protecting the townsfolk from threats to their safety. And Nova's a Hunter."

"She's not a Hunter," Bonnie countered. "She has a Hunter bloodline."

"What's the difference?" Nova said.

"Humans are Hunters. And everyone on your mother's side are Hunters," Bonnie explained.

"Everyone?" My eyes widened. "This shit keeps getting better and better. Her whole family is our mortal enemy."

Nova frowned. "So Hunters and Others are enemies?"

Bonnie nodded. "Yes. Hunters are members of a century-old organization of humans whose sole mission is to hunt and kill Others."

"Time-out. None of this makes sense," Quinn bellowed. "It's impossible for a male shifter to get a human female pregnant unless she's his fated mate. Are you saying Nova's mother was her father's mate?"

"Bingo!" Bonnie declared. "Don't ask me how or why, but Jackie was not only a hybrid but a Hunter."

"Who's Jackie?" I asked.

Bonnie arched a brow. "Nova's mother."

"Did you know my mother?" Nova asked.

"Personally, no." Bonnie's eyes tightened. "I only know what my son Nathan told me about her." She looked over at Nova. "You see, he and Jackie were freshmen in college when they met. After they fell in love, Nathan knew that she was his fated mate, so he revealed what he was—a jaguar-shifter—to her, and she admitted what she was, a Hunter. They knew their relationship would never be accepted by shifters or Hunters, so they made a pact to keep their true nature a secret from everyone."

"That makes no sense," Quinn stated. "They had to know their relationship would never work and that their secret would eventually get out. Why didn't they just walk away from each other?"

"She was his fated mate, Quinn!" Bonnie exploded. "When you found out Imani was your mate, could you walk away from her?"

"No." Quinn stared at Imani. "Never. Even when I tried to deny my true feelings for her, it was like my soul was being ripped from my body. She was mine even before I claimed and marked her."

"Exactly," Bonnie said. "Nathan was my only son, and I wanted to protect him. To beg him to run away from Jackie as fast as he could. To demand that he come back to the Ridge. But I knew he wouldn't listen to any of my demands, warnings, or advice because she was his fated mate."

She swallowed hard. "I felt helpless knowing that when Marcy eventually found out about what Nathan was, she would have him killed." Her eyes hardened. "Which she did."

"Who is Marcy?" I asked.

"Jackie's mother and the leader of all the Hunters in the United States," Bonnie explained.

"Oh God," Imani murmured. "This is bad."

"Fuck my life!" Quinn shouted. "It's bad enough to be a Hunter, but her other grandmother is the alpha of all the Hunters?"

I shook my head. "This shit is a horror movie."

"Wait," Nova interjected. "Are you telling me Marcy killed my father?"

"Yes," Bonnie answered. "When Marcy found out Jackie was pregnant, she lost her shit because she was grooming Jackie to take her place as the next leader of the Hunters. Marcy demanded that Jackie get rid of the baby. Jackie refused, which pissed her off more, then Marcy started digging into Nathan's life, and what she found out, she apparently didn't like."

"She found out that he was a shifter," Nova whispered.

Bonnie's fists clenched and unclenched. "Yes, but that was no surprise to Nathan, Jackie, or me," Bonnie disclosed. "Hunters have powerful connections. And their access to a vast amount of intel is what makes them so dangerous. Marcy had my son killed…" Her voice cracked on the word *killed*. "And Jackie ran because she knew that she would be killed next for betraying the Hunters by mating with their enemy… a shifter. I wanted my grandchild—you—so I tried to find Jackie by hiring the best Trackers money could buy, but she dropped off the end of the earth."

Bonnie eyed Quinn, Imani, and me. "Now do you understand why I need your help? Black Forest nearly imploded when they found out Imani was a hybrid. What do you think will happen when they find out that not only does Nova come from a Hunter bloodline, but her other grandmother is their leader?"

"But I don't have shit to do with that part of my family," Nova protested. "Hell, I didn't even know they existed until now."

"It doesn't matter," I fumed. "The hatred between Others and Hunters runs deep. To make matters worse, most people in this town, including me, have lost a loved one at the hand of a Hunter."

"Rhett is right," Quinn agreed. "Townsfolk are not going to see reason when they find out what Nova is." His eyes locked with Bonnie's. "I'm sorry, Bonnie. I know she's your kin, but for her protection, she has to go."

"I can protect myself," Nova exclaimed.

"Against a town filled with people who can shift into the most dangerous animals in the world?" I countered.

"She's not going anywhere," Bonnie declared. "I've waited years for this day. Nova is the only family I have left, and I'm not going to let anyone take her away from me."

"Bonnie, think with your head, not with your heart," Quinn pleaded.

"Is that what you did with Imani?" Bonnie demanded. "Because as I recall, when the town was in an uproar about a hybrid being in the Ridge, you called for a vote at the town hall meeting, asking to put her under the council's protection."

Quinn shook his head. "It's not the same."

Bonnie arched a brow. "Why not? Nova's a hybrid, just like your fated mate, Imani. To boot, the council recently passed a law making all hybrids official citizens of Black Forest."

Imani stared at Quinn. "Bonnie is right. All hybrids are now welcomed and protected in Black Forest. Including Nova."

"And you expect residents to accept that she has a Hunter bloodline?" Quinn demanded.

Bonnie looked him up and down. "I don't give a flying fuck what they accept. By law, Nova has a right to be here, just like all hybrids."

"But what about Jackie's bloodline?" I argued. "If Jackie is a hybrid, that could mean that she isn't the only one in her family, which means the Hunters can get past the Ridge's veil."

"No, they can't," Bonnie said. "Not according to what Nathan explained to me. Marcy adopted Jackie. They don't have the same blood."

"But how can we be sure that Nova's not here on some secret mission concocted by the Hunters?" I asked.

"Are you suspicious about everyone? Or just me?" Nova demanded.

I stared her down. "Just you."

Nova rolled her eyes. "Well, I'm not here on some secret Scooby-Doo mission. I'm here because when my mother passed away, I found my father's letter hidden in her jewelry box." She pulled the letter out of her bag, handing it to Bonnie, who scanned it.

"It's my son's handwriting," Bonnie confirmed. She smelled the paper. "And his scent is all over it."

"I was in Africa working as a volunteer midwife when my mother passed away," Nova explained. "I came back home to the United States to settle her estate, and that's when I found my father's letter."

Imani nodded. "Everyone in this room can smell that she's telling the truth."

"How?" Nova asked.

"When a person lies, it smells like burned rubber," Bonnie elaborated.

"Ah, interesting," Nova said.

Quinn rubbed his chin. "I hear what everyone's saying, but still there's a big damn difference between a hybrid and a hybrid with a Hunter bloodline."

"Why, when she could be someone in this town's mate?" Bonnie countered.

She was my mate, but I felt conflicted about saying it aloud—her bloodline was my sworn enemy; therefore, I had no intention of claiming her.

Bonnie continued. "Or you don't care because you found your happily-ever-after and couldn't give a shit about all the other unmated males in this town who are going feral without a mate?"

"That's a fucked-up thing to say, Bonnie," Quinn exploded. "I care about the well-being of everyone in Black Forest."

"Then stand firm on the law making all hybrids residents of Black Forest," Bonnie demanded.

"I agree," Imani said. "We can't start picking and choosing which hybrids are welcomed with open arms. That's not the kind of town I want to live in. None of us is perfect. We all come with baggage. Things we've done that weren't perfect. Family that we'd rather not fuck with. I consider every hybrid who comes into this town my sister, and I'll treat her as such." She clutched Quinn's hand. "We've overcome so much, baby, but we have to keep on fighting for equality in the Ridge."

Quinn sighed heavily. "You're right." He touched her cheek. "But I'm worried that the Nova backlash will come for you."

"Let them come," Imani gritted out. "I'm the alpha female of this town, and I'm ready to battle for what's right."

"Damn, that's hot, mate," Quinn said, nipping her bottom lip. "I love you."

"And I love you," Imani replied.

I cleared my throat loudly. "Hate to interrupt your Quinn-loves-Imani moment, but we have a big problem here." I nodded over at Nova. "She'll need protection until residents get used to her presence."

Bonnie nodded. "I agree. That's why she's staying at my house."

I snorted. "From the last census count, we've got about 773 Ridge residents. And you think you can take them all on if they decide to launch a mob attack on your house?"

"If they fuck with my granddaughter, I'll kill them," Bonnie said simply.

"One against many are not good odds," I countered.

"Agreed," Bonnie answered. "So if you feel that she needs additional protection, you're more than welcome to stake out in front of my place." She glanced over at Nova. "I think we're done here. It's getting late. I'm taking my granddaughter to my home."

As Bonnie guided Nova out of my office, I said, "I'll be seeing you, Nova."

"Not if I see you first, Sheriff Stick-Up-Your-Ass."

When my inner jaguar sensed her absence, he tore up my insides in a fit of rage.

*Why did you let her go?* my beast growled.

*Why do you care?* I snapped.

*She's our fated mate.*

*I can't claim her,* I retorted.

Rage raced through my veins after a lifetime of waiting for my other half. Why in the hell had Luna, the moon goddess, saddled me with the one thing I despised? A Hunter, for my soul mate.

Imani walked up and punched me in the arm. "What the fuck, Rhett?"

"Ouch!" I rubbed my arm. "What's that for?"

"The way you talked to and about Nova," she hissed. "That was cruel, even for you."

"I'm trying to protect her."

"By being rude?" Imani asked incredulously.

Quinn walked up to Imani, hugging her from behind. "Calm down, Imani." He kissed the top of her head.

"I won't calm down, Quinn," Imani cried. "For fuck's sake, I could smell the hurt, confusion, and anger all over Nova. Do you realize what a churning mess her mind and her emotions must be right now?"

"I'm doing my job as a Protector, Imani," I replied. "She could have a dark, hidden agenda."

"Nova wasn't lying, Rhett," Quinn rebutted. "She didn't know anything about her family."

I knew that Nova wasn't lying about anything she said. My shifter nose smelled the truth of her words. But I refused to back down from my stance. If Nova stayed in the Ridge, her safety was in jeopardy.

"I know that," I barked. "Yes, I admit I took it too far by saying the things I did, but we've got enough on our plate with tracking down two fugitives, Sam and Clancy. We don't need more work with protecting Nova."

"Wait a minute," Quinn barked. "Clancy's back in town?"

Clancy was a town resident and feral shifter who had ventured outside the Ridge and killed humans. He was on the Shifter Council's—a secretive group of alpha leaders from various shifter breeds that governed the shifter world across the globe—most wanted list.

I nodded. "Logan just reported that Clancy broke in and stole all his short loin. He smelled him all over his shop."

"So you're stressed about the workload?" Quinn eyed me suspiciously. "That's why you have a problem with letting Nova stay?"

"It's complicated," I admitted.

Quinn and Imani frowned.

"Look, despite her bloodline," I said, "I don't want anything to happen to her under my watch." That was half the story. The other part was that the moment I'd met her, I'd known that she was mine from her delicious scent that called to me in ways no other female had. I'd wanted her—well, before I'd found out she had a Hunter bloodline. Now my mind refused to cave in to the primal urge to claim my fated mate, and my inner beast was pissed about my decision.

"Wait a minute." Imani's nose twitched. "Are you attracted to her?"

"That's none of your business," I grumbled, shifting my eyes away.

"What's going on with you, Rhett?" she asked. "Being so rude to a female is not like you."

Tired of the back-and-forth about this subject, I blurted out, "She's my fated mate."

They both stared at me.

"I can't claim her," I rushed out. "She has Hunter blood. You both know what they did to my sister. I would never disrespect her memory by claiming a Hunter."

"She's not a Hunter, Rhett," Quinn said.

"It's not happening," I replied.

"None of what you said makes any sense, Rhett," Imani argued. "You forsaking your fated mate is unnatural."

"And it's utterly ridiculous," Quinn asserted. "I can't believe you'd rather not claim your mate over some vendetta with Hunters that she had nothing to do with."

"It's my decision," I answered.

"And the fact that you're sure to go feral without your fated mate—will that not persuade you to rethink your stance?" Imani asked.

I shook my head. "No."

"Quinn." She glared at me. "Talk sense to Rhett."

"I know him," Quinn replied. "His mind is made up about this." He shot me a look of disappointment. "But we still have to protect her. There's no doubt in my mind that, as we speak, the planning committee members are spreading gossip about Nova. She's under our protection while in the Ridge."

"Agreed," Imani said.

"I still think the better solution is kicking her out of town," I grumbled. She'd be safer anywhere but here.

Quinn frowned. "What the hell is wrong with you, Rhett? I can't make you claim her, but Nova is Bonnie's granddaughter, and she has the right to spend time getting to know her. They're family."

Anger and frustration bubbled to the surface. "Does anyone in this fucking room give a shit that her kind killed my sister?"

"It was her kind. Not Nova," Imani rebutted.

"Rhett," Quinn started, "we're not minimizing your hurt, but let's be fair to Nova. She shouldn't be held accountable for the sins of her bloodline." His eyes locked on mine. "Now… will you help the pack protect her?"

"Of course," I replied. "I'm not going to stand by and watch while they tear her to shreds. I don't have to claim her, but it's my job as the Protector of everyone in this town."

"Good." Quinn clapped my shoulder. "We're all in agreement. The pack will protect Nova in order to ensure that nothing happens to her while she's in the Ridge."

"Good luck with that shit," I murmured.

"I don't need luck," Quinn countered with a grin. "I have my pack."

# CHAPTER 6
## NOVA

I stared out the passenger's window as Bonnie's luxury SUV sliced through the darkness. My mind was racing a mile a minute, trying to process everything I had just discovered.

*Mom's family are cold-blooded killers called Hunters.*

*Marcy, my grandmother, killed my father.*

*I'm a hybrid jaguar-shifter.*

And Black Forest is not a town filled with aliens but with supernatural beings called Others.

*Damn, this is a shit-uation.*

"I still don't understand why Jackie didn't give you Nathan's letter when she was alive," Bonnie murmured.

I blinked back tears just remembering his words in the letter.

*Nova, my sweet baby girl. I'm writing this even before you are born. Know that I love you. And if anything should ever happen to me, I want you to go to Black Forest and find my mother, Bonnie King. She'll explain everything. Here are the detailed directions…*

My shoulders sagged. "I've been asking the same question over and over since I found his letter." Glancing over at Bonnie, I admitted, "The truth of the matter is that Jackie and I were never close."

Frankly, there were times I felt she didn't even love me.

The harder I tried to be the perfect daughter that she wanted, the more she despised me.

"She blamed me for every shitty job she had to take to put food on the table. Every man who rejected her. All the sacrifices she'd made for me." I swallowed hard, biting my bottom lip to hide the emotions—self-loathing, perfectionism, apathy, and sadness—I'd long buried. "Now I understand why our relationship was so fucked up," I said. "She hated what I was—a shifter—the monster that she and her family hunted and killed."

Bonnie clucked her tongue. "I'm sorry that you had it so hard, Nova."

"I survived." *Barely.* "Growing up, she taught me to believe that I had to earn her love, and when I didn't get it, I believed that I wasn't enough."

"But you know you're enough, right?" Bonnie asked. "Because you are."

"It took me eighteen years to believe that," I admitted. "I was eighteen when I realized that I had to get away from her in order to rebuild my confidence. My ticket away from her was when I received a full-ride scholarship from an Ivy League university. And instead of being proud of my achievement, she told me that I'd never make it on my own. That I'd come crawling back to her. But I didn't." I laughed bitterly. "After I graduated, I put myself through nursing school and became a midwife. All those years later, the daughter she thought wasn't good enough made it on her own."

With eyes still on the road, Bonnie grabbed my hand and squeezed it. "I'm proud of you. Your grit and determination made you the strong woman you are today."

*Proud of me?* I'd never heard those words from anyone about me.

"Thank you for saying that." I bit my bottom lip.

"There not just words, Nova. It's what I truly feel."

And somehow, I knew Bonnie was speaking the truth. I felt it.

Bonnie continued. "Jackie knew that I wanted to raise you, so if she didn't want to be a mother, then she knew how to get in contact with me," she confided. "My fucking email address hasn't changed."

I shook my head. "I can't tell you what she was thinking. She never talked about my father no matter how many questions I'd asked about him. So when I found his letter, I thought it was my chance to get answers about the man who walked away." I shrugged. "A small part of me hoped he wasn't some shitty man who didn't give a fuck about me. Maybe a part of me hoped to find why I've always felt so different from everyone else. Why I'd never fit in, despite my best efforts. Maybe feel a connection to you."

"We can make this work, Nova," Bonnie insisted. "You're my only family, and believe it or not, I love you."

"How can you not hate me?" I turned to face her. "My grandmother killed your son. My mother kept you from having a relationship with me."

She tightened her fingers around the steering wheel. "Because they did this—Jackie and Marcy. Not you. But that's history. You're here, and you don't know what a gift this is to me. I can't wait to teach you everything I know about our kind. You'll love living here."

I shook my head. "I'm not moving here, Bonnie. I have a life to get back to." Which was a lie. I didn't have friends or a romantic relationship because I traveled a lot—living a nomadic life—searching for what... I didn't know.

"You do remember that Others can smell a lie, Nova. It smells like burned rubber."

Embarrassed at being caught in a fib, I said, "Okay, that was a lie, but I can't live here, Bonnie. I don't want to live in a town that hates me because I have a Hunter bloodline."

"They'll learn to accept you like they did Imani."

*I highly doubt that.*

"How about we just take it one day at a time?" Bonnie suggested.

"Sure, we'll make the best of it while I'm here. But don't push, okay?"

"Fine. I won't push… much."

"Good. Which reminds me. My SUV broke down near Henry's place. Is there someone you can call to tow it to the nearest repair shop?"

"Yep. Let me call Emmett. He owns the only repair shop in town." Bonnie tapped a button on her steering wheel, and the sound of dialing echoed throughout her vehicle.

"Hi, Bo," a man's deep voice said. "What's up?"

"Hi, Emmett. I need a favor."

"If you're calling about your granddaughter's car, I'm already en route. Rhett asked me to pick up her vehicle."

"Well, that's nice of him," Bonnie exclaimed.

I snorted. *Rhett isn't nice. He's an asshole.*

"It's late, so I won't be able to look at her vehicle tonight," he said. "But first thing in the morning, I'll make it a priority."

"Thank you, Emmett. I'll bring Nova over to your shop in the morning."

"I'm looking forward to it," Emmett replied. "According to town gossip, she's a looker."

Bonnie laughed. "Damn right she is. Nova gets her looks from me." Their call ended.

"Thank you for making the call," I said.

"My pleasure." She drove through tall gates and meandered up a driveway, cruising past manicured gardens before parking in front of an impressive Victorian home set against a lush green forest.

I gasped. "Your home is beautiful."

"Thank you." She turned to smile at me. "Let me show you around."

She got out and I followed. Climbing up the stairs, Bonnie unlocked the door, ushered me inside, and flipped on the lights.

From the foyer, I could see the great room and the backyard. Her home was grand.

I followed her into the great room. Bonnie took off her elaborate kimono, revealing a skintight leather dress that looked like it cost a fortune. Her body was curvy but fit, and just like Heidi had remarked, I did look like a younger version of Bonnie.

We were family, so I asked, "How old are you?"

Bonnie popped her hands on her hips and grinned. "Eighty-one."

My mouth flopped open. Her ass-length jet-black braids were pulled back into a ponytail that clearly showcased the youthful appearance of her glowing sienna-hued skin. "You don't look older than thirty."

"That's the magic of being an Other," she explained. "We age slower." She kicked off her expensive-looking stilettos. I followed by taking off my sneakers.

I laughed. "I guess I have the fountain of youth to look forward to."

She winked at me. "And the ability to shift."

I swallowed, not sure if shifting into an animal was my thing. I scanned the large space, taking in all the artwork that was mostly nature-themed and generally of animals or mythological creatures.

I pointed to the artwork. "Are these your creations?"

Bonnie shook her head. "No. They're my clients' creations that I've purchased." She walked over to a miniature metal jaguar sculpture. "This piece was created by Rhett."

I came to her side, running a finger over the intricate work. "He's an artist?"

"Yes. In his spare time. Quinn Bane is a full-time blacksmith and owns a blacksmithing business, but his friends and pack— Mack, Emmett, Rhett, Brody, and Jasper—occasionally work on projects together that they sell through my art gallery. Their sculptures have gotten so popular, they can sell them and make some extra money for the town."

"Wow," I exclaimed. "All proceeds go to the town?"

"Yes."

"That's admirable."

"They're great guys. Quinn's great-grandfather purchased all the land the town stands on and built Black Forest with his money, blood, sweat, and tears. He spent his funds creating this oasis for the Bane family, and he could have kept this place for the Bane bloodline only, but he opened his heart and invited Others to take refuge here." She paused. "The Banes have always lived here. The first son of the Bane family has always ruled this town, and Quinn is the last descendant. So he makes sure that people's homes and vehicles and businesses all run smoothly."

I arched a brow. "So he's more than financially invested, he's emotionally invested in the workings of the Ridge."

"Yes. He's a little gruff, like most of his pack. But he really cares about the residents."

"Impressive," I said.

"It is, but enough about Quinn." Bonnie touched my cheek briefly. "Back to art." She pointed to a set of six prints. "My mate brought these home from a business trip. The artist is well-known for prints, so the ones he picked out are special."

"Are you and my grandfather divorced?"

The expression on her face turned sad. "He was killed in Thailand on a business trip."

"I'm sorry."

"It's been years, but I miss him like crazy. He died right before your dad went away to college." She sauntered over to a wall with tree silhouettes, a mirror, and a framed piece of art. "This one is a rubbing of a Mayan stone your father—an art history major—brought me back from the ruins near Cancún." Her lips curled up into a smile. "God, look at me, rambling away."

I grabbed her hand, squeezing it. "I love hearing about everything. So don't hold back." I released her hand.

"You don't know how happy I am that you're here." She

cupped my cheek. "Now let me make us tea while we chat some more. How do you take your tea?"

"Two teaspoons of honey."

"Got it," she chirped before striding away.

Spotting a large grand piano in the corner with lots of framed photos, I headed over to check them out.

All the photos were of Bonnie and a man that I knew instinctively was my father because they looked alike and I resembled both of them.

I smiled at the photos because they both looked so happy. Sadness settled over me when I thought about the animosity and hate toward shifters that had destroyed their happiness.

One by one, I scanned the photos that ranged from baby photos to photos of Nathan as an adult. I moved on to photos of a younger Bonnie in a swimsuit, with medals around her neck. After meandering around the large living room, I took a seat on her plush sofa.

A few minutes later, Bonnie walked in, handing me a mug before taking a seat on the sofa across from me.

Blowing into her own mug, Bonnie asked, "Do you have any questions for me?"

"Yes." I took a sip of tea, eyeing her over the rim of my mug. "Lots."

"Shoot."

"If I'm a hybrid, why haven't I shifted yet?"

"Because you haven't met your fated mate," she answered before sipping her tea.

"And a fated mate is the equivalent of a soul mate?"

"Exactly."

"I don't believe in soul mates," I admitted. "The concept is bizarre."

"And shifting from human to an animal isn't?" she argued.

I laughed. "You got me there. When I caught Henry shifting from horse to man, it blew my mind."

Bonnie choked on her tea. "You saw him shifting?"

"Yep. One minute, he was galloping across his property. The next, he was shifting into his human form. Believe me, he was none too happy that I caught him shifting. In fact, he chastised me for trespassing on his land. Then he called Rhett to come get me."

"Ah, I see. Henry gets ornery as hell about anyone on his land. But man, I would have paid anything to see that old coot's face when he realized you were a hybrid."

"But how did he know that I'm a hybrid?" I asked.

"This is a small town, so he knew that you weren't from here. Second, to Others, hybrids smell like both human and shifter. And third, only Others can get through the veil."

I frowned with confusion. "And what's a veil?"

"Centuries ago, the town's witch coven created a magical veil that hides the town from humans. For an added level of security, every human who has come in this direction gets confused and lost on the road, then ends up going back the way they came."

"I see." I stored that tidbit of information for dissection later. "Well anyway, Henry wasn't pleased to see me on his property." I laughed. "He's an eccentric man. He just stood butt naked while I tried not to stare at his massive junk. For an old dude, he's packing something powerful there."

Bonnie chuckled. "I've seen it, but it's pretty typical for a horse-shifter."

My eyes widened. I didn't even want to think about how and why she'd seen Henry's cock. I had a feeling it involved both of them being naked and sweaty.

Bonnie continued. "But I like them big, frankly."

I choked on my tea. "Bonnie! Too much information."

"What?" Bonnie batted her eyelashes playfully. "I'll never be too old to have sex. And even though sex will never be as good as it was with my fated mate, I enjoy it immensely."

"Okay. I guess this sex talk with my *grandmother*"—I emphasized the last word dramatically—"is going to happen whether I want it to or not."

"Yep." Her lips tilted into a small brief smile. "First thing you need to learn, I'm frank about everything. There's no need to sugarcoat shit around me. Second, nudity is the norm for shifters. It's quite common to see both males and females traipsing around town butt naked after shifting. Third, shifters love sex… lots of it. So consensual hookups are pretty standard."

"So there are no taboos about having sex with other races of Others?"

"It depends on who you ask," Bonnie explained. "I have no hang-ups about interspecies or interracial sex and dating. Others who disagree with my beliefs are frankly in the minority, but we have some in town." She sniffed the air. "You're not a virgin, and you're in your prime. Do you have a sexual partner who's waiting for you back in the human world?"

"How do you know I'm not a virgin?"

"I can smell it." She tapped her nose.

I blanched, not comfortable with the fact that shifters' sense of smell was that insightful.

"Shifters have an acute sense of smell," Bonnie said. "That's why it's hell for us to spend long periods of time in big cities. We can smell everything—foul odors, lies, anger, fear, desire, and whether you're unmated."

"To answer your question, no, I'm not in a relationship." It had been a long time since I'd had sex with anything other than my vibrator. "I'm focused on my career."

Bonnie frowned. "What's stopping you from having both?"

"I work long hours," I revealed. "Before deciding to take a job as a volunteer midwife in Africa, I worked twenty-four-hour on-call shifts. And none of the men I dated understood that they had to share me with my patients. So I stopped dating. Anyway, I'm not looking for romance right now."

She raised a dark brow. "Sounds like you haven't met the right man… yet."

I snorted. "Get that calculating look out of your eyes. I don't need a man in my life."

"Of course you don't need a man. Needing a man is the land of codependence. However, wanting a man is learning how to give and receive love. Don't you want to be around a man who makes you smile and makes you happier?"

"Sure, but I haven't met that man yet."

"The key word is yet." She placed her cup on the coffee table. "I suspect that your finding your father's letter after all these years has nothing to do with coincidence and everything to do with Freya's magical mating spell."

"What spell?" I asked.

Bonnie tucked her legs under her. "Unmated males in Black Forest are slowly going feral from not finding their fated mates. So Freya cast a spell that asked the universe to send the unmated males their fated mates."

"Feral as in killing one another?"

"No. Not yet. But it's a matter of time before shit hits the fan in the Ridge. A shifter without their fated mate loses touch with their human side, making them feral. That is what is happening to all the unmated males in Black Forest. That's why Quinn and Freya, the head of the witch coven, arranged for a little divine intervention by casting a spell."

"Magic is not real," I said evenly.

Bonnie lifted an eyebrow. "Of course it's real. Why do you think Black Forest is not on any map? Or why humans haven't found this place full of supernatural beings? The veil cloaks this town from humans. And the veil is pure magic."

I couldn't deny her logic. Black Forest Ridge wasn't on any maps that I'd checked. And after an exhaustive search, I found no references to the town on the internet.

"So you're saying that the spell brought me here to find my mate?"

"Yes. But my theory is that the true purpose of Freya's spell is to make the hybrid female whole. Without your mate, your inner animal is trapped inside, asleep. And when you meet your fated mate, the animal awakens. Your senses—sight, hearing, smell, taste, and touch—heighten. That's what happened to Imani, Quinn's mate."

"None of this makes sense to me. It's illogical." I stared at her with my lips pursed in disbelief.

"And a shifter who can shift from its human form to animal, that's logical?"

"No. It's not," I agreed. "But I'm not here to find a mate. I'm scheduled to renew my contract for another stint in Africa. I love being a midwife."

"We don't have a midwife in the Ridge. So this is your opportunity to provide a service that's desperately needed."

"No," I said.

Bonnie frowned. "But we need your help. Isn't that why you became a midwife? To help?"

"I love being a certified nurse midwife. But the type of work I do requires trust from my patients."

"Trust is built. You're my granddaughter, so I know that you're up to the challenge."

"Find someone else, Bonnie. It won't work. I'm a stranger in this town. And don't forget, I'm also a hybrid with an estranged family of Hunters. Do you really think women are going to flock to my clinic?"

The sound of an engine rumbled outside. Bonnie got to her feet. "I bet that's Sheriff Ward. We'll finish this conversation later." She went to the door, opening it. "Yup. It's him."

"Will you shut the door?" I hissed. "We don't need him coming in here, threatening to kick me out of town again."

Bonnie shut the door. "He's not going to do that." Her cell rang. "Hi, Freya," she answered. "Yes. Your spell brought my granddaughter to me. Hold on a sec." She looked over at me. "Nova, I have to take this. Can you bring the sheriff a slice of pie?"

I crossed my arms. "Nope."

"Be nice, Nova."

I arched a brow. "Who says that I'm nice?"

"I do." She pointed to the left of the room. "The kitchen is down the hall."

I rolled my eyes. "Fine." I got up with a huff and stormed toward the kitchen.

"Thank you!" Bonnie called out.

I grumbled all the way to the kitchen. Finding the pie in the refrigerator, I cut a piece, plopping it onto a plate before marching out of the kitchen. Bonnie opened the front door while continuing to talk on her cell. "Yes. Isn't it exciting? It's your spell… again."

Stepping out of the house, I stomped down the stairs, glaring at Sheriff Asshole, who was leaning against the hood of his cruiser.

"Here." I shoved the plate at him. My heart skipped a beat when his fingers grazed mine while taking the plate. "Bonnie says this is for you."

"Still upset with me, huh?" he asked, his eyes roaming over me from head to toe. My skin tingled as if he'd sensually stroked my skin.

My nipples throbbed and pebbled, and I crossed my arms to cover them.

"You threatened to toss me out of town," I grouched.

"I want to protect you." He took a big bite of pie. "Big difference."

I heaved a sigh. "I can protect myself."

He wiped his mouth with the back of his hand. "I'm sure you can, but I'm going to be here just in case."

His words eased a little tension. I had fighting skills that I'd learned over the years, but I wasn't sure I'd be much of a match against a shifter in animal form. And I wasn't going to admit it out loud because Rhett already had a big enough ego as it was, but his being here to protect Bonnie and me was a big relief.

"Whatever," I grumbled before walking away.

"And next time, you better serve me pie with a smile," he demanded with what I recognized as humor in his tone.

Despite the fact that his gravelly voice sent vibrations of lust throughout my body, I shot him the bird over my shoulder.

"Is that your age? Or your IQ?" he shouted with laughter still in his voice.

Ignoring him, I stepped inside the house, slamming the door behind me. "Fucker!"

# CHAPTER 7
## RHETT

"Damn," I hissed while running my hands through my sweat-dampened hair. "This shit is not happening." After I'd arrived home from my shift of keeping watch for trouble at Bonnie's house, sleep had been elusive.

Every damn time I shut my eyes, I was plagued by a dream of taking the hybrid against the wall while clutching a fistful of her thick hair as I fucked her hard.

Her skin glistened with sweat while her thick thighs gripped my waist. Her brown nipples jiggled from the thrusts of my cock pounding into her welcoming slit.

Her throaty voice screamed, "Rhett!" over and over. The sounds of our labored breathing and the slapping of our bodies in perfect synchrony rang in my ears before I released my seed inside her hot pussy.

I grunted aloud, "It will be a cold day in hell before I fuck that Hunter."

*I despise Hunters.*

*Always have, always will.*

Even before that damn Hunter had killed Maggie.

It didn't matter that Nova had no clue about her Hunter bloodline until she stepped into Black Forest.

She had Hunter DNA, which meant it was a matter of time before her sadistic, calculating, bloodthirsty side reared its head. At least that's what I'd convinced myself.

I didn't give a shit that she was my fated mate.

And I damn sure didn't have feelings for her.

My inner jaguar roared with displeasure. *Her scent calls to us. She's ours.*

*It calls to you,* I argued. *Not me.*

*Liar,* my jaguar said.

*Quiet,* I barked.

After years of my inner beast refusing to communicate with me, the grouchy animal had now decided to be social after getting one whiff of Nova's sultry aroma of vanilla, lavender, and citrus with soft floral.

*I will not be quiet,* my animal grumbled. *She's ours.*

My jaguar wanted Nova.

And normally, what he wanted, I wanted, but not this time.

*A Hunter cannot be our fated mate,* I argued.

*She is no Hunter,* my beast countered. *We have faced off and killed many Hunters. She does not act nor smell like any of them.*

*Enough!* I shouted, even though I couldn't refute his statement. Nova wasn't like any of the Hunters I'd encountered.

My inner beast retreated into silence, which was not a good sign of things to come. It was not in my beast's nature to take orders or to remain silent when he wanted something.

Swinging my legs over the edge of my sofa, I stood up, scrubbing my fingers over my face. Glancing around my spacious house, my eyes drifted toward the cardboard boxes scrawled on in broad strokes by a black felt-tip marker. Years of Maggie's personal possessions that I couldn't quite get up the fucking nerve to give away to charity.

Maybe Quinn was right. It was finally time to let her go.

I'd mourned her passing for years, even after I'd avenged her death by killing the Hunter who had slaughtered her.

But revenge hadn't quieted the inner demons within me, nor

had it brought me any closer to solace. And it damn sure hadn't been enough to help me move on with my life.

Years later, I was still standing in a house devoid of life, except for the boxes stuffed with memories of Maggie that I couldn't even bear to let go of. Or maybe I was just a sick fuck who loved to torture myself with the reminder that she was dead because I'd failed at my job as her protector.

*I was her shield.*

*Her protector.*

But I wasn't there for her the one time that she needed me.

I knew Maggie wouldn't have wanted me dwelling in a past that I couldn't change. She'd want me to live in the here and now and find happiness.

Striding upstairs, I ended up inside my bedroom. Except for the California king bed, the room was barren and unadorned, with sterile and dull white walls. The space was missing a woman's touch and vibrancy.

As I stripped off my clothes, my mind drifted to the vexing hybrid Nova and how sexy she would look draped across my bed with her hair spread across my pillows. My cock stiffened, craving the one thing that I'd desired for the longest time.

One woman to spend all my nights with.

My fated mate.

Running my fingers along my jaw, I strode naked to my bathroom. Turning on the shower, I adjusted the temperature to cold before stepping beneath the showerhead, hoping the frigid water would get rid of my aching arousal.

The jets beat against my body, but I was still at half-mast. Soaping myself up, I let my hand linger on my erection. I couldn't go to work in this condition.

I needed to stroke one out for sanity's sake.

Taking myself in my hand, I closed my eyes and tugged my thickness while the icy spray of the shower beat down on me like rain. I continued to rub my flesh. I thought about how Nova's glistening pussy would taste against my tongue as I licked her hard little nub. Her hands would tightly clutch my head against her hot…

My cock got even harder.

"Holy fuck," I muttered, throwing my head back, groaning, as I ejaculated until I had nothing left.

Breathless, I opened my eyes.

*Damn.* If I came that hard from just imagining doing those things to Nova, what would it be like if I touched her for real? I'd be lost.

My inner jaguar growled, *Claim. Mate. Mine.*

*Oh, fuck off. I'm not claiming her,* I snapped back.

My jaguar clawed at the edges of my mind, begging to come out and go find Nova. The struggle made my head pound. It took everything I had to fight the instinctive need tearing up my gut.

My jaguar's obsession with Nova had to stop.

There was no way in hell I was going to claim her.

No matter how much my inner beast wanted her.

Quickly, I washed my body and hair, rinsing away the shampoo and soap. Snatching one of my towels, I dried myself off before walking into my bedroom and then into my large walk-in closet, coming back out with a fresh black T-shirt and a pair of jeans. I pulled on my clothes and boots, then straightened my gold shield buckle that was hooked onto my leather belt.

Leaving my house, I hopped into my cruiser and drove over to Quinn's place. As I walked in the back door that led to the kitchen, my stomach growled loudly from the mouthwatering smell of sizzling steak, eggs, and biscuits that wafted through the air.

I glanced at the small gathering—Quinn, Mack, Emmett, Jasper, and Brody—my pack and band of brothers, assembled in the kitchen.

Even though each team member had his own house, it never failed that command central was always at our alpha's place. Despite the fact that in the Other world, it was uncommon for different species of shifters to form a pack, we were family. It didn't matter that I was a jaguar-shifter, Mack a lion, Emmett a rhino, Jasper a tiger, and Quinn, Imani, Brody, and Piper wolf-shifters. We had one another's backs, and that was all that mattered.

"Where are Imani and Piper?" I asked while pouring a cup of coffee.

"Left for the B and B," Quinn answered searing steaks.

"I'm happy to see you finally got up," Mack said around a mouthful of biscuit.

"Fuck off," I grumbled, leaning against the granite counter-top, gulping my coffee. "I'm not in the mood. I sat in my cruiser all night in front of Bonnie's place."

Mack swallowed his mouthful of food and exclaimed, "You're not the only one who's been working hard. After losing Sam's scent on the skunk-shifters' land, I spent all night chasing down leads on Sam's whereabouts. The fucker is slippery as an eel."

"Mack, cut Rhett some slack," Brody said. "He was probably releasing some stress by jacking off while thinking about that smoking-hot hybrid everyone's been talking about."

I leveled him with a stare. *Damn, the fucker knows me too well.* "Shut the fuck up, Brody." Pushing away from the counter, I slipped into the empty seat beside Emmett.

"Man, you're grouchy. You need to get laid… and fast," Brody countered while sliding a plate heavy with a huge steak, eggs, and biscuits toward me.

Giving Brody a warning stare, I dived into my plate. With this many shifters around, food tended to disappear quickly.

"And?" Jasper asked, not looking up from his cell. "Anything happen?"

I swallowed my mouthful of food. "Nothing," I replied.

Emmett arched a brow. "You sound disappointed about that."

"Shut up," I snapped. "I ain't disappointed. Just suspicious."

"That the town didn't launch an attack on the hybrid?" Brody asked, chewing on a bite of food.

"She's a Hunter, so I expected shenanigans." I guzzled my coffee.

"She's not a Hunter," Quinn said, dropping more steaks onto the platter on the counter. "The information about that already spread through the town's grapevine." He filled his plate and started eating.

I snorted. "You think they care about the difference?"

Jasper examined me with way-too-wise eyes. "They're not stupid, Rhett. Most townsfolk could give two shits about her estranged family."

"I heard she's beautiful," Emmett said, shoveling steak and eggs into his mouth like he hadn't eaten in days.

I stopped midchew, glaring at him. "What's with your hair?" I just noticed that instead of his normal scraggly ponytail, his locks were shiny and flowing around his shoulders like some damn model in a shampoo commercial.

He grinned. "I want to make a good impression when she comes to my repair shop today." He waggled his brows.

"She's not yours!" I shouted, barely stopping my canines from dropping.

"Why do you care?" Brody asked. "Quinn told us that you have no intention of claiming her," he said, tilting his head, studying me.

I gave Quinn an evil glare.

Quinn swallowed his bite of food. "What?" He shrugged. "You said it. So own it."

An uncomfortable sensation settled over me like a scratchy wool sweater.

"Well, since you ain't going to claim her, she's fair game," Emmett said.

"Like I said, she's not yours," I argued.

"And apparently she's not yours either," Quinn said.

Emmett, Mack, Jasper, and Brody nodded in agreement.

My mouth flopped open and then snapped closed. *What the hell?*

I eyed Emmett. "You haven't dated anyone since we came to the Ridge. I thought you're waiting for your mate?"

Emmett shrugged. "I am. I'm not trying to fuck her. But there ain't nothing wrong with being her guy BFF."

My jaguar growled with displeasure. *She's ours. Aren't you going to do something about this nonsense?*

"What the hell does that mean?" I sputtered.

"Everyone knows that I listen well," Emmett explained. "I know how and when to give advice."

I placed my fork on my plate, instantly losing my appetite. "Shouldn't we focus on protecting Nova?"

"We are," Emmett answered. "We're taking shifts protecting her. Hopefully, when she stops by my shop, I can wrangle a dinner invitation for tonight with my new BFF."

I had a feeling he was deliberately trying to provoke me. My fingers clenched around my cup so tight, I thought it would shatter.

"What's wrong with you?" Jasper asked with a smirk while examining me. "You look like you're a volcano about to blow."

They all turned to stare at me.

"Nothing's wrong." I slammed my cup down. "I just think we need to focus on protecting her instead of gossiping about her like girls, that's all."

"Uh-huh," Mack replied, eyeing me suspiciously.

"Whether I claim her or not is none of anyone's business," I fumed. "I'll still do my fucking job protecting her."

"Wowee," Emmett exclaimed. "What flew up your ass this morning?"

Brody nudged Mack with an elbow. "It seems like the sheriff wants to throw his hat into the ring for Nova."

"Yup." Mack leaned back in his chair with steepled fingers.

I scowled. "I'm not claiming her."

"He doth protest too much," Jasper observed.

"Maybe I should give her a call," Brody said. "To find out how she's doing and see if she's interested in crying on my shoulder." Brody gave me a devilish smile.

Jasper and Brody eyed me and laughed.

*Fuckers.*

Quinn's face was grim when he said, "Okay, guys. Enough. Nova will most likely come into Main Square with Bonnie today. So we need to keep sharp and ready to squash any attempts to cause trouble or hurt Nova."

"If they do, I'll throw their ass in jail," I said. "The law is on our side since the council voted to make all hybrids official residents of Black Forest. They're entitled to the same protection rights as all residents."

"Exactly," Quinn said. "I'm not putting up with any shit. The law is clear. A resident who perpetrates an unprovoked attack against another gets thrown in jail. They're entitled to a trial before me and the council, but if found guilty, sentencing is up to me."

"Sure as hell makes our job easier," Mack said.

"Well, I'm out." Emmett stood up. "Don't want to be late for my meeting with Nova." He walked over to the dishwasher, loading in his plate, cup, and utensils and saluting before striding out with a little too much swagger.

My eyes narrowed. "Are those new jeans Emmett's wearing?"

"Yup," Jasper answered. "He's pulling out the big guns for his new BFF."

*Fuck.* There was no way in hell I was going to let that happen. "See you at the station, Mack," I said, getting to my feet and heading out.

# CHAPTER 8
## NOVA

Sultriness lingered in the air as I hustled alongside Bonnie while we headed for her vehicle.

Lifting my hair away from my neck, I complained, "Why is it so hot? It's April."

"The Ridge has its own ecosystem," Bonnie explained. "It does what it wants, when it wants. It can be hot as hell in the morning, then snow like crazy at night."

I hopped inside her SUV, buckling up. "Well, sweat trickling between my breasts is not sexy."

After I had a restful night's sleep and a long, hot shower in the morning, Bonnie convinced me to wear her designer sundress that was so new it still had the price tag on it. Combined with my sneakers, I looked casual yet sexy.

She grinned at me after sliding behind the wheel. "That's why I told you that a dress would be cooler than your T-shirt and jeans." She pulled away from her house.

I took my cell from my handbag. "Still no signal," I grumbled.

"That's because the Ridge has its own private network." Bonnie rattled off the password and her cell number.

"Yes!" I exclaimed. "My cell is back and in effect."

In a cheerful mood, I stared at the scenery while Bonnie blasted music. It didn't take long to arrive at the crest of the long, winding road. From the top of the hill, I could see the town sprawling across the middle of the valley with a body of water surrounding it.

"What is the name of that river?" I asked, pointing over to the mass of water that seemed to extend for miles.

"It's called Bogbeast Lake. It's one of the Ridge's most scenic spots. The mermen-shifters and selkies claim the lake as theirs."

I turned to stare at her. "Mermen and selkies?"

"They're real and not just stuff from legends."

My mouth opened, then shut. "I thought those creatures were folklore. I mean, I've heard about mermaids, but I thought they were all female. And what the heck is a selkie?"

We descended onto a flat road and drove a few more minutes before reaching an area bursting with residents milling about.

"Mermen exist. We have a few that live in this town, but no mermaids," Bonnie said. "Just like most shifter breeds, they're going extinct. And far as selkies, they're seal-shifters. While in the sea, their bottom halves have a seal's tail, but their upper halves remain human."

"Others are fascinating," I exclaimed. "Just the existence of a town with supernatural beings is hard to believe."

Bonnie laughed. "That's the Ridge in a nutshell… fascinating and hard to believe." She continued driving. "This is Main Square. It's the center of activity. Shops and restaurants are here. Most of the townsfolk live inside the forest. There's plenty of land, so we tend to give each other wide berth. Others are finicky about encroaching on another's territory, so houses are spread out throughout the Ridge."

There were no high-rise buildings or streetlights.

"I love the small-town feel," I said while continuing to peer out the open window on my side of the vehicle.

"I do too. I'm fortunate to have the means to live anywhere in the world, and I have over the years—France, Italy, Thailand,

and New York. But I always come back to the Ridge. I grew up here."

The tree-lined street housed multiple shops, including Bessie's Coffee Shop, a posh-looking boutique named Rebellious Rose, a brightly painted storefront with a hanging Nyx's Yoga Studio sign, an herbal apothecary with a hand-painted window that promised Herbs, Oils, Teas, Tinctures, a whole block dedicated to a warehouse storefront named Sinner + Do Artisan Bakery & Smokehouse, and Panthera Onca Fine Art Gallery.

My heart sped up with excitement. "That's your business."

She nodded. "It is."

We drove past a few more businesses, including a tattoo parlor, hardware store, diner, and several bars. My eyes widened when I caught sight of several naked men, yelling and shoving one another by an enormous stone fountain with water cascading over the edges of the shell into the basin. There were four massive carved wolf heads around the pedestal and four shells around the basin that spilled water, creating a spectacular display.

"What's going on?" I asked, pointing to the ongoing scuffle.

She clucked her tongue. "It happens every day like clockwork. It's the otters-versus-the-penguins battle. They're fighting over who gets to swim in the fountain."

"Why don't they just swim in Bogbeast Lake?" I asked.

"The selkies and mermen already called dibs," she explained. "It's a long story."

She kept driving, and we passed more bustling residents wandering in and out of the open shops. Some waved; others stopped in their tracks to gawk at me like I had two heads.

"I guess the word is out that I'm here?" I asked.

"Tongues have been wagging since last night," she replied. "But I wouldn't worry about it. Hybrids are welcomed here."

*But am I? A woman with a Hunter bloodline?*

Not willing to ask that question, instead, I asked, "What's

going on over there?" I pointed toward a large grass clearing with tents, booths, and a large stage.

"Black Forest Ridge Festival starts on Saturday. It will have games, shows, cookouts, parties, and people selling various foods and items. A celebration of unity and peace among residents."

I glanced over at her. "I love festivals. I haven't been to one in a while."

"I was hoping you'd stay." She turned to stare at me briefly before returning her eyes to the road. "For the festival. Quinn and Imani have been planning it for a while." Driving for a bit more, she said, "We're here." And she pulled up in front of an enormous building with an EMMETT'S AUTO SHOP sign on the left and a BANE'S FORGE sign on the right. "Let's go." We hopped out and entered the large garage that looked like converted stables.

A tall tanned burly man with shoulder-length black hair greeted us. "Hey, Bonnie. I've been waiting for you." He wiped his large hand with a black cloth before sticking it out to me for a shake. "I'm Emmett. Nice to meet you, Nova."

*Jesus. Do they only make them tall, masculine, and gorgeous in this town?*

I grabbed his hand. "Hello," I replied.

His fingers lingered around mine a little longer than necessary.

"Emmett, you can let go of her hand now." Rhett's voice boomed from behind me.

Pulling my hand away, I turned around to see Rhett standing inside the shop with his muscles bunching inside his shirt. He was hot—well, hot and scary. He didn't even smile. In fact, he was scowling at me, menace hovering over him like a dark cloud.

"What are you doing here?" I asked, tilting my head, boldly glaring at him.

Emmett arched a brow. "Good question."

Rhett crossed his corded, muscular arms. "What are you talking about, Emmett? I always come here."

"Not this time of day, you don't," Emmett argued, glaring at him.

"Bonnie? Emmett?" a female voice called out. "Where is everyone?" Imani rounded the corner. "Hey, Nova. Bonnie, Emmett." She waved, then grinned at Rhett. "Hey, what are you doing here? Shouldn't you be at the station?"

"Exactly," Emmett said.

"I'm patrolling," Rhett answered.

Imani stared at him. "Patrolling for what?"

"Never mind that," Rhett said. "What are you doing here?"

"I saw Bonnie's SUV outside," Imani said. "And I was hoping Nova was with her so I could take her out to lunch." She smiled at me. "Interested?"

"Sure," I replied. "Let me get my luggage out of my SUV first." Pulling out my car keys from my handbag, I pressed the fob, popping open the back.

"That's a lot of luggage," Imani commented, examining the contents of my trunk.

"Yep, it is," I agreed. "I travel a lot for my job. I'm never in one place for more than a couple of months at most. Everything I own is in my SUV."

Stepping into my space, Emmett offered, "Let me get your luggage for you."

I gave him a slight smile. "Thank you, but—"

"I got it," Rhett declared, nudging Emmett aside.

Emmett and Rhett rushed to grab the same piece of luggage. "Let go," they hissed in unison.

"This is better than reality television," Bonnie mused, watching as the two men tussled over my luggage.

Rhett finally managed to tug my baggage away from Emmett. "Piss off," he growled.

Seeing enough of their ridiculous battle over my luggage, I

flung out my arms, pushing them apart. "Hey, there's enough luggage for both of you."

"This is between us," Emmett fumed, gently edging me aside.

I threw my arms in the air. "Whatever."

My eyes widened as they started pulling out my baggage in some weird race to see who could take out the most luggage the fastest.

Imani shook her head. "It's a shifter standoff."

Bonnie laughed. "I guess they're showing Nova's luggage who's boss."

"I don't know what's going on between them, and frankly, I don't care," I declared before walking over to the passenger's side, opening the door.

My skin tingled with discomfort as I peered into my vehicle. "What the hell?"

My backpack had been tossed onto my driver's seat with all the compartments unzipped. My laptop, camera, and tablet that I'd stowed inside the pack were on the floor on the passenger's side. Reaching for my backpack, I noticed the small pocket where I'd put my pendant was also unzipped. I stuck my fingers inside. It was empty. "My pendant is gone." Tears of anger welled in my eyes as I tried to process the fact that someone had stolen my jewelry.

"What pendant?" Rhett's voice boomed directly behind me.

Startled, I nearly banged the top of my head against the roof of my SUV. Looking over my shoulder at him, I snapped, "Will you stop sneaking up on me?"

"I'm not sneaking around," he countered.

Emmett, Imani, and Bonnie joined us at my passenger's side to see what was happening.

"What's going on?" Emmett asked.

"Someone rifled through my stuff," I said.

Rhett frowned. "Emmett, did you see anything strange when you picked up her vehicle?"

"No," Emmett replied, rubbing his chin. "There was no one around when I picked up her SUV. I did notice that her front windows were down, but I didn't pay that no never mind because it was parked on a deserted stretch of road."

"What about strange scents?" Rhett pressed.

"No, Rhett," he barked. "If there was something off, I would have said so."

"Calm down," Bonnie demanded. "What else is missing?" she asked me.

I shoved my tablet, camera, and laptop back inside my bag. "Just a black diamond-encrusted jaguar pendant that my father put inside his letter." I fought back angry tears. It was the only thing I had from my father, and now it was gone. "I was planning on getting a chain so that I could wear it as a necklace. I put it inside my backpack so that I wouldn't lose it. Why would anyone take my pendant and leave my tablet, camera, and a laptop?"

"Step aside please," Rhett requested.

I did as told, watching him lean inside the vehicle. "Sam," he exclaimed, then eased out of the vehicle. "His scent is inside your car."

"Who's Sam?" I asked.

Rhett's expression was thunderous. "A troublemaking wolf-shifter that I'm going to skin alive."

Bonnie cracked her knuckles. "Not if I catch him first."

"This shit has to stop, Rhett," Imani demanded. "Now he's stealing. What's next?"

"My pendant is a gift from my father," I reiterated. "I want it back, but Sam the thief probably pawned it. Are there any pawn shops in town?"

Emmett shook his head. "Shifters don't steal things for money. They take them because they can. The more sentimental, the better."

Anger coursed through my veins. "My pendant is his trophy? Why? He doesn't even know me."

"To make a long story short," Imani started, "he hates hybrids."

"Let me see your backpack," Rhett demanded.

I handed it over and watched him sniff it loudly. "Yep. Sam. His grimy fingers were all over your backpack." He eyed me. "Your backpack is evidence now, but everything inside, I'll make sure you get back."

I shrugged. "That's fine. Do you need me to file a report?"

"No, I'll take it from here."

Imani looped her arm through mine. "Let Rhett handle it. Let's go. I think you need a strong drink along with your lunch." She dragged me away.

"See you later, darling," Bonnie said. "I'll make sure your luggage gets to my home."

# CHAPTER 9
## NOVA

When we got outside, my body was still vibrating with anger.

"That asshole," I spat out.

"Don't worry about Sam," Imani said. "Rhett will find him and make him pay."

I took a deep, calming breath. She was right. I needed to calm down. Working myself into a froth over my pendant wasn't going to make it magically reappear.

"I do need a strong drink and good food," I said.

"Well, follow me," Imani replied.

"Yoo-hoo!" a blond woman shouted from across the street while waving frantically. "Imani."

Imani rolled her eyes. "Oh God. It's Josie." She glanced at me. "Gird your loins."

Josie swayed across the street with blond hair blowing in the wind. "Hello, Imani." Her smile was wide and plastic-looking.

"Hello, Josie." Imani wrapped her arm through mine. "Don't be rude. Say hello to Nova, Bonnie's granddaughter."

"Hello." Josie scrunched up her nose with obvious displeasure.

Not giving a shit that she didn't like me, I said, "Hey."

"Anyway," she said to Imani. "Have you given any thought

to my idea of serving your B and B guests my delicious biscuits?"

"Delicious?" The look on Imani's face was something close to disgust. "Your biscuits are dry and tasteless."

Josie's expression turned thunderous. "My biscuits are the best in this town."

"I disagree," Imani replied. "That's why Piper and I have decided to hold a baking competition. The winner will be given a monetary prize, a rent-free storefront, and a contract as the sole vendor providing baked goods to our B and B."

"What?" Josie yelled. "Why do you need a baking competition when I make the best biscuits in town?"

"Obviously, you don't," I chirped.

Josie gave me the evil eye. "Mind your business, Hunter."

"I'm just pointing out facts." I smirked, not the least perturbed by her Hunter jab.

Josie gave me one of those "Why are you still talking?" stares. Imani snickered. I nudged Imani with my elbow.

Imani cleared her throat. "You don't have a monopoly on biscuits, Josie. As the town alpha female, I have to be fair and give everyone a shot at making money. Now if you don't mind, we have to go." She dragged me away, leaving Josie fuming on the sidewalk.

"What's her deal?" I asked Imani.

"She's an owl-shifter who's territorial about everything, including her biscuits and Rhett."

My stomach churned with displeasure. "Are they dating?"

"No. But she's been angling for him to pull his cruiser up to her bumper." She stopped and stuck out her ass with exaggeration.

"He could like them blond and crazy." For some reason, I hoped he didn't.

"Ooh, I know that look," Imani said. "You like Rhett."

I sputtered. "I do not like Sheriff Stick-Up-His-Ass."

Imani arched a brow. "What's wrong with Rhett?"

"Everything! He's domineering, arrogant, and rude."

"So you don't find him attractive?"

I eyed her as if she were crazy. "I'm not blind. Of course I find him attractive."

"You ain't saying something I don't already know."

I glanced at her with surprise.

"Everyone in the damn office smelled the undercurrents of your mutual attraction last night."

I snorted. "Don't know how you smelled that when his anger and distaste for what I am were clearly evident." Which, frankly, hurt a little, given our flirtatious banter prior to him finding out I had a Hunter bloodline.

"Welcome to the club. Rhett took a while to warm up to me when I first got to the Ridge. But now he'd give up his life for me, and I'd do the same for him. Put it this way—you have to look past Rhett's abrasiveness to see his caring and nurturing side."

My eyes widened. "Caring and nurturing side? Every time he opens his foul mouth, he inserts his foot. Rhett doesn't like what I am. He's made that abundantly clear every opportunity he could."

"That's because he's scared and confused."

"About what?" I replied.

"What he feels for you."

I arched a brow.

Imani continued. "He's attracted to you, but you represent something he's spent a lifetime hating… Hunters. As he said last night, Hunters killed his sister, so he has a hell of a lot of anger and guilt about her death. It's been years, but he hasn't worked through his feelings."

"I understand loss," I said but it didn't mean that being an asshole to me was acceptable. "My mother died from a heart attack."

"I'm sorry for your loss, Nova."

"Thank you."

Even though Mom and I didn't have the best or closest relationship, I'd mourned her passing. At times, I'd felt anger and guilt over the fact that we'd rarely talked since I'd left for college. Part of me would always wonder if, had I tried to mend fences with her prior to her death, maybe we both could have gotten closure.

As we continued walking, I carried on. "I'm intimately aware of all the complicated emotions that come with a deceased loved one. But I refuse to be held accountable for the sins of my Hunter family. I'm not like them. I don't have a prejudiced bone in my body. Hell, I'm a Black woman who knows personally how destructive racist people can be."

Imani nodded. "As a Black woman too, I can tell you you're preaching to the choir. But thank goodness shifters don't give a shit about the color of anyone's skin."

"So they're just prejudiced against hybrids and Hunters?" I spat. "Prejudice is prejudice, Imani."

"You're right, Nova. But not everyone in the Ridge is antihybrid or will hold your bloodline against you."

Across the street, a very pregnant woman—whom I recognized from last night—stepped out of the police station, propping the door open. "Hi, Imani. Hi, Nova," she called out, adding a cheerful wave.

We both waved back and stopped.

"Hi, Heidi," Imani said. "You going to the festival on Saturday?"

"Wouldn't miss it for the world." She rubbed her belly. "But my mate is worried about me being overdue."

The midwife in me instantly rose to the surface. "How overdue?"

"We're guessing two weeks."

I frowned, not liking the fact that she was guessing about something so important. "Make sure you check in with your doctor. But it's normal to give birth before or after your due date. In fact, your pregnancy should continue two weeks past your due date to earn the official label of post-term pregnancy."

"You sure know a lot about pregnancy." She rubbed her stomach in circles. "Are you a doctor or something?"

"I'm a certified nurse midwife."

She grinned. "We sure need one of those in the Ridge." She swung her head toward the station. "Oh, that's the phone. I better go answer it. See you two at the festival." Given her condition, I was surprised at how fast she disappeared into the station.

Imani urged me along, and it didn't take long for us to arrive at our destination.

She grinned at me before opening a nondescript black door. "This is where we're meeting my bestie Nyx for lunch. Sinner + Do Smokehouse is a farm-to-table restaurant with the most delicious food in town. Next to mine of course."

Crossing the threshold, I scanned the large open space with couches and tables on both sides leading up to a bar along the wall.

"This sure isn't small-town dining," I remarked, panning my eyes across the area, stopping on the large plush U-shaped communal couch anchoring the space. "It has a swanky, big-city vibe."

"There's more than meets the eye in the Ridge. We have a little bit of everything here, from small-town feel to upscale, doing-it-like-a-baller vibe."

A monstrous man swooped out of nowhere, looking like Thor except with black hair. "Hello, Imani," he said with a thick Irish accent.

"Hi, Donovan." She reached up to hug him, then stepped back. "When did you get back in town?"

"This morning," he replied, but his eyes were glued to me like I was a tasty steak he wanted to gobble up.

A voluptuous brunette wearing skintight leather leggings and a red corset that pushed up her ample cleavage approached us with a huge smile. "Scoot, Donovan. Greeting guests is my job."

"Hi, Odessa," Imani said. "Donovan. Odessa. This is Nova."

"Hello, Nova," Odessa said. "Welcome to the Ridge."

"Aren't you a beauty?" Donovan remarked with eyes locked on mine. "I've heard a lot about you."

"Good or bad?" I grinned.

"I tend to ignore the bad shit." He winked.

Odessa rolled her eyes. "My brother is a horrible flirt. Go away, Donovan." She pushed him, but he didn't budge. "Okay. Then we'll go." She gestured to Imani and me. "Follow me."

When we trailed behind Odessa, I whispered to Imani, "Seriously, what's in the Ridge water? Why are all the men smoking hot?"

Imani laughed. "You ain't seen anything yet. Wait until you go to the festival. There will be man candy galore, and all of them will be flirting outrageously with you."

Odessa stopped at a booth where a woman with dark skin and short, natural hair sat. "Your server will be here shortly." She winked at us. "Enjoy." Then she walked away.

"Hi, Nyx," Imani said, sliding into the booth. "This is Nova."

Nyx waved at me. "Hey, Nova."

"Hi," I said, taking a seat, sandwiching her between Imani and me.

A server rushed over to our table, filling our glasses with water.

"What took you so long?" Nyx complained. "I'm starving."

"Josie accosted me about her biscuits… again." Imani took a gulp from her glass.

Nyx rolled her eyes. "Her biscuits, aka hockey pucks, are terrible."

"Ain't that the truth. But she keeps trying to peddle them like drugs. Hell, Rhett and I can make better biscuits than her with our eyes closed, but I'd like to spread the wealth. We need new businesses here. It's not fair for the established businesses like

Josie's to monopolize all the economic opportunities in this town. That's why Piper and I decided to hold the baking competition."

The server came over and asked, "Would you like to order today's special? It's family-style roasted pig head, served on a platter with tortillas, salsa, and other taco condiments."

"I'm game," I answered. "If you two are."

"Sounds delicious," Imani said.

"And what would you like to drink?" the server inquired.

"I'll have a Moscow Mule," I said.

"Oh, that sounds great. I'll have the same," Imani added.

"Make that three," Nyx said.

The server roamed away.

"Anyhoo," Imani said. "Let's move on to more entertaining matters." She grinned at me, then Nyx. "There was some man drama between Rhett and Emmett involving lots of luggage."

"Ooh, pack drama." Nyx rubbed her palms together. "Spill."

I chuckled. "It's not that interesting. Just a lot of grunting, shoving, and posturing. I'm still not sure what the testosterone-fueled standoff between Rhett and Emmett was about."

"They were fighting about who gets to court Nova," Imani told Nyx.

I choked on my sip of water. "Is that what they were doing?"

"Uh-huh," Imani answered while sipping her own water.

"Wow!" Nyx waggled her brows at me. "Not one but two alpha shifters vying to court you."

"Court me?" I declared. "There's no courting happening. I'm out of here on Sunday."

Nyx frowned. "But what about Rhett? Bonnie told my mom that she thinks Rhett likes you."

I frowned. "Likes me? He's always snarling, snapping, and scowling at me. And like I told Imani, Rhett's pointed out several times that he hates Hunters."

The server arrived with our Moscow Mules served in copper mugs and placed them in front of us.

Imani took a sip of her drink before saying, "Like I said, Rhett is just grumpy, so I wouldn't take it personally. He's a great guy once he gets to know you. He just takes his job as Protector of the Ridge seriously. That's why I know he'll take care of your Sam issue."

"What Sam issue?" Nyx asked while drinking her mule.

"Sam broke into Nova's SUV and stole her pendant."

"Now he's stealing?" Nyx scrunched up her nose. "I swear, that fucker needs to be put out of his misery."

I put my napkin in my lap. "What's wrong with him?"

"Too many issues to count," Nyx said.

"When I first came to the Ridge, he tried to attack me," Imani said to me. "The fucker chased me all the way to Quinn's house. But the upside to that terrifying event was that's how I met my fated mate, Quinn."

"He also stirred up a shitload of trouble because Imani's a hybrid," Nyx interjected. "He tried to get the town to rally around him with torches and pitchforks, but the council voted to let Imani stay. Sam's a selfish bastard. Everyone in the Ridge knows that without Freya's mating spell, unmated males in this town will never find their fated mate and get their happily-ever-after."

I gave her the side-eye. *Happily-ever-after?* I'd stopped believing in that shit when I turned forty.

"That's why I'm so relieved the council voted to make hybrids official residents of Black Forest," Imani stated. "Nova, you're welcome here for as long as you want to stay. Don't let anyone convince you otherwise."

Nyx nodded. "Agreed. Pay no attention to any bullshit anyone gives you about having Hunter blood. Especially when we have bigger issues to worry about, like the lack of mates for our unmated males."

"Bonnie told me about the feral situation." I took a sip of my mule, enjoying the flavors of fiery ginger beer, vodka, and fresh lime.

"It's a fucked-up predicament," Imani stated. "I'm hoping the spell brings more fated mates."

"That's the plan," Nyx said, tapping her copper mug against mine, then Imani's.

"I'm not staying in the Ridge, y'all."

The server arrived, placing a huge silver platter onto the table. "Enjoy," he said, then walked away.

My eyes widened at the sight of the roasted pig head on the platter with tortillas and condiments in small glass jars.

"What do you mean, you're not staying?" Imani asked, taking a fork and filling her tortilla with all the fixings. Nyx and I followed suit.

Between chews, I said, "I'm renewing my contract for another year in Africa. Midwives are in short supply."

"Black Forest needs you," Imani said. "And so does your mate. Rhett."

I nearly choked. "What are you talking about?"

"Okay." Imani sighed heavily. "I didn't want to tell you because, well, it's really not my place. But Rhett's your fated mate."

My eyes widened. "But how do you know?"

"Your scent," she replied. "A shifter knows his or her fated mate by their distinctive, alluring scent that calls to them like no other."

My stomach flip-flopped. "But he doesn't like me."

"Not true," Imani countered.

"I beg to differ with you," I argued. "Anyway, I'm not giving up my life for a town that hates what I am."

Nyx and Imani eyed each other silently.

I stopped chewing and asked, "What?"

"I felt the same way when I arrived in the Ridge and found out what I am." Imani spread her arms wide. "But here I am. Not only am I the part owner of a B and B, I'm working in the career that I adore, and I found the love of my life."

Nyx took another chug from her mug. "You see, having love and a career are not mutually exclusive."

"Exactly," Imani chimed in. "The Ridge is in desperate need of a midwife, and Rhett needs his fated mate… you."

Nyx nodded. "That's a win-win situation, if you ask me."

I frowned. "And what about what I need?"

"It's apparent that your career is important to you," Imani said. "You can have that easily here." She popped a morsel of pork into her mouth. "The question remains, do you want a good man in your life?"

"Good man?" I asked. "Is there such a thing?"

"In this town," Nyx replied, "plenty… like Rhett."

I snorted.

"When Quinn and I met, we argued, pushed each other away even when we knew that we belonged together."

Nyx shook her head. "I don't know why fated mates waste so much time fighting the inevitable, but they do."

Imani answered, "Maybe it's to see how much bullshit both the man and woman can take before realizing they belong together."

I loaded up another tortilla. "That sounds like more drama than I'm up for. Honestly, y'all, I'm not interested in Rhett." I took a bite of the succulent pork. "Or being his fated mate."

"Famous last words," Nyx said. "Until the mating heat starts."

"Ain't that the truth," Imani agreed.

I choked on my mouthful of food. "Mating heat?"

Imani and Nyx slapped my back.

"You okay?" they both asked while I chugged water.

"Yes," I replied. "Go on about the mating heat."

"It's when a female becomes highly sexually receptive to her mate," Imani answered. "Signaling him she's ready for mating."

"Basically, the couple has sex until the heat haze goes away." Nyx waggled her eyebrows. "Imani says it's exhausting but very satisfying."

Imani grinned. "Sure is."

"So you fuck until one of you taps out?"

Nyx and Imani laughed.

"Nova, it's not just about sex," Nyx said. "Even though shifters love to fuck."

"We do," Imani chimed in with a waggle of her eyebrows. "A lot. It's been over two years since Quinn and I were mated, and we're still going at it like rabbits. And when I'm in heat, we go at it nonstop for days."

"Days?" I squeaked.

"Typically," Imani said. "But it depends on the female."

I rubbed my forehead. "Sounds like sex aerobics."

"But according to Imani, it's a lot more fun," Nyx chirped.

The two women nodded with lips curled up into smiles.

I burst out laughing. "This is crazy."

"But true," Nyx said before taking a drink. "But before the heating game begins, both shifters have to recognize each other as mates."

I wiped my mouth with my napkin. "And how does that happen?"

"Shifters recognize their mates by scent and attraction," Nyx informed me.

My eyebrows rose. "Instantly?"

"Unfortunately, no," Imani said. "It took a while for my inner animal to wake up and choose Quinn."

I swallowed my mouthful of food. "And what happened when your animal awoke?"

"My eyes turned amber, and so did his. That is nature's sign that the mating is true. After that, the fireworks began." She waggled her brows. "Mating heat. During sex with your mate, his incisors will drop, and he'll bite you on the spot between your neck and shoulder. It's called the mating bite."

*Mating bite?* I choked on my drink mid gulp. Nyx patted my back.

"The mark shows other males that he's claimed his female,"

Imani stated. "That she's his to love, protect, and keep happy for the rest of her life. The mark seals the mating bond. And for hybrids, the bite can speed up the process of them shifting into their true animal form. The female also reciprocates and marks her male during the mating ceremony."

"What's that?" I asked.

"It's a Black Forest tradition. After the mating bite, you're not fully mated until your union is witnessed at a mating ceremony. Freya conducts this ceremony, and she asks Luna, the moon goddess, whether the mating between the couple is true. The goddess must approve of the mating."

"It's Others' version of a wedding," Nyx said, chomping on her tortilla. "Except instead of rings being exchanged, bites are exchanged."

"But what if this goddess disapproves of the mating?" I asked.

Nyx pursed her lips. "I've never heard of that happening, but that's a good question."

"Anyway," Imani interrupted. "My mating ceremony was in front of the town. But that's because Quinn's town alpha. Yours can be small and intimate with friends and family."

I didn't bother telling her there would be no ceremony because I wasn't going to mate Rhett.

"But the getting naked in the forest and having freaky, naughty sex is not optional," Nyx added. "That's a must."

"Sex in the forest?" I remarked over a mouthful of food. "Not happening."

"I said the same thing," Imani said. "But I did it. It's amazing the things you'll do for your soul mate."

"No to finding a mate." I glared at them. "No to the mating heat. And a hell no to the mating ceremony."

Imani peered over at Nyx. "She's in denial."

"This going to be fun...," Nyx said in a singsong voice.

"Let the mating games begin," they said in unison while clinking their mugs together.

# CHAPTER 10
## NOVA

Hours later, after lunch and Imani dropping me back over at Bonnie's house, I jolted awake from my nap at the sound of an eerie shriek.

My heart raced as I scrambled into a sitting position. "What the hell?" Pressing my back against the upholstered headboard, I tried to clear my sleep-fogged brain.

With trembling fingers, I pushed my tangled hair off my forehead and screamed when I spotted the large furry animal with brown, white, gray, and black markings perched at the end of my bed.

"Holy shit!"

It was a gigantic owl with large tufts of feathers on its head that looked like horns. Its big catlike yellow eyes were locked on me.

My heart raced faster. I had been terrified of birds ever since I was ten and had a scary incident at the Bronx Zoo involving a flock of pigeons that attacked me for my salted soft pretzel. After that debacle, I had to wear an eye patch for a week.

Blinking rapidly, I tried not to make any sudden movements. But all bets were off when the gigantic owl snapped its beak before muttering "hoo-hoo-hoo-hoo" in a series of hoots.

"Oh hell no!" Rolling over the edge of the bed, I flopped onto the floor, faceup, with a painful thud. I screamed at the top of my lungs at the sight of the gigantic owl with a wing-span that looked to be over four feet flying around the bedroom.

"Oh God," I pleaded while yanking at the tangled sheets. "Please don't let this be a death-by-owl situation." Finally getting free from my cocoon of cotton sheets, I got flat onto my stomach and low-crawled—hugging the floor as close as possible—until I made it into the hallway.

The owl was still inside the bedroom when I stood on shaky legs, hightailing it down the stairs, somehow managing not to break my neck in my haste to get away from the killer owl.

I breathed out a sigh when my bare feet hit the landing. "I made... Ouch," I finished when I felt a sharp tug on the hair at the back of my head. Glancing over my shoulder, I screamed when I saw the owl had my hair in its talons.

"Shoo!" I yelled, swinging around and punching it. The owl shrieked and released its grip on me.

"Nova!" someone shouted while banging on the front door.

The owl rose higher into the air above me and then dived for another attack.

Outside, someone banged and rattled the front door. The owl hooted and flew back upstairs. The door slammed open, sending shards of wood everywhere. Rhett charged inside with sharp and dangerous canines lengthened past his lip.

"An owl attacked me," I blubbered as my legs buckled. Rhett caught me before I crashed to the floor.

His canines retracted before he asked, "What did it look like?"

"Big catlike eyes. Large tufts of feathers on its head that looked like horns."

"That's a damn great horned owl," he roared so loud that I felt it in my bones. "Wait here," he demanded before taking the stairs two at a time. I heard footsteps above, then silence.

Nervously, I shifted from one foot to the other. Then I heard footsteps again, and Rhett came thumping down the stairs.

He walked up to me, wrapping his arms around me. "You okay?"

Breathing hard, I held on to him like a life preserver. "Yes."

Releasing me, he stepped back, examining me. "No injuries. That's good. Tell me what happened."

"I was sleeping and heard this loud noise. When I awoke, it was that…" I swallowed hard. "Damn creepy owl sitting on my bed, just staring at me with yellow eyes." I shuddered. "Why would an owl want to attack me?"

His eyes tightened. "That owl was Josie. She's a great horned owl-shifter, and I scented her all over the bedroom."

I gaped at him. "The psycho biscuit lady?"

"Yes."

Now I was pissed. When I saw her ass again, I was going to cunt punt her across Main Square.

"Why the hell would she want to attack me? I don't even know the bitch."

"I suspect it's because of me." He scowled.

Utterly mystified, I stared at him. "Why?"

"There's a rumor going around town that I like you."

"Is that true?"

"You're not bad," he said simply.

"Not bad?" I pursed my lips. "What the hell does that mean?"

"Irrelevant right now, don't you think? Especially when we have bigger fish to fry with this whole Josie attack."

With an aggrieved sigh, I said, "I guess so." Then I eyed him suspiciously. "What are you doing here anyway?" Not that I wasn't grateful for his presence, just curious.

"I dropped by the gallery to check on you, but Bonnie said Imani dropped you off here at the house after lunch. I called you several times just to make sure you were all right, but when you didn't answer, I got worried. So I drove over here." His stoic expression turned grim. "Why the hell didn't you answer your cell?" He lifted an eyebrow and waited.

I glared up at him, but my resolve faltered beneath his steady, authoritative stare.

"When Imani dropped me here after lunch, I crawled into bed to take a quick nap before Bonnie came home. I just didn't realize how tired I was until my head hit the pillow." I shrugged. "I'm a sound sleeper when I'm exhausted."

He glowered. "You're in a town with shifters that might want to hurt you because of your Hunter bloodline, and that's your answer?"

"Yes." I sensed his anger simmering just below the surface. "Why are you so angry, Rhett?"

"Because when I drove up to the house, I heard your blood-curdling screams." He paused as if trying to calm down. "I thought you were being killed." He clenched his fists. "Why didn't you stay with Bonnie instead of telling Imani to drop you here?"

"Because I'm not a baby, Rhett," I said between clenched teeth. "I don't want Bonnie putting her life on hold to babysit me."

"It's called protecting you, Nova," he bit the words out, tight-lipped.

"I'm not stupid or reckless. Once I got inside, I made sure all the doors were locked."

He folded his arms across his chest. "Yet, Josie somehow slipped inside."

I finally threw my arms up in the air in exasperation. "I don't know how she did it. How about you go ask your psycho girlfriend how she broke into Bonnie's house?"

"First, she's not my girlfriend. Never was. Never will be. Second, if I hadn't arrived when I did, Josie could have killed you."

"Injure me, yes," I admitted. "Kill me, no. She's an owl."

"Don't let Josie's shifter size fool you. Great horned owls

have strong, lethal talons that can pierce organs. They strike so hard that even larger animals are helpless before they know what hit them."

*Is that why Josie grabbed my hair?*

*Was she trying to gouge the back of my head?*

I shuddered at the thought of the extensive damage she could have done if she'd accomplished her sinister goal.

I rubbed the goose pimples on my arms, and that was when I realized that I was standing in front of the sheriff with bare feet and in my underwear.

"Oh, for fuck's sake," I hissed. "I'm practically naked."

"I don't mind." His eyes raked over me from head to toe, making my skin tingle as though he'd stroked me. I watched him with apprehension, not comfortable with my physical response to him.

"I bet you don't," I replied. "For the record, my ass is not for your amusement."

He winked at me. "Your ass is beautiful, not amusing."

I pointed at him. "Keep your eyes off my ass, shifter."

He laughed. "I'm not making any promises." He tugged off his T-shirt, handing it to me. "Here."

"Thank you," I grumbled.

When I put on his shirt, my heart rate sped up. I closed my eyes briefly, breathing deeply his wonderful, captivating scent. Sandalwood. Pastries. Coffee. It was as if his scent were reaching out, pulling me to him.

"Nova?" His voice snapped me out of my internal musing. "Are you okay?" He reached over, taking my hand in his and touched his lips to it. I stiffened at the jolt of heat that raced through me. Tightening my thighs, I fought against the need to climb him like a tree.

I yanked my hand away. "Ummm." I heard my voice croak. "I have to make a call," I blurted out. "To Bonnie. You know, to tell her what happened."

"I already texted her and Quinn while I was upstairs and

briefed them both about what happened." His eyes were like lasers aimed at me. "She wanted to cut her meeting short, heading home, but I told her I'd stay with you until she got back." His nostrils flared as he breathed deeply. "Your scent has changed."

Struggling to breathe normally while my heart nearly pounded out of my chest, I replied, "Are you saying that I stink?"

"Quite the opposite." A low growl sounded deep in his throat. He reached over and brushed his hand down my back. My body tingled with awareness and my nipples throbbed.

He growled again. My insides fluttered, and I became hotter, needy for him.

*He's ours,* a female voice inside my head declared.

*What the hell?*

*Am I going crazy?*

I stepped back so fast that I tripped over my feet. Lightning fast, Rhett caught me. Heat raced up my arm, and I gasped and attempted to pull away, but his other hand closed over my other arm.

*You're not crazy,* the voice replied. *I'm your other side. Your inner animal. And this male is our fated mate.*

My heart pounded faster, and my breath quickened.

*This can't be happening.*

*It's true? Rhett's my mate?*

*Tell him,* the voice demanded.

*No!* I snapped.

*Why?*

*Because you're wrong. Rhett will never accept me because of my Hunter bloodline.*

*He will,* my animal replied. *And I am never wrong.*

# CHAPTER 11
## RHETT

Nova shoved at my chest. I took a few steps back, even as the savage need to take her raced through me.

Nova's scent had transformed into a captivating fragrance that nearly brought me to my knees. I knew with every ounce of my being that her delicious, sweet smell was calling to me.

My cock stirred and stiffened, straining against my jeans.

My mouth watered with the need to taste Nova.

All of her.

Every inch.

Her fragrance called to me, trying its damnedest to link us together. I was scenting her animal. Her jaguar was awake.

*Mine. Claim. Mine,* my inner beast demanded.

*Shut up, beast,* I groused. There was no way in hell I was claiming a Hunter.

"You should go." She bit the words out, tight-lipped.

I released her. "That's not happening."

She licked her bottom lip. The gesture made me tremble with the urge to nibble it.

"Why?" She pinned me with a glare. "This time I swear to double-check the doors and windows."

"No." I tightened my hands into fists as I fought the overwhelming urge to strip her naked, exploring every inch of her.

"Maybe if I left the Ridge," she murmured, "it will solve everything."

I ruthlessly swallowed a growl before it could erupt. "Solve what?"

"Shit!" Her eyes widened. "I didn't mean to say that aloud."

"Are you talking to your jaguar?" My eyes narrowed, waiting for her to tell me the truth.

Her lips parted, then closed, then parted again. "That's none of your business."

"So that's a yes." I reached out, grazing the side of her cheek with the back of my hand. "Talk to me, Nova. Tell me what's going on."

"I… ugh." She threw her arms in the air. "Okay, fuck it." She started pacing back and forth. "I might be suffering from a delusional disorder brought on by the owl-shifter attack. That has to be the problem, because hearing a voice in my head cannot be real unless I'm losing my shit."

She slapped her hand against her chest. "Oh God. My heart is racing so fast that I'm feeling light-headed." She stopped in her tracks, peering over at me with panicked eyes. "Is this normal?" Her breathing became loud and heavy. "Oh God. My skin feels tingly." She held out her arms in front of her, examining them as if they were foreign objects. "Am I shifting right now?"

I blinked, trying to tamp down my beast clawing its way to the surface to soothe her.

"Nova, you are not shifting."

She ignored me and mumbled, "My muscle just twitched."

She jumped when I settled my hands on her shoulders. "No. It didn't."

She glared at me. "How would you know anyway?"

"Because I'm a shifter."

She rolled her eyes heavenward. "You don't know shit."

"Nova, take a deep breath. Calm your mind."

"What makes you think I'm not calm?"

"Because your eyes are dilated like you've just seen Bigfoot." I paused. "And I can hear your heart beating faster and breath quickening. Your body is preparing to fight or flee a threat by boosting adrenaline production."

Her hands were trembling. "How about you mind your business and turn down the volume on your shifter hearing?"

"It doesn't work like that, Nova." Closing one hand over hers, I held her trembling one cupped between us. She struggled against my firm but gentle grip. "Talk to me."

I could hear her heart pounding faster, but she stopped fighting my grip. "My animal is talking to me, and it's freaking me out."

"And what is your animal saying?" I asked.

Nova scrunched up her nose. "She thinks you're my fated mate."

"That's what I suspected. I can smell you. Correction, I could always smell you, but now your scent has changed."

She blinked rapidly. "Changed into what?"

"Into a scent that makes my mouth water with the need to know what every inch of your skin tastes like." My nostrils flared as the scent of her arousal reached me. I fought the need to bury my face between her thighs and taste her sweet nectar. "But we both know that our mating would be a fucking disaster," I said, still determined to deny with every ounce of my being that she was my fated mate.

"You're damn right," she snapped. "Besides, Imani and Nyx told me that our eyes are supposed to turn amber. Yours are still blue. Have mine changed?" She squared her shoulders and took a deep breath as if waiting for bad news.

"No."

Her shoulders sagged with obvious relief. "Good. You're not my mate."

*What the fuck!*

I frowned. "You don't have to look so relieved about the possibility of me not being your mate."

She snatched her hand away. "Why not?" She glared at me. "You've made it abundantly clear, several times, that you hate me because of my Hunter bloodline."

I rolled my shoulders to relieve the tension. "I don't hate you. Never have. Never will. I—"

She cut me off. "It doesn't matter. No amber eyes. No mate match. My animal is wrong, so…"

"Nova!" Bonnie's voice bellowed from outside the house before pushing at the broken door that was barely hanging on to its hinges.

Nova sidestepped me and moved toward Bonnie.

"Are you okay?" Bonnie asked, pulling her in for a brief hug.

Nova nodded. "Yes. Josie didn't complete her 'claw the Hunter to death' mission."

I winced when Bonnie leveled me with a *What the fuck!* glare. "Why did she attack my granddaughter?"

I crossed my arms, widening my stance. I didn't like her accusatory stare. "I don't know, but I intend to find out."

"And you best believe that I'm pressing charges," Nova said.

"I can't arrest her, Nova," I replied. "According to Others law, you're presumed innocent until proven guilty."

"Innocent?" Nova's lips pressed into a thin line, and then she said, "She attacked me in my bedroom. Are you calling me a liar, Sheriff?"

Nova stared at me like she was seeing me for the first time and didn't like what she saw.

"Don't go twisting my words," I clipped out. "All I'm saying is that according to Others law, I can't arrest Josie for attacking you without evidence and/or a witness to the crime."

"He's right, Nova. If he arrests her without proof, that would set off a powder keg of trouble we don't want."

"Exactly," I replied. "The owl-shifters would accuse my pack of breaking Others law, and they would be right, because the law is clear."

"Oh, I see." Nova's eyes narrowed and her nostrils flared. "I'm a Hunter, so my word doesn't count in this town."

Bonnie patted her arm. "We just have to work harder to convince the residents that you mean no harm."

Nova snatched her arm away and glared at Bonnie. "Convince them that I mean no harm? Are you fucking kidding me?"

"Calm down, Nova," Bonnie soothed.

"I will not calm down." She made air quotes. "I'm the victim here."

Bonnie's fists clenched. "All I'm saying—"

Nova cut her off. "I'm not interested in hearing what you meant, Bonnie," she retorted. "Once my car is fixed, I'm out of here."

"Nova, Others law—" I started to explain.

"Fuck your law!" she shouted before storming up to me.

The hurt that I saw shining in her eyes made my stomach plummet.

She tugged off my T-shirt and threw it in my face. The garment landed at my feet.

"Go fuck yourself, Sheriff Stick-Up-Your-Ass." She bit the words out from between tight lips before stalking away and up the stairs.

"We messed that up big-time," Bonnie murmured.

"Our hands are tied." I ran my fingers through my hair. "This is a damned-if-I-do-and-damned-if-I-don't situation." Which was why being the town's Protector wasn't an easy job. "If I arrest Josie, it would spark a war within the Ridge. Everyone is already whispering about Nova being a Hunter. Do you really think they'll take Nova's side against Josie's?"

"I know whose side they'll take, Rhett, but it doesn't make it right."

"It makes no sense debating right or wrong when we're

dealing with townsfolk with so much pent-up resentment against Hunters."

"Including you?" Challenge dripped from the words.

"Yes." My gaze bored into hers. "But the big difference between me and them is that I give a shit whether she lives or dies."

I stormed out of Bonnie's house without another word.

# CHAPTER 12
## RHETT

With blood boiling, I banged on Josie's front door.

Josie opened it with a huge grin on her face.

"Oh my goodness," she said in a singsong voice. "I've been inviting you to my place for years, and here you are." She eyed me like I was a side of beef. "Come on in, Sheriff." Stepping aside, she beckoned me with her index finger. "How can I be of service to you?" She batted her eyelashes.

"This is not a social visit." I plodded inside, a frown on my face. "What were you doing at Bonnie's house tonight?" I asked, stopping in the foyer.

"I was paying a social visit." A smile twitched across her lips.

I narrowed my eyes, not bothering to hide the rage building within me. "Don't play games, Josie. Nova said that you attacked her."

"Me?" She gave me a coy smile. "Never. I was just being neighborly."

My irritation swelled. "So let me get this straight. You broke into Bonnie's…"

"The bedroom window was wide open." She sounded so incredulous. "I took that as an invitation."

"To attack Nova?" I asked in a low tone.

"Attack?" She tried to look innocent but failed. "She attacked me. I could have fucked her up, but I didn't. She was screaming and hollering like she saw Jesus. I was trying to get away, and she grabbed my talons. I thought she was trying to kill me. I got scared and I defended myself. Is that against the law, Sheriff?"

"That's not what Nova said."

"Well, it's her word against mine. Who do you think the townsfolk are going to believe? Me or your Hunter girlfriend?"

And that was what I was afraid of, a town riot over conflicting opinions about what happened between Nova and Josie tonight.

"You know that I can smell a lie, right?" I said.

"Can you also smell my pussy, Sheriff?" She trailed her fingers across my chest.

Everything inside me recoiled. "Don't touch me," I said between clenched teeth.

She snatched her hand away.

I carried on. "I'm here on official business. I'm not here to smell your pussy."

Josie's lips pressed into a thin line, and then she said, "You mean that you're here to tell me to stay away from your Hunter girlfriend."

"I'm only going to warn you once. Stay the fuck away from Nova." I kept my voice low and soft, but I left no room for doubt that I'd issued a command.

She raised her chin in a gesture of defiance and met my gaze. "And if I don't?"

"I'll pluck those damn feathers from your wings, so you better take me seriously." Steel laced my tone. "Understand?"

"I understand you, Sheriff," she mumbled, smiling slyly.

I turned on my heel and walked out of her house, knowing I'd just painted a bull's-eye on Nova's back.

*Fuck. My. Life.*

# CHAPTER 13
## NOVA

"Nova?" Bonnie called out.

"In the library," I replied.

Bonnie stepped into the room with a tentative smile on her lips. "Emmett just dropped off your car."

I sat up, nearly toppling the book on my lap. "How much do I owe him?"

"I took care of it."

I arched a brow. "Thanks, but I feel more comfortable paying my own way."

"Nova, it's been two days." She sighed heavily, taking a seat in the chair across from me. "How long are you going to stay mad at me?"

Bonnie's house was so huge that it didn't take much effort to avoid bumping into her for days. It also helped that she gave me my space to sulk and lick my wounds.

"I'm not mad," I replied, slipping the book off my lap and onto the coffee table. "But if you think that I'm going to grovel to a bunch of Hunter-hating fuckers in the hope that they'll accept me, then you are sadly mistaken."

"You didn't let me clarify my statement from a couple of days ago."

"Then explain," I said.

"Most of the residents in this town are here because they were driven here out of fear. The residents mistrust you, and mistrust is really fear."

"Sorry. Not sorry." I shrugged. "Not my problem."

"Okay," Bonnie continued. "Then think of it this way. If a Hunter killed your family member, wouldn't you be scared if that person showed up at your front door? A place that you considered safe?"

"But this situation is different. My mother's family are the killers. I have nothing to do with them."

"But they don't know that. Others fear what they don't understand, and I don't think they will ever understand Hunters. That's why I made that statement about working to let them see the real you."

"When I was younger," I said, "I spent all my time being worried about what people thought of me. It was exhausting. And now you want me to go on some roadshow to convince people in this town that I'm not a killer? Hell no. Look, I understand your position, but none of this matters. I'm leaving Black Forest."

"I really wish you'd reconsider." She leaned forward. "The spell brought you here for a reason."

"To meet you. And I did."

She arched a brow. "And you're not even going to mention the fact that your animal is awake now?"

My heart thumped. "How did you know? Did Rhett tell you?"

"No. Your scent has changed. I've been around long enough to know what that means. You've met your fated mate. Rhett."

"Rhett and I would never work. He can't get past the fact that I have a Hunter bloodline, and I can't give two shits to convince him otherwise." I paused. "Bonnie, I'm leaving the Ridge on Sunday."

Her jaw dropped. "But that's in two days."

"You can visit me in Africa if you want."

"Your animal awoke for him, which means Luna—goddess of the moon—has deemed you two a fated-mate match. You can't run away from your fate, Nova."

"After the crazy shit that I've experienced in this town, I don't believe in fate." I stood. "I don't even believe in love." I walked out of the library without another word.

I shut the bedroom door and fell onto the plush bed. I hated walking away from Bonnie, but she was pushing me too hard.

Yes, I wanted to get to know her more but not at the expense of my sanity, and that meant I had to leave the Ridge.

My cell rang. "Hi, Imani," I answered.

"Finally, you answered your cell. I've been calling and sending texts for two days. I wanted to check in with you. Rhett told us about the Josie incident."

"Is nothing secret?" I snapped.

"Not in a small town." She laughed. "Welcome to Black Forest."

I sighed heavily. "I'm fine. I just didn't feel like speaking to anyone." I shoved a pillow under my head. "I was shaken up after the owl clusterfuck."

"Well, it's time to come out of hibernation. Tonight's ladies' night at Mama June's, and you're coming."

"I really don't feel like it."

"You're coming. A few drinks and a ride on the bull should take care of everything."

"Ride on a bull?" I laughed.

"I'm not explaining anything. Just get ready by eight. I'll be there to pick you up." Our call ended.

"Pushy woman," I grumbled, even though the idea of hanging out with her filled me with excitement. I didn't have any besties, and the vibe with the three of us was great. It was just too bad that I'd be leaving all that behind on Sunday.

# CHAPTER 14
# RHETT

After getting a call from Mack about an incident at the Sleepy Skunk Motel, I hopped into my cruiser with Quinn and high-tailed it over there.

"Why won't Mack say what's going on?" Quinn asked from the passenger's seat.

"All he said was that we had to see it to believe it," I replied.

"I don't like this shit," Quinn growled. "There's never been trouble with the skunk-shifters."

"Times are changing, that's for sure," I said.

Quinn's cell rang. "Hi, darling. What's going on?" There was a beat of silence. "Sure, I can pick you up from Mama June's later." More silence. "That's interesting." He turned to stare at me. "You've invited Nova."

My body stiffened at the mention of Nova's name. It had been days since the owl-shifter incident, and so many times I had found myself wanting to call her or ring the doorbell to see her but stopped myself. There was no future for the two of us. So I just did my job of sitting outside her home when it was my turn to keep watch.

Quinn continued. "Yes. I do think it was a great idea inviting her to hang out with you and Nyx at ladies' night, given how much you like her. Okay. Yes. See you later, baby."

When his call ended, I said, "I don't think it's a good idea for Nova to go to Mama June's."

"Nova can't stay cooped up in the house. She needs to socialize with the townsfolk."

I gripped the steering wheel so hard I swore I'd crush it. "Townsfolk who might be plotting to hurt and kill her."

"She's safe at Mama June's. Everyone knows that June will not stand for any shenanigans at her bar."

"I don't like it, not after Josie attacked her."

"Well, aren't you protective of Nova," Quinn commented.

"Just doing my job."

"Are you now…"

"What are you implying?" I asked.

"That your interest in Nova is more than just as the Protector." He paused. "That ever since the Josie incident, you've been grumpier than usual. And people in town have been talking."

"Talking about what?" I inquired.

"That you're interested in Nova."

"Well, they need to mind their business," I grouched.

"Since you didn't deny it, I'll assume they're right."

"She's attractive," I snapped.

"And?"

I sighed heavily. "Her scent changed when I was with her last time."

"And do you finally admit that Nova's your mate?"

"Yes." I was done fighting that fact.

"Why the hell aren't you shouting it to the world?"

I shrugged. "Because I can't claim her."

"Can't? Or won't?"

"Same thing," I replied.

"So let me get this straight. You've waited your entire life to find your fated mate, and you still refuse to claim her?"

"Yes."

"That's bullshit. I know you. There's more to this than you're saying."

"It ain't complicated, Quinn. I'm not claiming a Hunter."

"This has nothing to do with her bloodline and everything to do with you still feeling guilty about Maggie's death."

"I failed at my one job, which was protecting her." I white-knuckled the steering wheel. "There ain't no way I want to go through that shit with Nova."

He sighed heavily. "You were young, overseas serving your country, when Maggie died. Even if you were here at the time, there was no way you could have known that a Hunter was stalking her. How could you?" He huffed out a breath. "You, of all people, know that when my dad got killed, I was messed up in the head for years. I felt guilt and blame because I was serving, just like you. I wasn't here for him, and lastly, our parting words when I left the Ridge for the military were angry and bitter. But I learned to cope with my guilt. The bottom line was I learned that I was blaming myself because if I didn't, then I'd have to accept that the universe is unpredictable. There was nothing I could have done differently that would have changed the outcome of his loss. You have to accept that you never could have known or changed the outcome of Maggie's passing because things happen every fucking day that are completely outside our control."

"It's been years, but the guilt and blame are eating me alive," I admitted.

"I've been there. You know I have. But by holding on to your guilt, you hold on to the misperception that you could have controlled the outcome. Consider what Maggie would tell you about your guilt and blame."

I knew she wouldn't want me blaming myself for her death.

"She'd be pissing mad at me using my guilt and blame as a shield to protect myself from claiming Nova."

"Well, that's your answer. If you want Nova, claim her. Don't let fear get in your way."

I frowned. "How do you deal with being fearful for Imani's safety all the time?"

"Because I'm not the only one looking out for her safety. The town has you as our Protector. We all were young and inexperienced before the military. We came back as the Protectors of this town. We're brothers-in-arms, and you always have our back, as we have yours. You will never be alone again. But you have to make up your mind what you're going to do about Nova. Whether you're going to court her or not. You're either all in or all out."

He was right. For so long, I'd let fear of losing another person I loved rule my life.

He kept talking. "When I met Imani, my wolf was tearing me up inside to claim her. But I made all kinds of stupid excuses about why I shouldn't pursue her, even when my heart, mind, and animal wanted her. But when I decided to put my heart on the line and tell her what I felt for her, her animal awoke and deemed me a worthy mate. You need to do the same with Nova. If you don't, you'll just push her into another shifter's arms."

"That shit is not going to happen." My eyes narrowed. "Nova is mine. If she'll have me."

"Well, man up, Protector, and prove that you're worthy of being her mate."

I nodded. "That's exactly what I intend to do."

We pulled up to the motel, and when we both got out of my cruiser, the stench of blood and skunk spray nearly knocked me on my ass.

"This ain't going to be good," I told Quinn.

"No. It ain't," he agreed.

"Get back," Mack ordered the crowd of onlookers. "This is a crime scene."

The area outside of the motel was littered with body parts, blood, and guts.

"He's dead!" Agnes, Dean's mate, screamed, with tears running down her face. "Sam killed my mate."

I strode over to Agnes to console her and to find out what the hell had happened. "Agnes, I'm sorry for your loss. We're going to find Sam and get you justice."

"Dean could be an ornery skunk." She sniffled. "And sometimes he smelled all to hell, but I loved that skunk with all my heart."

"I'm sorry for your loss, Agnes," Quinn said.

"Thank you, Alpha. Dean and me were mated for forty years. He didn't deserve to die like that. But he put up a hell of a fight protecting me, giving me enough time to get away." She sobbed harder. "He was a good skunk."

"I need to know exactly what transpired," I demanded.

"Sam came to the motel. His eyes were red like fire, and he was foaming at the mouth. I was so scared." Her hands trembled. "He was half shifted. Half man, half wolf. I ain't never seen nothing like that before." Her eyes widened. "Dean tried to send him away, but Sam started talking gibberish. Sam tried to grab me and said he was going to kill everyone in the motel, starting with me." Her eyes darted from me to Quinn, then back again. "When he grabbed me, Dean put up such a fight. I ain't never in our forty years together seen him so spitting mad. But Sam was just plumb crazy and ripped my Dean apart. Dean's kin tried to help, but Sam was feral and tore them apart too. When he was done, he took off running toward the forest." She sniffled again. "I will never forget the way Sam looked. He was feral. Protector, you've got to catch him. I demand justice for my Dean and his kin."

I patted her back. "Justice will be swift."

"Thank you, Protector."

Quinn and I moved over to the side, allowing the skunk-shifters to collect the remains of their kin.

Quinn's expression was bleak. "This needs to be taken care of now. Sam's gone feral."

I nodded. "Yup. There's no going back once a shifter turns feral. He'll continue killing unless he's stopped."

# CHAPTER 15
## NOVA

It was unclear whom I blamed more—Imani or Nyx—for my current predicament. But here I was, straddling a mechanical bull in the dimly lit hole-in-the-wall bar called Mama June's.

"Don't touch anything," I ordered the guy in charge of starting the bull. "I'm not ready."

After watching Nyx and Imani take turns riding the bull, I thought it looked fun and easy. But now that I was sitting astride the monstrosity, I was questioning my decision to give the bull a try.

He scowled. "I ain't got all night. I've got a bunch of women waiting for their turn."

Ignoring him, I yelled to be heard by Imani and Nyx over the loud music. "How the hell do I ride this bull without looking like a jackass?"

"Grab the handle," Imani instructed.

"I am," I said while awkwardly using both hands, holding on for dear life.

Imani and Nyx cackled.

"Stop laughing," I ordered.

"Grab the handle with your nondominant hand," Imani answered. "Reach underneath the strap, not over it."

I did as instructed while moving my crotch closer to the front of the saddle to prevent me from catapulting off once it got moving.

Nyx instructed, "Don't forget to keep your feet forward and turned out. When the bull goes forward, lean back. When it goes back, lean forward."

"Once it gets going," Imani said, "for balance, put your dominant hand near the head, palm out, then make your hand an L-shape."

"Are you ready now?" the bull operator asked me.

"Anything else?" I directed to them.

"Yes," Imani said. "Have fun!"

I sighed, still not liking my odds of not falling off the bull. I glanced around. At least if I did topple, the thick, heavily padded red area surrounding the bull would prevent me from injuring myself.

"Okay, I'm ready," I told the operator.

"Alrighty," he said. "Stay on the bull for as long as possible. If you are concerned at any time, say stop while extending your arm with a flat hand forward to communicate to me you are ready for the ride to end."

When the bull started, it wasn't as hard as I thought it would be. I just mirrored its movements and rode for what seemed like a lifetime before saying stop to the operator. He had a huge grin on his face when he helped me off.

"Good job," he complimented me. "You rode for eleven seconds. For a newbie, that's good."

When I reached Imani and Nyx, they each gave me a high five.

"You mastered the bull," Nyx said, looping an arm through mine.

"Now let's see how you do against the BF Home Brew," Imani said, clutching my other arm and dragging Nyx and me toward an unoccupied tall, round bar table with four chairs. Once we arrived at the table, we each plopped into a chair.

The air inside June's was like a steam room, hot even with the AC on. "God, it's hot as hell in here," I complained, wiping the perspiration from my forehead. I was glad I'd made the choice to wear light clothing—a black tube top, designer shorts, ankle boots, and a drapey fishnet jacket. But now my thighs stuck to the red leather seat.

The music from the bar's DJ was loud, and he'd played the same pelvic-thrusting reggaeton song three times in a row. People were on the dance floor, gyrating like it was their last day on earth.

A guy wearing a black T-shirt with Mama June's written in gold on the front arrived at our table with a tray and promptly set out two platters—one stacked with hot wings, another with fried golden mozzarella sticks.

I arched a brow because we hadn't ordered yet. He laid out small plates and napkins.

Imani snatched a wing. "Our door fee comes with unlimited bull rides, wings, and sticks."

I grabbed a piece of fried cheese. "I'm not complaining," I replied around a mouthful of melted cheesy perfection.

A petite older woman wearing a skintight T-shirt with Mama June's written across it, jeans, and ass-length braids swayed over to our table.

"Well, if it isn't my favorite ladies," her hoarse voice called out.

"Hi, Mama June," Nyx and Imani said in unison.

"Meet Nova," Imani said. "Our newest resident."

"Visitor," I said. "Nice to meet you, Mama June."

June's lips curled up into a genuine smile. "Ditto. I came over here because I wanted to officially welcome you to the Ridge and Mama June's." She leaned closer. "Bo told me that you're a midwife. We need one of them in town, especially if you lovely hybrids keep showing up."

"I don't think townsfolk will be receptive to me being here."

She fanned me. "Who gives a damn about a few ornery

fuckers? Don't let them chase you away, darling." She looked me up and down. "You belong here." She winked at me, then looked at the three of us. "Drinks on me tonight. What can I get you?"

"A round of BF Home Brew shots," Nyx replied. "And keep them coming until the newbie"—she eyed me—"passes out."

"You got it!" She chuckled and sauntered away.

"She seems nice," I said.

Between bites of chicken, Imani said, "See, not all townsfolk are certified nutjobs."

"Yeah, I'm calling bullshit on your statement," I retorted.

"Why?"

"Because I've been in the Ridge a total of five days." I held up five fingers. "And I've had a run-in with a nude horse-shifter who insisted on showing me his dick. An asshole sheriff who wants to kick me out of town. I got my pendant stolen by a sketchy shifter named Sam, and I was attacked by a deranged owl-shifter."

"She has a point," Nyx agreed.

"We're trying to convince her to stay, Nyx," Imani growled.

Nyx shrugged. "I'm just giving her credit for a factual assessment."

"Well, I can up your crazy," Imani said, peering at me. "My Welcome to the Ridge experience was me being chased and almost mauled to death by said sketchy shifter Sam. And then I was mindfucked by her"—she jabbed a finger in Nyx's direction—"mother."

"Oh, stop whining. It was a harmless pulse."

"What's a pulse?" I asked.

"Witches like Mom and me can see a person's aura," Nyx answered. "Everyone's aura has a color. Shifters are blue. Vampires are orange. Humans are yellow. Well, you get the point. But what we can't do is tell what type of shifter an Other is unless we pulse the aura. Pretty much, it's like tapping on the glass of a fish tank, annoying the fuck out of a fish. For example, we tap on the aura to provoke the shifter's animal to reveal itself."

"Yes, all of what Nyx explained," Imani said. "But when Freya tried to pulse me, she said something blocked her magic from digging and finding out what type of Other I was."

I arched a brow. "So the question is"—I glared at Nyx—"have you tried to pulse me too?"

Nyx shook her head. "Nope." She waved at the server and yelled, "Another round! Thank you!" Then she said to me, "Unlike my mother, I don't pulse without permission." She leaned closer to me. "You want me to try?"

Curious, I said, "Yes."

Nyx's eyes focused on me. My brain got fuzzy for a second. My limbs stiffened as if being held involuntarily immobile, then my brain kicked into top gear, breaking the trance.

"That's weird," I blurted out.

"Damn." Nyx slammed her palm against the table. "I just lost a bet."

"What bet?" Imani asked.

"My mom thinks we probably can't pulse all hybrids. I thought Imani was a fluke." She eyed me. "I couldn't pulse you. It's like a wall is erected around your body, protecting you from my magic."

"Can we move back to my tirade?" Imani asked.

Nyx rolled her eyes. "If you must."

I laughed. "She must."

Imani pointed at us. "I don't need attitude from the likes of you two."

Nyx and I eyed each other and laughed.

Imani continued. "I was challenged to a duel by Quinn's skanky stalker one-night stand."

"You mean an Old West gun duel?" I asked.

Nyx shook her head. "No. A duel is a bloody fight between shifters."

My eyes widened. "Just for the record, don't sign me up for that shit."

Imani pursed her lips. "May I continue?"

I waved my hand. "Go on."

"I had to visit a hot but, frankly, a little scary leader of the vampire coven and convince him to vote in my favor to let me stay in the Ridge."

I shook my hand. "I still can't believe vampires exist."

"And they're hotter than what's described in supernatural movies," Nyx pointed out.

Imani gave us a mock glare. "If you two interrupt me one more time, no more wings for you."

We mimed zipping our mouths.

She carried on. "I had to endure a vote by the town council to let me stay in the Ridge and put me under their protection. I had an encounter with a group of displeased rioting town idiots after said vote." She paused. "Learned how to shift for the first time at the duel where I was fighting for my life. Oh, and last but not least, I fucked my mate in the forest."

"Okay. You win the Most Crazy Shit to Happen to Me award." I handed her a shot glass.

She accepted and air-kissed it. "Thank you." She grinned. "And I dedicate my award to you and all my beautiful sisters soon to come to Black Forest, finding their fated mates and happily-ever-afters."

Nyx clapped loudly. "Bravo!"

I snorted. "I'm forty. I stopped believing in happily ever after years ago."

"Well, we haven't," Imani replied. "And we"—she gestured to herself and Nyx—"are in our forties too."

The server arrived with more shots. We clinked our glasses and chugged the contents.

I waited for the burning in my tummy to lessen before asking them, "What's in this Brew?"

"It's a special concoction crafted by Brody Thornbern's brewstillery," Imani said, putting her empty glass on the table. "Others love it because it's the only thing that can get us drunk."

Nyx explained, "Others' metabolisms churn through human alcohol like water."

Still feeling the afterburn, I replied, "Well, it sure packs a wallop."

Imani winked at me. "That's the point."

"So what do you think about Mama June's?" Nyx asked me.

"I love it." I panned June's, with its glowing red lights. The crowd was diverse, which I liked, but the place was packed with more men than women. I gave Imani the side-eye and flat-out asked her, "Did you low-key bring me to a pickup spot?"

Imani waggled her eyebrows. "Maybe."

I rolled my eyes. "Well, you wasted your time." I swallowed another mouthful of Brew. "Because I'm not looking."

"Is that because of Rhett?" she asked.

Nyx leaned closer to me. "There's a rumor circulating that you and the sheriff are a thing."

I sputtered. "We are *not* a thing."

"Well, the nose don't lie," Imani said, tapping her nose. "Your scent has changed. And since I've heard that the last man you were with was Rhett two days ago…"

"And who told you that?" I asked.

"It's a small town, Nova," Nyx said.

Imani cut in. "I'm betting your animal is awake and she chose him."

"My animal is wrong." I emptied my glass and glared at Imani, then Nyx.

I ignored my inner animal when she shouted, *For the last time, I am not wrong!*

Nyx eyed Imani. "She's still in the denial phase."

"Yup," Imani replied.

"Are you telling me that my animal can't be wrong?" I demanded.

"Yes!" they said in unison.

I crossed my arms and glared. "I disagree. No one is 100 percent accurate."

"Lordy." Nyx shook her head. "There are too many reasons to count why what you just said is utter bullshit."

I pursed my lips. "That's my stance, and I'm sticking with it."

The server showed up again with another round of Brew.

"Thank God," Imani said, grabbing a glass. "We're going to need lots of Brew to tackle her stubbornness."

I took a sip of Brew. "Since the three of us are well on our way to being intoxicated, who will be driving us home?"

"Quinn," Imani declared.

"Thank goodness it's not Rhett," I said.

"I don't know why you and Rhett are fighting your obvious attraction to each other," Nyx complained, shoving a cheese stick into her mouth.

"Obvious?" I arched a brow. "You haven't seen us together."

Imani and Nyx exchanged knowing looks with each other.

"What?" I commented.

"She told me"—Nyx gave Imani a playful pinch—"that you and Rhett are like a sparkling bottle of 'hot, angry, sweaty sex waiting to happen' wine."

I snorted. "If such a wine did exist, give me five bottles please."

Nyx raised her hand. "Ditto."

"Second"—I gave Imani a bemused smile—"snitches get stitches."

"Don't shoot the messenger." Imani chuckled, holding her hands up in surrender. "All I'm saying is that you and Rhett most definitely have a sexy vibe."

"Chemistry cannot be denied," Nyx chimed in.

"Chemistry is overrated," I retorted.

"That's like saying sex is overrated." Nyx's eyes lit with a twinkle of mischief.

"And we all know that's not true." Imani waggled her eyebrows.

"All I'm saying is that Rhett and I are never going to be a thing." I leaned back in my seat when my whole body started feeling warm and cozy.

"He can't help the fact that he's an alpha shifter," Nyx said.

"He's alpha, all right." I knocked back another shot, even though I was well on my way to being tipsy. "He loves imposing his will on me."

"Rhett is more bark than bite," Imani commented.

"Exactly," Nyx said. "Rhett is a great guy. He just hides it most of the time."

I blinked dramatically. "So his grunting and scowling is part of his alpha love language?"

"Yeah. Pretty much." Imani sighed heavily. "I'm not going to lie. When Quinn and I met, we argued and pushed each other away even when we knew that we belonged together."

Nyx piped up. "God, I don't miss those angst-filled 'will they get their shit together and mate' moments between you two."

Imani jabbed her in the side.

"Ouch!" Nyx gave her the evil eye. "What was that for?"

"Because it wasn't that dramatic between Quinn and me."

Her eyes widened. "Yes, it was." She grabbed another piece of chicken. "I'm telling you right now if I have to go through all this drama with every damn woman who shows up in this town, I'm going to start randomly cunt punting newcomers until you hags get your shit together."

I choked on my bite of chicken. "Present company not included, right?"

"I might start with you just to set a precedent."

I laughed so hard my stomach hurt. "You two are crazy… but I love it."

"What's not to love?" Imani replied sassily. "But all joking aside. Do you like him?"

I bit my bottom lip. "My body says yes. My mind says run. It's not remotely possible for me to contemplate exploring anything with Rhett when he's holding such a grudge against Hunters."

They reached across the table, each grabbing one of my hands.

"Drop your guard the next time you see him," Nyx implored.

"Listen to what your heart is saying," Imani continued. "And take it from there."

They released my hands, grabbing a glass. I followed suit.

"To possibilities," Imani toasted. Then we clinked glasses and tossed back our shots.

The sounds of a hip-hop song blasted through the air. "The dance floor is calling us," Imani said while jumping to her feet and beckoning us with a finger.

We joined the crowd of gyrating bargoers. Everyone clapped to the beat as Imani moved her body like a snake. Nyx air-slapped my ass while I twerked. It was unadulterated fun with no judgment or filters.

After dancing to back-to-back songs, we returned to our table for more rounds of Brew.

"Don't you care if people talk about the mate of the town alpha dropping it like it's hot on the dance floor?" I asked Imani.

Imani smirked. "Nope. First thing you'll have to learn about shifters is that anything goes." She pointed to the cavorting patrons. "See that woman with short red hair gyrating against that male like they're reenacting a porno scene?"

I nodded.

"The redhead is a billionaire who owns the number-one makeup brand in America. She lives in the Ridge part time, like most residents."

Nyx nodded. "Almost half the population work in the human world and have a vacation home here. This is the place where they can let loose and relax."

"Exactly," Imani chimed in. "And second, even if they were judging me, I wouldn't give a shit. I am who I am. You either accept me, or you don't."

"That's how I feel," I declared.

Nyx raised her hand. "Ditto."

"But don't you find it ironic that they can accept everything except hybrids and a woman with a Hunter bloodline?" I asked.

"Just as in the human world, people have their quirks." Imani shrugged. "But I don't care what they think about me. I let that shit go when I mated Quinn." She eyed me. "And if you decide to stay and mate Rhett, you should do the same."

Her words were food for thought.

The server brought us more rounds, and I face-planted on the table from too much Brew.

"Who's ready for more bull riding?" they both chirped.

Buzzed from Brew and feeling like one giant vibrating being, I said, "Not me."

"Come on," they whined playfully, trying to yank me off my chair, but I refused to budge.

"Go away," I grumbled. "My head's spinning. Just leave me here to die."

"Nope," Nyx said. "We would never leave a drunk sister behind."

"Go. I'll watch her," Rhett volunteered.

I jerked upright, nearly toppling off my chair.

Rhett gently caught me, settling me back onto my seat.

"What are you doing here?" My heart thumped hard in my chest. "Wait." My eyes narrowed. "Are you stalking me?" I stared at him with my lips pursed.

"I'm just doing my job by making sure you're not getting yourself in trouble." He scowled. "Again."

"Oh, shut up, Sheriff Stick-Up-Your-Ass!" I bellowed.

"You're right, Imani," Nyx broke in loudly. "They are like a bottle of 'hot, angry, sweaty sex waiting to happen' wine."

"Yep," Imani boasted, then pointed to us. "Come on, you two. Just make out already."

Rhett frowned at them. "You two are drunk."

Imani wobbled on her feet. "No, we're not."

When Quinn appeared at the table, he said, "Yes, you are, baby."

Imani wrapped her arms around his neck. "Yay! You're here."

"Hi, Nyx. Hi, Nova," Quinn said.

I saluted. Nyx waved.

"What about me?" Imani asked, batting her eyelashes almost comically. "You didn't greet me properly."

"Apologies, mate." He leaned down, kissing Imani in a slow, tender, but smoking-hot manner that showed me how much he loved her.

When he pulled back, Imani said, "Love you, mate."

"Love you too, mate," Quinn said. He rubbed her back in slow circles. "Time to go home."

Imani released her grip on him and nearly stumbled, but he wrapped an arm around her waist.

"One more bull ride," she urged.

"Nope. First, I'm driving Nyx home, and then we're heading home."

"What about Nova?" Nyx pointed out.

"Rhett's taking her home," Quinn said.

I frowned, not liking the idea of Rhett and me being stuck in a car. "I don't want to send Rhett out of his way."

"I have no issues unless you do." Rhett spoke in a rough voice, taking a seat across from me.

"Fine," I said as Nyx and Imani gave me a hug before being escorted out of the club by Quinn.

I groaned when my head started pounding while seeing double of Rhett.

Rhett beckoned the server. "One glass of wake-up juice."

The server nodded before plodding away.

As the music throbbed around us, Rhett ran a hand over his chin while he tapped the fingers of his other hand on the table.

"How many rounds did you have?" he clipped out.

"Too many," I replied, rubbing my forehead.

The server came over and said, "Wake-up juice," placing a tall glass of green juice and a bottle of water in front of me.

Lifting the glass to my nose, I nearly gagged from the horrid smell of a compost pile.

I wrinkled my nose before pushing the glass away. "I'm not drinking this shit."

He slid the glass back in front of me. "It's a miracle worker for hangovers."

I smelled the juice again, scrunching up my nose. "Oh hell no!"

"Drink it, or you'll be passed out drunk in a few minutes." He held my stare, unwilling to relent. "Come to think of it, if you do the latter, it would make it all the easier to lug your ass out of here, caveman-style."

I made a face. "I bet you'd like that."

"At least you'd be silent." He eased back, his crystal-blue eyes searching my face. "For once."

Not relishing giving him the satisfaction of the opportunity to manhandle me like a side of beef in front of the partiers, I gulped the juice, which had a bitter, earthy flavor that made me wince. Once the glass was empty, I opened the bottle of water, taking a sip, and nearly choked. The water was a fizzy combination of bitter and sweet.

"What type of water is this?" I demanded.

"It comes from the town's hot springs. It's an elixir. The water is touted as having medicinal properties—both for bathing and drinking."

I arched a brow. "Are you telling me that this"—I held up the bottle—"has magical healing powers?"

"Yep. We have hot springs water fountains at various locations around the Ridge."

"God, this place is weird," I murmured even as I chugged more of the water. Placing the half-empty bottle on the table, I sighed as my stomach started to settle and the room stopped spinning. The fog in my head cleared. My headache was now nonexistent.

I gasped. "Holy shit! It worked."

"I told you so." His lips twitched into a mockery of a smile. "Now time to go home, woman."

*Wait. What?*

*His home?*

*Or mine?*

# CHAPTER 16
## NOVA

Sultriness lingered in the air as Rhett hustled me out of Mama June's while partiers lingered outside the bar.

I glanced around and didn't see his cruiser. "Where's your ride?"

"At the police station. I dropped my vehicle there and rode over here with Quinn." He peered over at me. "Do you mind walking a bit? It won't take long to get to the station."

I shrugged. "Nope. I could use a bit of fresh air to clear my Brew haze."

Pressing his hand to the small of my back, he directed me to the left. "This way."

As we walked through Main Square, I noticed that it was jumping with townsfolk milling around despite the fact that it was past ten at night.

"I never imagined that a small town could have the nightlife of Manhattan."

"But none of the crime," Rhett replied. "The most excitement you'd find in the Ridge is the daily fight between the otters and penguins about who has the right to skinny-dip in the town's fountain."

I laughed. "Sounds amusing."

A smile twitched across his lips. "For the bystanders, it is, but for Mack and me, who have to take turns breaking up the ruckus, it's not."

We walked another block.

"Damn, it feels like August not April," I complained. "Why is it so hot in Alaska?" I pulled my hair away from my neck. Every muscle in my body was fatigued from the combination of drinking way too much Brew and bull riding.

"The theory is that having such a high concentration of Others living in such a small town affects the weather and temperature."

I arched a brow. "And do you believe that theory?"

He nodded. "Yup. Of course it's not a scientific fact, but while in the military, I traveled all over the world, and I noticed areas with a high population of Others had abnormal temperature fluctuations."

He pointed across the street. "My cruiser and the station are over there."

We stepped into the crosswalk, making it halfway across the street, when I heard squealing tires.

As I peered to my left, my eyes widened at the sight of the motorcycle rider weaving dangerously. Midmotion, he fell off, dropping his motorcycle. It landed sideways, skidding down the middle of the street and heading toward us.

"Nova. Move!" Rhett barked.

I froze, not sure which direction to run—left or right—to escape getting hit by the runaway bike. Bracing for the worst, I felt my heartbeat race so fast it caused pains in my chest.

Rhett shoved me behind him so quickly the momentum of the movement made me topple to the street and onto my side.

I flinched at the sound of hissing and the screeching of metal scraping the street while the motorcycle continued its riderless joyride.

Moving gingerly onto my elbow, I watched in horror as Rhett

crouched like a warrior, putting himself protectively between me and the out-of-control bike.

*What the hell?* He was going to get mowed down by the motorcycle.

*No. I can't lose him.*

And just the thought of him dying, of not being in my world, made me dizzy and weak.

I was already on my feet, though I couldn't remember standing. I watched Rhett's hands shoot out so fast, it was a blur. The sound of groaning metal thudded in my ears.

Somehow, Rhett stopped the trajectory of the motorcycle.

Now motionless, the bike was a mess of metal and rubber. I swayed slightly at the sight of a seemingly unharmed Rhett straightening, then wiping his palms against his jeans.

I pushed through the crowd of townsfolk now gathered around me. Both Rhett and I rushed toward each other. His gaze raked over me, heating every inch of my skin in its path.

"Nova?" Concern glistened in his eyes. "Are you okay?" He grasped my chin, tipping my face up to the moonlight.

"Yes," I answered, gazing up at his tanned face. "You?"

"Don't worry about me."

"But I am." I curled my fingers, fisting the fabric of his shirt. "I don't understand. How in the world did you stop that motorcycle?"

He brushed his fingers across my cheek. "I'm a shifter with enhanced speed, agility, and strength. I'm invincible." He winked.

"Invincible?" Anger burst to the surface. "Are you crazy?" I pounded my fists against his chest. "You could have been killed."

He growled, and every erogenous zone on my body tingled with awareness. "You're mine to protect."

"That was reckless. You should have saved yourself."

"I could have, but there was no way in hell that I was leaving you to die. I know now—there is no me without you."

His words, combined with the emotion that I heard in his tone, floored me. "Rhett. You saved me at the expense of your own life."

"And I'd do it again, Nova," he said, never taking his eyes off me for a second.

My throat tightened with emotions. I wasn't used to anyone caring about me, but to put my life before his… that selfless act of bravery blew my mind.

"Rhett…"

My words were cut short by a barrage of screaming and yelling residents, barreling toward the now-standing motorcycle rider.

"I made a mistake," Motorcycle Guy yelled, his body swaying side to side. "Too much Brew."

"Drinking and driving is against the law," a man said.

A female said, "Let's beat his ass for almost killing the sheriff and that hybrid."

The crowd yelled and clapped like they were at some damn football game.

"Stay here," Rhett demanded. "I've got to break this up before they tear him apart." Charging over to the crowd, he started issuing orders. "Go home. I'll deal with Kirk."

They grumbled with dissent but moved. Some walked away, but most just backed up a bit and watched like spectators.

A huge man strode up to me. "I'm Mack, Rhett's deputy." He looked me up and down. "You okay?"

"Surprisingly, yes. No injuries, thanks to Rhett. He saved my life."

"Kirk! You idiot!" Rhett barked at the motorcycle rider. "You can't even walk, much less ride a motorcycle."

"I'm sorry," Kirk blubbered. "I thought I could make it home, but my bike just got away from me."

Rhett was shaking with rage while he stared pointedly at Kirk. "You could have killed my mate."

Kirk swayed, tipping sideways.

"Timber!" someone yelled. The crowd laughed.

Rhett caught Kirk, righting him.

"Since you appear to be all right," Mack said to me, "I best be getting over to Rhett to calm this situation down before he rips Kirk a new asshole."

Rhett shoved Kirk toward Mack when he arrived. "He's spending the night in jail." He jabbed a finger in Kirk's face. "When you're sober in the morning, you'll be brought before the council for sentencing."

"What?" Kirk cried, trying with no success to free himself from Mack's grip. "No. Please. Sheriff, have mercy," he begged. "This is my second offense. They'll punish me this time."

"And that's what you deserve," Rhett countered. "Now go on. Get."

Mack dragged a whimpering Kirk away.

Rhett stormed over to me. "Are you sure you're okay?" He scanned me with his hands and eyes.

"Yes. I'm just rattled." I swallowed hard, and I bit my bottom lip to hide the emotions that had set it trembling.

His nostrils flared, every muscle in his body seeming tense, straining against his shirt and jeans. "Just in case, I'll text Izzy, the town's healer, and have her check in with you first thing in the morning."

"No Izzy. I'm fine. Now let's go. It's getting late."

I nearly jumped out of my skin when he clutched my hand, entwining his fingers with mine. My mind warred between the thoughts of how nice his touch felt and how I shouldn't be enjoying this moment with him as much as I was.

"Now let's get you home," he said before escorting me across the street and into his parked cruiser. Slamming the passenger's door, he strode around his vehicle before getting in.

The crowd dispersed, and Rhett pulled out from his parking spot, taking off down the now-empty street.

The tension hanging in the air between us was suffocating. "Rhett—"

He cut me off. "I spoke to Josie and warned her to stay away from you."

I turned to stare at him. "So she admitted attacking me?"

"No. She didn't. But there is no doubt in my mind that she did."

"No doubt?" I scoffed. "It seems like you had a lot of doubt that night."

"All I did was explain why I couldn't arrest her, Nova. It may have sounded harsh, but it's Others law."

"This town is so strange." I glanced through the passenger's window. "I don't understand anything, including—" I stopped short, not wanting to get dragged into an argument with him, especially after he'd just saved my life.

"Were you going to say that you don't understand me?"

I bit my bottom lip, hesitating while contemplating Imani's advice to be open with him.

*Oh, fuck it.*

*What could it hurt to be truthful?*

"Yes," I answered, watching as he finally drove away from Main Square, continuing up the sloping road that led through the forest. "I don't understand you or why I feel the way I do about you. I'm attracted to you, but frankly, I don't like half the shit that comes out of your mouth. Or the way you've treated me since I stepped into this town." I pursed my lips. "And now there's this thing with my animal, who has been protesting rather loudly because I won't accept you as my mate." I rubbed my forehead. "God, I'm dreading how she'll react when I leave the Ridge on Sunday."

"You're leaving?"

"Yes."

"You can't leave," he argued.

"I can and I will," I asserted.

He took his eyes from the road briefly. "I'll fight for you, Nova."

"There's no future for us, Rhett."

"There is if you're willing to fight for it… for us."

"I'm getting whiplash from your emotional windstorm. One minute, you want me gone. The next, you want me to stay. I don't have time for games, Rhett. What do you want?"

"You."

"Why now?"

"You are mine to claim. My fated mate. Don't you see?" He flexed his fingers around the wheel. "I could have lost you. You could have lost me. I don't know about you, but that was a big wake-up call for me. I can't—" His voice broke. "No. I won't continue to deny what we are to each other. Fated mates."

"That's lust speaking," I countered.

"It's not."

"Maybe if we just fuck it out, you know, get it out of our system, then we could walk away with no regrets."

"Do you really believe that?"

"No." I sighed heavily. "But I had to put that option on the table."

"Nova, I know this sounds crazy, but how about if we just hit restart on our relationship?"

"It's not that easy, Rhett. You said some horrible things to me."

"And I'm man enough to say I'm sorry." He placed a hand on my thigh. "And if you give us a shot, I will never make you regret it."

Part of me wanted to agree, but the other part—the scared and wary side of me—was terrified of opening my heart to a man who could break it easily.

"I don't do romantic relationships, Rhett. I don't want to hurt or be hurt."

"So you don't feel anything for me?"

I could lie, but it wasn't who I was. "I do, but it scares the shit out of me." I swallowed hard.

"I won't hurt you, Nova."

"In relationships, someone always gets hurt." Placing my

palms into my lap, I clasped them together to prevent my fingers from trembling.

"Did you have a recent breakup that went bad?"

"No." I nibbled on my bottom lip. "I have lots of baggage because of my toxic relationship with my mother. She…" I allowed the words to trail off. I didn't want to open that sealed-with-caution-tape box of hurt.

I sighed with relief when he pulled up to Bonnie's house. *Saved by the bell.*

He parked the cruiser and turned it off. "Talk to me, Nova." He turned and stared at me.

Glancing away, I peered through the window into the inky darkness of the night.

Minutes ticked away before I said, "For as long as I could remember, my mother's love was conditional."

Turning to study him, I carried on. "She expected perfection at all times, and if I failed, her wrath was like an emotional tsunami."

He reached over, entwining his fingers with mine.

"I had a very lonely childhood, and even at school, I never fit in. When I left for college, leaving my mother behind, it was for the best because I knew that I had to say goodbye to a relationship that would never be."

"Sounds like she hated herself and took it out on you. Nova, her pain is not yours, and it most definitely was not your fault that she chose to walk away from her family and Hunter life."

"Deep down inside"—I tapped my chest—"I know that, but she inflicted so much emotional damage that the wounds are still there, just scabbed over, visible to anyone cruel enough to pick at the flesh, reopening them."

He brought my fingers to his lips, kissing them. "I would never hurt you, Nova."

"You already did by rejecting me because of my bloodline. I want to love and be loved, Rhett, but not with a man who believes I'm not enough because I'm a hybrid with a Hunter bloodline."

Letting go of my hand, he rubbed his hand over his face. "God, I fucked this up big-time, all because I was too pigheaded to acknowledge the fact that I felt guilty about my sister Maggie's death."

I grabbed his hand when I heard the anguish in his voice. "Can you tell me about her?"

"She was funny, beautiful inside and out, intelligent, and stubborn." His lips curled up. "She was older than me and thought I could do no wrong. Our parents died when we were young, so we only had each other. She was a lot older than me, so she took one dead-end job after another just to put food on the table. She wanted more for me, so when I decided to join the military, she had my back, unlike the naysayers who balked at a shifter joining the armed forces."

"She sounds like a good woman," I said.

"She was. It killed me emotionally when I got the call while serving overseas that she was killed."

"If you don't mind my asking, what happened?"

"She was killed by Hunters while on a shifter full-moon run." He rubbed his eyes. "I wasn't there for her when she needed me. I failed at my one fucking job, and that was protecting her."

"You can't blame yourself for something completely outside your control."

He nodded. "I'm coming to terms with that now, Nova. I've beat myself up for years, accusing myself of being a bad brother and Protector because I *should* have been there. Seeing how hard I was being on myself, Quinn made me realize that Maggie didn't care if I was there or not when she died. She knew I loved her because when she was alive, I showed her that over and over again."

I realized from his heartbreakingly beautiful words that when this man loved, he did so unconditionally and completely. *What more could a woman hope for?*

But there was so much I had to ponder tonight.

*Should I give Rhett another chance?*

*And if I do, will that mean sacrificing my work?*

*My life as I know it?*

The light in one of Bonnie's rooms flicked on.

"It's getting late," I whispered. "I should go."

He nodded before hopping out of the vehicle, then opening my door. He clasped my hand in his, and the sweet smell of pine filled my nose while we walked toward the house. Making it up the stairs, we stood by the front door, staring at each other.

"Thank you for sharing that part of you with me, Rhett."

"I should be thanking you, Nova. I know how painful it was for you to tell me about your mother."

"We're starting over, right?" My lips curled up slightly.

"Yes, we are."

He circled my nape with his hand. His touch set my skin aflame. Leaning against his fingers, I ached for more. He dipped his head, planting his gorgeous lips on mine. I wrapped my arms around his neck, clinging to him as he deepened our kiss, coaxing his tongue into my mouth. He groaned, and I moved my tongue with his. My breath became ragged, my nipples strained against my bra, and warmth pooled between my thighs.

As he broke off our kiss, his breathing was heavy. "So does that mean that you're going to give me a chance to redeem myself?" He reached over, brushing his hand down my back.

I'd seen another side of Rhett tonight, and I couldn't lie to myself, I wanted to discover more about the man behind the mask.

"Yes." I slid my arm around Rhett's waist. "But I'm not making any long-term promises."

"I don't need promises." He spoke in his quiet, rough voice. "I just need a chance to show you that you're mine and that I'm yours."

"Rhett…" I swallowed hard, biting my bottom lip to hide the emotion that had set it to trembling.

Catching my chin, he bored his eyes into mine. "I'm not pushing you, Nova. I'm just stating straight-up facts." He released me, then stepped back, watching me closely, making me feel precious and beautiful.

Moving forward, I pressed a quick kiss against his lips before breaking it off. I turned my back to him, my fingers trembling with emotion as I unlocked and shoved the door open.

Spinning around to face him, I asked, "Are you going to the festival tomorrow?"

He tilted his head and studied me. "Yes."

"Well, I'll see you there, Sheriff."

His face dissolved into a delicious grin. "I look forward to it."

"Good night, Rhett."

"Good night, Nova."

Shutting the door, I pressed my back against it, scared to death of all the feelings for Rhett rushing to the surface, making me hope for more with a man I was just getting to know.

I nearly jumped out of my skin when I heard the loud clearing of a throat. Bonnie was sitting on the couch with a glass of milk clutched in each hand.

I strode over and took a seat next to her. "How long have you been sitting there?" I asked, accepting the glass she extended to me.

"Long enough." She took a sip from her glass. "So ladies' night ends with making out with Rhett on my front porch?"

My lips curled up into a smile. "Nosy much?" I gulped the cool beverage.

"I'm your grandmother. It's my business to snoop into your business. Besides, I haven't given you the sex talk."

I choked out a laugh. "I'm forty. I've had sex before." Not recently, but it still counted.

"But sex with a shifter is different."

I really didn't want to ask, but my curiosity was piqued. "How?"

"Wilder. Hotter. Kinky. Biting. And that's just foreplay." She grinned.

"It was only a kiss," I replied.

"Even from spying on you through the window, I felt the sparks between you two." She drained her glass. "He's a good man, you know."

I folded my legs under me. "I know."

She eyed me. "Are you still upset with me about what I said two nights ago?"

"No. I'm not. I can admit that I got a little sensitive about what you two said. Emotions were high, and I needed time to come to terms with the rules of this crazy town."

"Good." She grinned and patted my thigh. "I'm relieved that we're back on speaking terms. Now about Rhett… Is he a good kisser? Because there's a betting pool in my wine-tasting club that says—"

I cut her off. "Stop right there. I will not gossip with my grandmother about a man I may"—I eyed her pointedly—"or may not be thinking about starting a relationship with."

"Why not? I'll have you know that I'm very open about sex. Shit. I can give you lots of tips about what shifter men love in bed."

I laughed. "And that's the end of this conversation." I drained my glass, placing it on the coffee table. "Good night, Bonnie." I gave her a kiss on the cheek and stood up, brushing past her.

After heading upstairs, I entered my bedroom, shutting the door behind me. Sauntering over to the window, I started to open it, then hesitated, not wanting another owl-shifter incident.

"Fuck it." I pushed it open. "There is no way I'm living my life in fear."

I sighed with contentment when a fresh breeze rushed into the room. The night air was heavy with a multitude of noises, and I heard them all with my heightened senses.

Sounds saturated the room around me—insects buzzed, frogs

croaked, mammals scuttled. Even the trees seemed to pulsate with sound as the din ricocheted off the high canopy and cascaded back to earth on a tidal wave of noise. Every muscle in my body tightened as primal instincts rose to the surface within me.

*I'm changing.*

*I can feel it.*

My senses were heightened, sharpened. There was no denying it. My inner animal had awoken because Rhett was mine.

Now I wondered how much longer until my animal demanded to be released to claim and be claimed by him.

# CHAPTER 17
## NOVA

"Nova, we're here," Bonnie said.

"Ow, Bonnie." I slapped my hands against my ears. "Why are you yelling?"

"What's wrong with you?" She yanked my hands away from my ears. "You've been jumpy all day."

"Everything sounds so loud," I grumbled, rubbing my eyes. "It's like the volume of my hearing has been turned up tenfold." I pointed to the bee flying outside in front of the windshield. "I can hear the buzzing." And it was annoying.

"Why didn't you say something before?"

I shrugged. "I'm changing. Transforming into the beast."

"Transforming?" She arched a brow.

"Yes. You know, becoming one of you. A shifter."

"Becoming?" She burst out laughing. "Dramatic much?"

I fanned her. "All I know is that my senses are on fire."

"That's what happens when a hybrid shifter meets her fated mate. All her senses start firing at a faster rate."

"All I hear is blah, blah, blah. Nyx and Imani gave me crib notes."

"So…" She batted her eyelashes dramatically. "You and Rhett, huh?"

"Yup. I guess the sheriff might be mine."

"I'm so excited," Bonnie squealed while rubbing her palms together.

"Don't start planning the wedding. I'm not sure where this thing with Rhett is headed."

"Okay, I'm not going to push." She pursed her lips. "Or say I told you so."

I gave her the evil eye. "How about you just tell me how to deal with my sensitivity to sound?"

"The first thing you have to learn is to modulate the sounds in your surroundings. You have to center yourself by taking slow, deep breaths." She mimicked the instructions. "In. Out. In. Out."

I did as instructed, but it took a bit of practice to focus. Eventually, the volume of sounds became almost normal.

"It's working," I said, relief flooding through my body.

"Anytime you feel your senses are heightening to a level that you feel is out of control, just take a deep breath and focus. It takes practice to calm the mind, but that's one of the first lessons jaguars teach our cubs."

"So you're saying I'm as inexperienced as a cub?"

"Yup." Bonnie agreed. "Now that your animal is coming awake, you'll have to learn basic skills like modulating some of your instincts and senses. And how to shift into your animal."

"This shifter thing is definitely going to be challenging," I admitted.

"But you're my strong granddaughter." She pinched my cheek. "So I know that you're up for the challenge." She opened the driver's door. "Now let's go. There's a funnel cake out there calling my name."

We hopped out of Bonnie's car, weaving our way through the throng of people milling around or dancing to the music playing.

It was night. Tiki torches illuminated the festival. Residents were seated on haystacks and benches, laughing, eating, and having a good time. My mouth watered from the smells of delicious foods, like funnel cake and pizza, wafting through the air.

Two women with wide smiles walked up to Bonnie and me.

"She looks like the spitting image of you, Bo," the female with thick white hair that contrasted sharply against her beautiful ebony-hued skin said.

Bonnie preened. "Yes, she does." She wrapped her arm around my waist. "Nova, this is Freya." She pointed to the woman with white hair. "She's the leader of the witches and Nyx's mother." Then she gestured to the other woman with dark hair and a face that looked like an older version of Quinn's. "And this is Piper, Quinn's mother."

I stuck out my hand to Freya, who used my outstretched hand to pull me in for a hug. "Welcome, Nova." I hugged her back quickly. "We wanted to meet you days ago." She pointed at Bonnie. "But your grandmother said that she didn't want us scaring you off with our wacky behavior." She rolled her eyes.

"My turn," Piper chirped, giving me a strong hug. She stepped back to admire me. "You are beautiful. I can see why my son Rhett is so taken with you."

Puzzled, I asked, "Your Rhett's mother too?"

"Not by blood, but I consider him my son."

"Can I pulse you?" Freya blurted out.

"Nyx already tried last night," I admitted. "She couldn't sense my animal."

"I'd still like to try," Freya pressed with an excited gleam in her eyes.

"Oh, let her do it," Bonnie begged. "Or she'll obsess about pulsing you for weeks."

"Don't exaggerate." Freya shot her a dirty look. "I don't obsess, Bo."

Bonnie gave her an "I beg to differ" stare.

"Your middle name is obsession," Piper argued. "Remember when we were in high school? The horse-shifter thing?"

"Why do you always have to bring that shit up?" Freya complained.

Curious, I asked, "What horse-shifter thing?"

Bonnie laughed. "When we were in high school, Freya heard a rumor that horse-shifters were hung like horses."

Piper chimed in, "So she became fixated on finding out if the rumor was true."

"Fixated?" Freya arched a well-manicured brow. "That's harsh. It was scientific research."

Bonnie batted her eyelashes. "Henry thought it was love."

"Old Man Henry?" I asked.

"Yep," Bonnie confirmed.

Piper pointed at Freya. "She convinced Henry to go skinny-dipping with her in Bogbeast Lake."

"What happened?" I asked.

Bonnie gave me a wicked grin. "She discovered that he was gloriously hung like a horse, even in icy water."

"He sure was, and he fucked like a stallion." Freya winked at me. "So young lady. Are you going to let me pulse you or not?"

I grinned. "After hearing that story, hell yes."

As Freya got closer, it was her almond-shaped emerald-green eyes that captured my attention—they were almost hypnotic when they focused on me. My brain got fuzzy for a second. My extremities felt like an invisible force was holding me captive, then mysteriously, the trance was broken, along with my brain fog.

"That's so strange," I blurted out.

Freya arched a brow. "That confirms it."

"Confirms what?" I asked.

"That I can't pulse hybrids for as long as I can with full-blood Others. When I first pulsed Imani, something blocked my magic from digging further into what type of Other she was. You just did the same thing. My magic could not penetrate what felt like an invisible perimeter you erected around your body."

I shrugged. "That's what happened to Nyx last night."

"I need to get to the bottom of this hybrid-pulsing situation," Freya murmured.

Piper jabbed Freya in the side. "Stop digging for shit that ain't none of your business."

"Ouch!" Freya gave Piper the stink eye. "Will you quit poking me with that bony elbow of yours?"

"Stop being so damn grumpy," Piper complained before looping her arm through mine. "So Bo told us you're planning on staying in the Ridge."

"I haven't decided." I glared pointedly at Bonnie.

A smile twitched across Bonnie's lips. "I don't see what the holdup is. We all know that you and Rhett are mates."

"Who's we?" I squeaked.

"The whole town," Piper confided. "Gossip travels fast around here."

"I see," I commented.

"That's right," Freya added. "Bo already let everyone know that you're a midwife and you'll be opening a clinic to treat our females."

My eyes widened. "What?"

Piper grinned. "Lord knows we need you in the Ridge, especially if the spell calls more fated mates and they settle down with their mates."

I gave Bonnie a dirty look. "It seems my grandmother has been very busy stirring the gossip pot. But I'm not sure what my plans are when it comes to the Ridge."

All three of them stared at me.

"But we need you," Piper said.

I frowned. "But don't you already have pregnancy health care?"

"What health care?" Piper arched a brow. "Most females rely on Izzy's magic-laced remedies or the town's hot springs to get them through any hiccups during and after their pregnancy."

I frowned. "What about prenatal care, delivery, and post-partum care?"

"Nova, remember we're talking about female shifters, not human females," Bonnie reminded me. "Pregnant shifters don't trust the human world for health care."

"It doesn't matter if they're a human or shifter. Everyone is entitled to health care." I fumed, frustration coursing through my body. "No one should have to choose between the health of their baby and the fear of being captured and dissected by humans."

"We're just explaining the situation," Freya said. "Most female shifters give birth at home or in their birthing dens, with their mates providing comfort and support during the birthing process."

"With no trained medical attention?" My eyes widened.

"None," they said in unison.

"That's not safe for the mother or the baby." My heart was racing with fear, just thinking about all the women in this town who had no trained medical experts. "I've helped bring many babies into this world safely as a certified nurse midwife. My focus is educating and empowering women to make their own health care decisions based on knowledge, not fear. That's why what I do is so important. Women should be empowered to make decisions about their own bodies and be educated to know what's going on."

"And that's why the Ridge needs you," Bonnie said.

Piper touched my shoulder. "Won't you just think about it?"

I nodded. "I'll think about it." I looked at them pointedly. "But you have to stop spreading rumors about a clinic." I'd always wanted to open my own clinic someday. *Is the Ridge the place where I'll finally make my dream come true?*

They looked at one another.

"Um..." Piper scratched her chin. "It's too late for that. Quinn and Imani are planning to announce the news to the town."

"Without confirming it with me?" I threw my hands in the air.

"What confirmation? They heard it from her." They pointed to Bonnie.

"Grandma," I growled.

"What?" She gave me a not-too-innocent stare.

A tall, thin man with black eyes, a potbelly, and a brown cowlick strode up to us and glared at me. "I don't know why the Hunter's here at our festival."

His words ignited my temper. "Excuse me?"

"You know full well that she isn't a Hunter." Bonnie bit out the words. "So go on. Get, Weasel. We don't have time for you or your silly games."

"That's right. Don't be rude," Piper snapped.

He puffed out his chest. "I have a right to my opinion."

Freya snorted. "Opinions are like assholes. Everybody's got one, right?"

"Now get out of here before I tear you a new asshole," Bonnie delivered between clenched teeth.

"You women are plain old ornery," he said before scuttling away.

"Who was that?" I asked.

"Chester. He's a weasel-shifter," Bonnie said. "So we just call him Weasel."

"He's a pain in everyone's ass." Piper scrunched up her nose. "He loves to complain and hear himself talk."

"Attention, everyone." A man's voice boomed over a microphone.

"Let's go," Freya said. "Quinn is about to open the festival."

The four of us made our way to the front of the stage. There was a band sitting on the stage, and Quinn and Imani were standing by the microphone. Imani waved at me, and I waved back.

"Good evening, everyone," Quinn said. "Welcome to the Black Forest Ridge Festival. Tonight's event signifies the return to tradition. The return of unity among our kind."

The crowd clapped, and I nearly jumped out of my skin from

the noise until I remembered Bonnie's tip about modulating sound. Taking a deep breath, I focused on turning down the volume, and it worked.

Quinn continued. "The council and I had considered canceling tonight's festivities in light of the tragic loss last night of a few of our own, Dean and some of his kin. But we decided that the significance of this festival is too important to everyone in this town."

Imani added, "Our Black Forest Ridge Festival is a celebration of our connectedness. No matter our Other race, we are one."

More clapping mixed with cheers.

"We would also like to take this opportunity to share some good news," Quinn said. "Nova King has decided to become our newest resident. She's a certified nurse midwife, and it is our good fortune that she's decided to open a health and wellness center for our expecting females." The crowd cheered, agreeing with Quinn's words.

I hadn't decided shit, but I wasn't going to raise my hand in the middle of his speech and correct him.

When the noise died down, Weasel yelled, "What is this tomfoolery? Town Alpha, why do we need a center?"

Imani rolled her eyes heavenward. "Quinn just told you that she's a midwife. She delivers babies."

"Oh," Weasel said, his cheeks turning red.

"Let the festivities begin!" Quinn shouted. "Dueling banjos, take it away."

Three banjo players began plucking their instruments, and then the rest of the band joined in.

"Come on, Nova." Bonnie looped her arm through mine. "Let's check out the food. I'm hungry."

A young boy ran up to us. "Hi Piper, Bonnie, Freya."

"Hello, Jacob," they said in unison.

"You enjoying the festival, Jacob?" Piper asked.

"Yes, ma'am," he answered, then stared at me.

"This is Nova," Freya said.

"I know," he said. "I need to speak to her…" He peered at Piper, Bonnie, and Freya. "Alone."

Bonnie looked at me. I shrugged.

"Okay," Bonnie agreed, then glanced over at me. "We'll be checking out the food. Come find us when you're done." They waved goodbye and walked away.

"What would you like to talk about, Jacob?"

"Can I have my photos back?"

"What photos?" I asked.

"The ones you took of me by the river."

"So you're the ferret?" I asked.

"Yes, ma'am. That's me. I want my photos back because my grandma says Hunters can't be trusted." He scuffed his sneaker against the grass. "But is that true?"

"Jacob, I can be trusted. And for the record, I'm not a Hunter."

"Okay, lady. Then you can go ahead and keep one, but I need the rest of them for my grandma."

"Okay, that's a deal." I stuck out my hand and said, "Let's shake on it."

"Okay, Nova." He grabbed my hand, shaking it exuberantly.

I nearly jumped out of my skin when my inner animal said in my head, *He's here.*

"Who's here?" I asked aloud.

"What?" Jacob asked, frowning at me.

"Uh, nothing," I stammered.

*Our mate. Rhett. I smell him.*

A few minutes later, Rhett strolled over to us.

"Hi, Nova. Hi, Jacob."

Jacob grinned. "Hey, Protector. Nova and me just cleared up the whole photo thing. Despite what Grandma says, I like her." He stared up at Rhett. "She's my friend now, and I think she needs protecting. When are you going to hire me as a deputy?"

"I'm not." Rhett ruffled his hair. "Now go on. I want to dance with Nova."

He grinned. "See ya, Nova." He ran away.

The band started playing slow music.

"Can I have this dance?" Rhett asked in a low, rough voice.

"Yes."

He pulled me into his arms, and we swayed to the music.

He tilted his head and studied me. "So you're staying and opening a clinic?"

"That's the rumor my grandmother, Piper, and Freya have been spreading."

He smiled, and my heart skipped a beat. "Well, everyone's happy, especially me."

"How happy?"

"This happy." He leaned down, brushing his lips against mine before his tongue darted into my mouth. I sucked on his tongue, and he growled low in his chest before he broke off our kiss.

Wrapping my arms around his neck, I clung to him, wanting this moment to last forever.

"I'm still deciding whether I'm staying. But I can be bribed with food." A smile curved my lips.

He chuckled deep in his chest. The sound was delightful and sexy. "Well, I better feed my female."

Rhett grabbed my hand, lacing his fingers through mine as we sliced through the excited crowd. When we finally made it to the red-and-white booths that lined the massive grassy area, we saw Josie yelling from her booth, "Piping-hot biscuits!" But no matter how loud she got, there were no takers. In fact, pedestrians seemed to be deliberately giving her booth a wide berth, as if they were trying to avoid contact with her and her biscuits.

"Her biscuits must be horrible," I commented. "Because everyone loves biscuits."

"According to town gossip, they're the worst," Rhett confirmed.

"Then how is she still in business?"

"She's an heiress. She doesn't need to make money from her business. Her biscuit shop is some weird hobby."

We stopped at a booth with a Thornbern Brewstillery sign. "Nova, this is Brody, my brother-in-arms. He's also a member of the Bane pack."

Brody winked at me. He was incredibly attractive, with a physical perfection that made him model-worthy. "Wowee, she's definitely a looker."

Rhett frowned at him. "Just serve up the BF Home Brew, and stop eye-fucking my woman."

"All right. All right," Brody said. "Just remember, all I have is strong, stronger, and strongest. Which would you like, Nova?"

"After all the Brew shots I drank last night, I'll take the strong."

"Here you go." He handed me a small cup. Shooting back the amber liquid that burned my throat going down, I felt my eyes start to water. "Holy hell," I choked out. "This stuff is stronger than what I had last night at Mama June's."

Rhett and Brody laughed.

"June tends to water down the Brew so the ladies don't get too drunk and tear her place up," Rhett confided. "After that, you need something to eat." Placing a hand on the small of my back, he gently nudged me away from Brody's booth.

"Don't forget to come back later," Brody called out. "Enjoy yourself."

"Bye, Brody," I said over my shoulder.

"I like him," I said to Rhett. "What type of shifter is he?" I stopped in my tracks. "Or is that impolite to ask?"

"Not in the Ridge." He nudged me along. "Brody, Quinn, and Piper are wolf-shifters. Mack, my deputy, is a lion-shifter. Emmett is a rhino, and Jasper, a tiger."

"Is it common in the Other world to form a pack with different species?"

"No. That's why most residents in this town call us the misfits."

"Misfits? That sounds derogatory."

He shrugged. "We don't care what people say about us. We're more than friends. We're a band of brothers who served in an elite military unit together, and we're inseparable."

We passed a funnel cake booth, and my stomach grumbled. "Why did you decide to settle in the Ridge?"

"When Quinn's father died, he retired—well, we all did—and he came back here to take over as the alpha of this town and alpha of the Bane pack. So instead of going our separate ways, he talked us into making Black Forest our home, and we've never looked back."

We stopped at a booth with a THINGS ON A STICK sign.

"Hey, Darcy. How's it going?" Rhett asked the rotund woman grilling an assortment of meats. The aroma curling up from the grill made me practically tipsy.

"It's going," Darcy replied, then looked over at me. "Welcome, Nova. What can I get you?"

I smiled. "Hi, Darcy. Just surprise me."

"Serving it up," Darcy replied in a singsong voice. She pulled two skewers of sizzling meat off the grill, wrapping them in foil before handing them over to us.

"And two lemonades," Rhett requested, then paid for everything.

We took our food and drinks over to an empty picnic table and sat side by side.

I bit into the succulent, rich smoked meat. "Goodness, it's scrumptious. What is it?"

Rhett ripped a chunk off the skewer. "Don't ever ask what kind of meat Darcy is cooking up. You might not like the answer. Just enjoy." He took another chunk off his skewer and chewed with a look of pure enjoyment on his face.

*He smells better than that meat you're eating,* my inner beast said.

I chewed faster. *Quiet,* I snapped. *Just let me figure this out.*

*What's to figure out?* my beast asked. *We choose him. Now bite him.*

"Question," I squeaked.

"Huh?" He stopped midchew.

"Does your animal talk to you?"

He laughed. "All the time… lately."

"What do you mean by lately?"

"My jaguar has been pissed at me for years. He stopped talking to me. Well, correction, he communicated only when he was complaining about one thing or another. And let me tell you, he's a big complainer. But other than that, he was angry at me because he thought I'd given up on searching for our fated mate." He grabbed my hand. "Now I can't get him to shut up. He's been saying that you're ours from the first moment he got a whiff of your scent." He pressed his muscular thigh against mine.

Picking up my cup, I sucked lemonade through the red-and-white straw. "And did you agree with him?"

"Nope." He shrugged. "I fought my attraction to you because I'm stubborn and a little bit of an asshole."

I arched a brow. "A little bit?"

He laughed. "Okay. Let's split the difference." He cocked his head. "Has your animal been talking to you a lot?"

"Yes," I confessed. "And my bossy beast is making me nuts."

"What's she been saying?"

"Yapping about you. For God's sake, she wants me to bite you… like, right now. Is that normal?"

"The biting, yes. But I bite you first, then you reciprocate."

"I see."

"Your beast is trying to speed up the process because she's chosen me." He grinned. "That makes me extremely happy."

*See? Now bite him.*

*Bite him where?* I asked.

*Do I have to show you everything?* my beast hissed.

*Don't be so rude.*

Rhett said in his quiet, rough voice. "There's no ifs, ands, or buts. You are the missing piece in my life, Nova King. You. Are. Mine." Rhett brought my fingers to his mouth, kissing them one by one. His touch was like a shock of electricity, setting my body aflame. Shamelessly, I ached for more, knowing that I had to maintain my composure because we were out in public. "But the most important question is, what do you want, Nova?"

"Despite the fact that my animal is a bossy chick, I can honestly say that I want you, Sheriff."

His face dissolved into a delicious grin. "Despite the fact that I was an asshole to you when we first met?"

"You were, but let's get past that." I squeezed his hand. "Just don't let it happen again."

"Believe me, I won't."

A tall man with a bushy beard stopped his cart by our table. "Hello, Protector. Hi, Nova."

"Hey, Pete," Rhett replied.

I waved at him.

Pete gestured to his cart. "I'm selling slices of powdered honeycomb. Would you like to try a piece?"

"Pete's a beekeeper," Rhett said. "And sells the best honey in town, hands down."

"Thank you for the compliment." Pete grinned, puffing out his big barrel chest. "You want to taste it?" he asked me.

I raised my hand. "Yes please."

"Let me get two, Pete," Rhett said, handing him the money.

"Thank you kindly," Pete said, sliding the parcels onto our table along with packets of wet napkins before moving on.

I drank some lemonade before asking, "Why does everyone call you Protector?"

"It's an old-school term that shifters in this town still use. Basically, it means because I'm the sheriff, I'm responsible for defending and guarding the residents of this town. But technically, I'm not the only Protector. My pack are all Protectors, and we all care about the well-being of everyone in this town."

"I guess that's what makes this town so special. Well, that and the fact that everyone is Other."

"Yup." He scooted the parcels across to me. "Try the honeycomb."

"Aren't you going to eat one?"

"No, I bought it for you. I'm not a big sweet fan."

"I am. Sweets are my jam." I opened the parcel, revealing a small slice of honeycomb covered with powdered sugar. "I can eat the whole honeycomb, including the honey and waxy cells surrounding it?"

"Yup. Biting into a fresh piece of raw honeycomb is a special experience."

I tore off a piece, and the flavor burst into my mouth. "It's a little bit sweeter than plain old honey. It reminds me of one of those wax-bottle candies, but instead of juice, there's honey inside."

"Exactly," Rhett said before dipping his head and planting his gorgeous lips on mine. I moaned when he nibbled my bottom lip.

Someone cleared his or her throat loudly. We broke apart, glancing over to see a short plump woman with gray hair pulled into a tight bun, wearing a bubblegum-colored sweater set paired with jeans. She stood by our table, staring at me with her lips curled up into a sneer.

"Hello, Sheriff Ward," the woman cooed, angling her body in a position that clearly said she was deliberately snubbing me. "Nice festival, ain't it?"

"Gertrude, I don't take kindly to you ignoring Nova." His nostrils flared. "So please move on."

Gertrude clutched her pearls. "You don't have to be so rude, Sheriff."

Rhett shook his head, the look on his face something close to disgust. "Neither do you."

She tapped her foot. "You can't talk to me like that. I'm a member of the council."

"Which means nothing, especially since you're not the town alpha."

"Yet," she purred.

"Never." He drained his cup of lemonade. "Have a nice evening, you hear."

I burst out laughing when Gertrude nearly tripped in her haste to get away from us.

"What's her deal?" I asked. "Besides her obvious dislike of me."

"Gertrude is a member of the town council, just like Bonnie is."

"And the council rules the town?"

"Not exactly." He glanced at the last piece of my meat. "You going to eat that?"

"Nope. Help yourself."

He popped the bite into his mouth. "Anyway, back to what I was saying. There are nine members on the council, and each are highly respected leaders of their kind. Your grandmother, Bonnie. Isabella, who is a dragon-shifter. Shane is the alpha of the honey badgers. Gertrude is the leader of the ferret-shifters. Freya is the head of the witch coven. The brothers—Wilder and Hugo—are wolf-shifters. Atticus is the leader of the vampire coven. And last but not least, Quinn, the alpha of the Bane pack. The council are advisers to the town alpha, and two of them—Gertrude and Shane—are full-blood snobs."

"So Gertrude has issues with me because I'm a hybrid?"

"Most likely, but I'd pay her no never mind. She's just a bitter woman who has issues with everyone and everything in this town."

Over the loudspeaker, a woman said, "Come on over, folks. It's time for the slippery pig contest."

"A slippery pig contest?" I laughed. "I have to see this."

"Let's go." He cleaned off our table and grabbed my hand,

guiding us over to a large pen filled with pig muck and pigs whose skin was completely oiled up. So trying to catch a pig didn't seem like an easy task for man, woman, or beast.

All the contestants, including Nyx and Imani, were lined up outside the stall. Quinn was standing at the side of the pen with a huge grin on his face.

Nyx called out to me, "Hey, Nova. You participating?"

I shook my head. "Hell no. I'm just here for the entertainment."

Imani laughed. "Chickenshit."

"No, pig shit," Nyx said.

The contestants entered the stall, and the pigs were released.

"Go, Imani!" Quinn yelled, cheering her on from the sidelines. "Get that pig."

I laughed until my stomach cramped as I watched two men try to catch one of the pigs, only to end up facedown in the muck.

I turned to Rhett. "Maybe you should have tried."

"Hell no. I learned a long time ago not to play in pig shit."

Nyx and Imani were hilarious as they tried a two-woman strategy to corral a pig, which was an epic fail. They both ended up facedown in the muck.

Nyx wobbled to her knees while Imani rolled over faceup.

"Get that pig, baby," Quinn said.

The crowd cheered, "Imani. Nyx," over and over.

They both got to their feet, covered in muck.

I chuckled. "I can't watch any more of this."

Rhett shook his head. "Once you see one slippery pig contest, you've seen them all. Let's take a stroll over to the axe-throwing contest to see how good you are."

We walked over to an area set up with throwing targets and a bunch of axes. Three men were lined up in front of each target with three axes lying in front of them by their feet.

"Oh, that's Emmett and Mack," I pointed out.

"The third is Jasper," Rhett informed me.

A referee said, "Go!" and Emmett, Mack, and Jasper picked up their axes and threw each one with spot-on precision, hitting the center of the target.

"They're good." I clapped loudly, then eyed Rhett. "Why don't you try?"

"I'll try if you try."

"I'm game."

We walked up to Emmett, Mack, and Jasper, who greeted both of us. None of them compared to Rhett's bad-boy veneer, but they were certainly handsome, with bodies that looked like they were sculpted out of marble.

*Are all male shifters genetically blessed with good looks and well-honed bodies?*

"Stand here." Rhett positioned me on a spot, then took his place. "This is the twelve-foot line." Mack handed each of us an axe.

"Here are the rules," Jasper told me. "Each game is five throws. You get the highest point value that the blade of your axe touches. Our bull's-eye is worth six points, and each surrounding ring decreases to five, four, three, two, and one points. On the last throw, you can call the eight-ball."

Emmett spoke next. "The target has a small circle with an eight in each corner. If you call the eight-ball on the last throw and hit one of them, you score eight points. If you hit anywhere else, it's worth zero. At the end of the game, the higher score wins."

"Is there a superninja technique to doing this?" I asked Rhett.

"Since you're a beginner, hold the axe with two hands, bring your axe back directly over your head as if throwing a soccer ball, then bring your arms forward, releasing the axe at eye level."

Emmett said, "Go."

Rhett's axe hit the bull's-eye. My axe landed three feet from where I was standing in the dirt. "Shit."

"Six for Rhett. Zero for Nova," Mack said.

Rhett went to his target, pulling out his axe, then coming back to the line.

"Would you like a couple of practice throws before we start?" Rhett asked, his lips curled up into a grin.

I picked up my fallen axe. "Hell no. Let's do this, Sheriff Ward."

By the time I threw my third axe, I launched it with all my might. It landed at the side of the bull's-eye. "Close." My fifth one landed directly into the bull's-eye. "Yes!" I jumped up and down, fists pumping in the air.

"You were supposed to hit your bull's-eye, not mine," Rhett grumbled.

I winked at him. "No one said that. You just said throw it at the target."

"I guess so, my Viking princess warrior." He laughed. "But I hit the bull's-eye five times, which means I got more points than you. So I won." He gave me a quick kiss.

"My, my, my," Josie said. "Ain't this quaint? The sheriff and his hybrid."

"What do you want?" Rhett said, taking a position between Josie and me.

Oh hell no! I appreciated his protective sentiment, but there was no way I wanted Josie to believe that I was weak and afraid of her.

Stepping around him, I stood by his side, earning a *What the fuck?* glare from Rhett.

"Oh, there she is," Josie sneered. "Couldn't see you from your cowering position behind Rhett."

I looked her up and down. "That's some tough talking coming from a woman who snuck into my bedroom while I was sleeping to attack me."

"Attack you?" Josie's eyes widened with fake shock. "I would never do such a thing."

"Lies." I rolled my eyes. "You're just mad because everything about me makes you feel this"—I wiggled my pinkie finger—"small."

A crowd gathered around us in curiosity.

Josie tossed her blond hair before giving me a plastic, beauty-contestant smile. "Nothing about you is better than me, hybrid." She glanced at the axe on the ground. "How about we put that to the test with a little axe-throwing competition?"

"No," Rhett said.

"Let's go," I countered, refusing to back down to Josie.

"Uh, can I have a word with you?" Rhett pulled me to the side and whispered, "What are you doing? You just learned the basics of axe throwing."

"So are you saying you don't think I can beat her?"

"I'm saying don't let her bait you into a pissing contest," he snapped.

"Too late. She's going down." I stomped away from him, back over to the axes.

Our audience was larger. I guess everyone was interested in the shifter vs. hybrid axe-throwing battle.

Josie took a position in front of a target with her axe in hand.

I took the spot to her left.

Rhett turned me to face him. "Throw with two hands," he instructed before giving me a quick kiss. "Kick her ass," he finished.

"Go," Mack instructed.

I threw my axe with two hands. Josie threw one-handed.

"Six points Josie. One point Nova."

After the fourth throw, Josie was winning with twenty points. I had nineteen.

Josie grinned at me. "Last throw, hybrid."

There was no way I was going down without a fight. Then I remembered what Mack had said about the eight-ball. The target had a small circle with an eight in each corner. If I hit one of them, I'd score eight points. If I hit anywhere else, it was worth zero. It was a gamble, but I had to take it.

"I call the eight-ball," I said.

The audience clapped and cheered.

We both threw our axes.

It seemed like time stopped while watching my axe sail through the air until it hit the target.

"Six for Josie. Eight for Nova!" Mack yelled. "Total points—twenty-six for Josie. Twenty-seven for Nova. Declaring Nova the winner!"

The gathering roared with delight.

I fist-pumped the air. "Yes."

"That's my mate." Rhett lifted me up, giving me a loud, smacking kiss.

"Whatever," Josie snapped before stomping off like I had stolen her bike.

"Bye, loser!" I yelled after her.

# CHAPTER 18
## NOVA

"Who knew you were a gambler," Rhett said, ushering me through the gathering. "Calling the eight-ball was risky." He winked at me. "I love your sassiness, darling."

"That's me. Midwife sassy-pants."

"So how shall we celebrate your victory?" he asked.

I pointed to the ice cream booth. "Yummy sweet goodness."

We arrived at the station. I ordered a cup of cookies and cream. Rhett picked chocolate. We strolled around the festival while gobbling the lush cold creaminess.

"Are you enjoying yourself?" he asked, dumping our now-empty cups into a receptacle.

"Yes, Sheriff, I am." I stopped, smiling up at him. "And you?"

"Yes, Nova. You bring me joy." Wicked intent shone in his eyes. He settled his warm hands on my shoulders.

Pleasure raced through me. *Jesus, he's potent.*

His gaze raked over me, heating every inch of my skin.

"Oh my goodness!" someone screamed. "Heidi's water broke, and she's having her baby right in the middle of the festival."

My eyes panned around to find the source of the commotion. Across the grass by a large tent marked Hospitality I saw a crowd gathering. I ran in that direction with Rhett right behind me.

Heidi was on the ground, panting, with a man by her side.

"Clear the space," I ordered. "Back up."

"You heard her," Rhett said. "Move."

Crouching by Heidi, I noticed her water had broken. "How far apart are your contractions?"

She grabbed her stomach. "Every four minutes, and they last for one minute."

"Breathe," the man clutching her hand ordered.

"Shut it, Bruce!" Heidi shouted. "Can't you see that I'm trying?"

"I'm only helping, darling," Bruce offered.

Heidi's face was beet red as she huffed and puffed. "Well, zip it."

Bruce rubbed her shoulders.

Eyeing Bruce, I said, "I presume you're her mate."

"You presume correctly, little lady, and I need to take her home to our birthing nest."

"Bruce, I hate to break it to you, but your baby is on its way now." I peered at Rhett. "We're going to need to move her somewhere close that's big and relatively clean."

He gestured to the tent to our left. "This hospitality tent should do the trick."

The audience continued pressing toward us.

"People, please step back," Rhett ordered.

Heidi wailed.

I glanced over at Bruce and Rhett. "We need to move her quickly into the tent." They both did as ordered, carefully carrying her inside.

"Get her on the cot in the corner," I directed. "Bruce, sit down behind her, then ease her between your legs. We need to help her into a position to get her through contractions." Once that was accomplished, I said, "Rhett, I'm going to need some clean cloths and a sharp instrument to cut the cord."

He nodded and left the tent to handle his assignment.

Heidi wasn't coping well with her contractions.

I patted her arm. "Heidi, I know this is not the best of circumstances, but we have to make do." I took a deep breath, worried because I didn't have any of my medical instruments needed to check her vitals and listen to the baby's as well, but I had to roll with it.

Rhett returned with the things I had asked for.

I heard lots of noise outside, too close to the tent.

"Rhett, can you please keep everyone out of here?" I requested.

He nodded. "Will do." He marched out of the tent. "Go on, people. Move. Everything's being handled."

Heidi wailed in pain again. Removing her panties, I checked her vagina. The head was crowning. Heidi was ready to deliver.

"Push!" I ordered. "Heidi, push."

Hours later, Rhett and I stood by his cruiser, watching partiers dancing the night away.

"You were amazing back there," Rhett praised. "You were solid as a rock and so confident. Are you sure this was your first time delivering shifters?"

"Hell yes." I emptied my water bottle, tossing it into the nearby recycling bin. "I've helped deliver lots of babies but never triplet rabbit-shifters. That was a whole different experience for me."

"Bad or good?"

"Good, but strange. Especially when Heidi shifted into a gigantic bunny after giving birth."

"She had to shift in order to start her body's healing process."

I sighed heavily. "I have a lot to learn about shifters." Regardless of Heidi's shifter healing abilities, tomorrow I planned on visiting her to make sure her newborns transitioned well and that Heidi was recovering.

"But you will," he reassured me with a rub on my shoulder. "From what I've heard, most shifters giving birth just push and hope for the best. What you did with Heidi was guide her through the birthing process, making sure the bleeding was appropriate. Believe me, townsfolk will be talking about what you did for Heidi for days to come."

After the delivery, Rhett had told me that everyone had gathered outside the tent and used their shifter hearing to eavesdrop on Heidi's birthing process.

Gently, he tugged me to stand in front of him. "I'm proud of you, Nova."

"Thank you, but I'm just doing my job as the town's midwife." I trailed my fingers across his chest.

He tilted his head and studied me. "So that means you've decided to stay?"

"Yes. In all good conscience, there's no way in hell I can walk away from women who can use my help." I sighed heavily. "No doubt, it will probably be rough in the beginning gaining the trust of the women in this town, but I'm up for the challenge. Besides, I've always wanted to open my own clinic, and this town just feels right to build my dream."

"This dream..." He reached down and took my hand, squeezing it softly. "Does it include me... us?" He watched me closely, the look in his eyes making me feel beautiful and precious.

"Yes, Sheriff, it does."

His hungry eyes scanned me, making me tremble and yearn for him. "I don't want to push, but I want you to spend the night with me."

"Push, shifter." I backed him against his cruiser.

He growled, grabbing the back of my hair, nipping my lips.

"Sheriff," a woman's voice called out.

With an aggrieved sigh, he pressed his forehead against mine. "What now?" he mumbled.

The woman called again, "Yoo-hoo, Protector."

"Hi, Trudy," he said while turning me around, pressing my back against his chest. "How can I help you?"

Trudy ran up to us with a flustered expression. "Hi, Nova. Great job back there with delivering Heidi's babies."

"Thank you," I replied, deliberately pressing my ass against Rhett's hard cock. Trudy gave me a wide smile. "This town sure needs a midwife like you. I was just talking to Bo, Piper, and Freya—"

"Trudy?" Rhett interjected. "You came over here because you wanted something?"

"Oh yes." Her face flushed. "Sorry, I almost forgot what I came over here for. It's about Henry."

"What about him?" Rhett said.

"Well, it's not like him to miss tonight's festival. And I've been asking around, and folks haven't seen him in days. I'm worried about him. Can you ride over to his place and check on him?"

"Sure. No problem, Trudy," he replied.

"Thanks, Sheriff. Night, you two." Trudy waved before bustling away.

"I'm sorry, Nova."

Turning around, I wrapped my arms around his neck. "I know, duty calls."

"Rain check?" he asked.

"Definitely," I agreed.

# CHAPTER 19
# RHETT

Pulling up to Henry's place, I parked and hopped out. As I glanced around, I noticed Henry's truck parked at the side of his house. From the light shining through his windows, he had to be home, especially since country music was blaring from inside.

I frowned when I strode up to the wide-open front door. "Henry?" I called out.

No one answered.

"Henry?" I yelled again, stepping inside his house.

Still no response.

I ventured into the kitchen. On top of his table was an opened bottle of beer and a plate full of untouched food. It looked like he was about to settle down for dinner, but I could tell the food had been sitting there for quite a while.

"Fuck. Something's wrong."

Pulling out my cell, I called Mack. "Hey, it looks like there's trouble over here at Old Man Henry's place."

"On my way," Mack replied.

Making my way out of the kitchen, I headed toward the sound of blaring country music and ended up in Henry's living room. Turning off the radio, I peered around the space.

"Yeah. This ain't right."

Furniture was tossed about like there had been a scuffle. But the most damning clue that Henry was in trouble was the scent and sight of his blood that was splattered across the floor.

Sniffing loudly, I also scented the horrible odor of Sam. I followed the trail of blood out of the living room, down the hallway, and out the back door. The droplets of blood were heavier outside on the grass.

I continued following the blood across Henry's lush green pasture. That was when I saw it. Henry's body was splayed out in the center of the pasture. Sprinting over, I knew by the smell of decomposition wafting through the air that Henry was dead.

Careful not to destroy evidence, I circled his body. From the wolf claw marks on what was left of his corpse, he had been mauled to death. And the scent of Sam was unmistakable—the stench of the unwashed body burned the hairs in my nose.

Anger coursed through my veins.

Henry was a kind man who didn't deserve this brutal death.

I heard a vehicle drive up, and a few minutes later, Mack called out, "Rhett?"

"Back of the house," I answered. "In the pasture."

It didn't take Mack long to locate me, and when he did, sniffing the air loudly, he declared, "Dammit, Sam strikes again. His scent is all over Henry's body."

Sam had tossed Henry's legs a few feet from his torso. "Sam's escalating," I muttered.

"But why Henry?" Mack asked as he crouched down, examining the torso. "He didn't have a bad bone in his body."

"Only Sam can tell us that. Let me call Quinn to tell him what's going on." I pulled out my cell.

"Wait!" Mack shouted. He pointed to Henry. "What's that shiny thing in his right hand?"

We both stepped closer, hovering over his body. "You got gloves?" I asked Mack.

Mack pulled out black latex gloves from the emergency case

he'd brought with him. A set for him and one for me. Both of us donned gloves, and Mack pulled the object out of Henry's hand.

"What's this?" Mack asked, eyeing the object.

"I think it's a woman's pendant." It was an expensive-looking, diamond-encrusted black pendant in the shape of a jaguar.

I sniffed the pendant, and I stiffened at the scents of Sam, Henry, and Nova. "Wait a minute." I eyed Mack. "Remember when I told you that Sam broke into Nova's car and stole her pendant? This pendant belongs to her."

"Why would Sam try to frame Nova?"

"Who the hell knows?" I countered. "It could be because she has Hunter blood or that she's hybrid. Maybe he has a vendetta against Bonnie. Maybe he's just fucking crazy. But until I catch his ass, I'm in a real fucked-up predicament."

"What are you talking about, in a predicament?"

"Henry was found dead with Nova's pendant clutched in his hand. We have to put that in our report. Don't you think the town is going to find out about that?"

"What if we just left that part out?" Mack asked. "From the way you and Nova were acting back there at the festival, I'm assuming you plan to claim her as your mate. Do you really want that kind of trouble right now?"

He was right. I didn't want trouble. Not when I knew with all my heart that Nova was mine. I'd wasted so much time since she'd arrived in town, fighting our attraction. Fighting the proof that she was my fated mate. Our time together at the festival proved that it was more than her scent linking us together. We had chemistry, and at the festival, I'd found myself relaxing, enjoying her touch and her humor.

I clenched my fists. "I swore to uphold the law and protect the citizens of this town." I looked at him pointedly. "You did too. We can't just go bending the law. We have to reveal the truth. Regardless of the fact that we know it was Sam who committed this crime. We have to present all the evidence and let the chips fall where they may."

Mack shook his head. "That's your call. But you know that the townsfolk will automatically blame Nova because she has a Hunter bloodline."

Everything in me yelled to protect her by hightailing it out of town with her, but that would only cast a shadow of guilt over her when Nova didn't commit this crime.

Pacing back and forth, I said, "It may be to our advantage to go ahead to hold her in jail for her own protection against the townsfolk and maybe even Sam. Think about it. It's the perfect scenario. We don't have to lie to the residents, and she'll be protected at the same time."

Mack crossed his arms. "Do you really think Nova's going to like being locked up?"

"It's for her own safety," I countered.

Mack shook his head. "I can already see this shit between you and Nova going downhill fast."

"She'll understand."

But I knew she wouldn't.

In fact, she'd probably hate me for putting her in jail. But as Protector of this town, hard decisions had to be made, and I was making them.

# CHAPTER 20
## RHETT

Parking my cruiser in front of Bonnie's house, I sat there staring at nothing in particular while my inner beast was throwing a tantrum. He was pissed with me for coming here, and I didn't blame him. But if I didn't do this, Nova wouldn't be safe.

My cell buzzed with a text. Swiping it, I read the group text Quinn sent out to the residents, detailing my report about Henry's death and the evidence found at the scene, including signs that Sam was the killer and mentioning Nova's pendant.

"Fuck!" I shoved my cell into the cup holder. I knew this was going to be the hardest thing I'd ever done in my life, but it had to be done… for Nova's protection.

*Don't do this,* my jaguar begged.

*And if I don't, how do I protect her from the wrath of the Ridge residents?*

*We fight,* he grumbled.

*No, we find Sam, get a confession, proving to the town that she's innocent. I will not have my mate living under a cloud of suspicion.*

*I don't like this,* my animal snapped.

Neither did I, but I wasn't going to admit that to him. Getting through what I had to do next was hard enough.

Stepping out of the cruiser, I walked up to Bonnie's door and banged on it. It took a couple of minutes before she opened it.

"Hi, Bonnie. Can I come in?" I stepped in. She slammed the door and glared at me.

"What is this shit about Nova's pendant?" She held up her cell. "It's all over town. Do you really think she could do something like that?"

"No. But we had to disclose everything, Bonnie." I panned my gaze around, searching for Nova.

"Bonnie?" Nova called, coming into the living room. She smiled when she saw me. "Hi, Rhett. What are you doing here?" She frowned. "Why are you so tense?"

"I'm here to put you under protective custody," I answered. "At the station."

Bonnie shook her fist. "Oh fuck no."

"Bonnie, calm down." Nova touched her arm. "Let's hear him out." She stared at me. "What's going on, Rhett?"

"Sam killed Henry," I revealed.

Tears welled up in Nova's eyes. "Why would he kill that poor man?"

"We don't know for sure, but your pendant was found at the crime scene and it was clutched in Henry's hand."

"But you know Sam stole my pendant," Nova countered. "It's obvious that he's trying to frame me for the murder."

"There is no doubt in my mind that you're innocent, Nova. But the residents of this town won't give a shit about the truth. All they'll focus on is that your pendant was found on Henry. Quinn sent out a group text to the residents, laying out the details from my report. But I guarantee you, they won't give a shit about logic. You have Hunter blood, and prejudices run deep."

"Why the fuck would they think that I would kill Henry?" Nova argued.

"Because you come from a Hunter bloodline," Bonnie fumed. "Which gives the racist fuckers an excuse to blame you for his death." She glared at me. "What's next? Torches and pitchforks on my damn porch?"

Touching Nova's elbow, I said, "That's exactly why I need to put you in protective custody down at the jail."

"I thought we went through this shit once," Nova said. "I don't need protecting."

Turning her to face me, I cupped her cheek. "Yes, you do, darling. I need to keep you safe while I hunt down Sam. We need his confession to clear your name."

"Bullshit," Bonnie argued. "If you haven't found him yet, what makes you think you can now?"

Heat flushed through my body as I whipped my head around to face Bonnie.

Bonnie flexed her fingers. "Some fucking Protector you are. You couldn't protect Dean, his kin, or Henry. What makes you think you can protect my granddaughter?"

I flinched as if she'd slapped me.

"Bonnie!" Nova exclaimed. "Take that back."

"No." Bonnie's lips flattened.

Planting my feet wide, I stared Bonnie down. "That's a low damn blow, Bonnie."

With her chin held high, Bonnie said, "I don't give a shit." She pointed a trembling finger over at Nova. "My granddaughter is in danger because you and your pack of Protectors can't stop a fucking feral wolf-shifter from his murderous spree."

"Grandma, stop," Nova begged. "Enough."

"No, I won't stop." Her voice croaked. "He wants to put you in jail."

"For her own damn protection," I repeated. "Do you fucking think that I would put my mate in protective custody unless it was absolutely necessary?"

Wrapping an arm around Nova's waist, I pinned her to my side. "She's mine, and I'd fucking lay down my life for her in a heartbeat. But you and I know that if I don't bring her down to the station, residents will tear this house apart just to get to her.

Do you want Nova hurt or, God forbid, killed during their wild tear to hand out their form of justice?"

"Bonnie, he's right," Nova said. "With me in jail, cooler heads might prevail with the residents thinking justice is being served." She walked over to Bonnie, grabbing her hand. "I don't like this shit, but we have to give Rhett time to find Sam." She made eye contact with me. "And he will find him."

The muscles in my body relaxed when I heard the trust and belief in Nova's voice.

Bonnie pulled Nova into a tight hug. "I don't like this, but I'll go along with it because I have to." She released Nova, peering at me. "Forgive me for throwing a tantrum. I let my fear do the talking. I know by your actions and not just words that you've always done right by this town. So I know that you'll do right by my granddaughter."

"Damn right, I will," I asserted. "It's tearing me up inside that I have to do this, but if the townsfolk get their hands on Nova, I won't be able to stop myself from retaliating." And I would, ripping apart anyone who dared to hurt Nova. "Let's play this by the book."

Bonnie nodded. "Agreed."

I walked up to Nova, placing my hands on her shoulders. "I'm sorry, baby."

"I know," she whispered, cupping my cheek. "Let's get this over with."

Stepping back, Nova turned, and we all slowly walked out of the house. Opening the door to my cruiser for Nova, I slammed the door after she was safely inside, then hopped in, taking off. Bonnie followed in her vehicle.

Inside my cruiser, it was silent all the way to the station, each of us lost in our own thoughts until we finally reached our destination.

"Well, that didn't take long," I growled, staring at the crowd thronged around the station.

"There the Hunter is!" someone shouted.

"About time," another person replied.

My pack—Quinn, Imani, Piper, Mack, Emmett, Brody, and Jasper—was out in force, corralling the crowd, pushing them away from the station's entrance, giving us a safe path inside. Freya, Nyx, Izzy, Rose, and June were arguing with the residents stupid enough to actually bring fucking torches.

"Rhett," Nova said softly, placing a hand on my thigh and squeezing. "Get your shit together. You have to do this."

I was in a fucked-up predicament. Torn between protecting the town and protecting my woman.

"What I have to do," I snarled, releasing my death grip on the steering wheel, "and what I want to do are two different things." I glanced over at her, lacing my fingers through hers. "They'll try to kill you if we don't find Sam, bringing him in for justice."

"Then find him, Protector." She leaned over, giving me a tender kiss. "Now let's go." She unlaced her fingers from mine. "My mob is waiting."

I loved Nova's strength, courage, and humor in the face of this explosive and dangerous situation. It fortified me for what I had to do. Put my female in jail for a damn crime she didn't commit.

Taking a deep breath, I exited my cruiser, ignoring the screaming and yelling crowd as I came around to open Nova's door.

"Go home," Quinn boomed to the people.

"We have a right to be here," Blanche, the owner of the town's gas station, said.

"And I have the right to rip those ugly rollers out of your hair," Freya countered.

The crowd began chanting, "Justice. Justice. Justice" while surging forward.

"Get back!" Mack shouted, pushing the residents. "And Josie, if you don't put away that rolling pin, I'm going to arrest you."

"She better put it away," Bonnie shouted. "Because I'm one step away from beating her ass with it."

Nova held out her hands to me.

"What are you doing?" I asked.

"You have to do this by the book, Rhett. Handcuff me."

I scowled. "No. I'm not doing that shit."

"Rhett, just fucking do it," Nova argued. "Have you forgotten your job?"

She was right. I had to do this by the book. Reluctantly, I handcuffed her wrists in front of her body. Nova and I walked around the cruiser to face the belligerent crowd.

"I can't believe they actually brought torches," Nova complained. "Well, ain't they bringing medieval back?"

The horde pushed forward. My pack shoved them back.

"I knew there was something not right with that Hunter girl," Weasel bragged with a smug expression that I wanted to rip off his face.

Josie's hand flew out to grab Nova's hair. I caught her movement midmotion, gripping her wrist. "If you touch my woman," I growled, pushing her arm away, "so help me, I'll fucking kill you." Josie swallowed hard, stepping back.

I angled my face in a silent warning to anyone who would dare try to attack Nova. The gang parted like the Red Sea as I continued to usher her along the path. I breathed a sigh of relief when we got inside to safety. Heidi was standing at her desk with tears running down her cheeks.

Nova walked up to Heidi. "What are you doing here? You just had triplets. You should be resting."

"Bruce is home with the babies. I had to be here." She sobbed. "What they're doing to you is not right."

Sally crossed her arms. "Heidi's right. I came here in support of Nova."

"Heidi. Sally." I patted their shoulders. "Thank you, but go home. It's dangerous right now. In fact, take the day off tomorrow."

"No," Heidi and Sally said in unison.

"I can't just sit at home with my thumb up my ass while those jackasses outside are acting the fool," Sally said.

"Me neither," Heidi agreed.

"I appreciate you, but go home," I ordered.

The last thing I needed was my staff getting attacked for standing in solidarity with Nova and me. They nodded, walking away reluctantly.

Pressing my palm against Nova's lower back, I said, "Let's go." We made our way to the back of the station, where the cells were located.

I unlocked her handcuffs. "You okay, darling?" I rubbed her wrists.

"I'm okay," she replied.

I brought her wrists up to my lips, kissing every inch of her skin slowly.

"Uh, Rhett..." Her pink tongue snaked out to wet her full lips, and that was when I saw the transformation of her eyes. "Your eyes," Nova whispered. "They're amber."

"As are yours. If you needed proof that I'm yours and you're mine, then here it is."

Quinn yelled, "Rhett?" from the front of the station.

We broke apart, and I sighed heavily. "Duty calls," I grumbled before opening the cell door.

Nova walked into the cell, plopping down on the edge of the bed. "You better find that killer fast, Protector, because you and I have some unfinished business."

# CHAPTER 21
## RHETT

I stood at the side of the town hall's stage, staring out at the irate crowd chanting, "Justice. Justice. Justice." All rational thought had flown out the window. Residents were acting like piranhas that smelled blood in the water.

"You can take your justice and shove it up your ass," I grumbled.

"Enough!" Quinn exploded, glaring at the crowd.

Silence echoed throughout the space.

"Your behavior is deplorable," he continued. "Because of your mob-like antics, I had to leave my pack behind at the station to keep the rest of the hooligans at bay."

He crossed his arms, glowering at the audience that included five council members, Freya, Isabella, and the two perpetual troublemakers—Gertrude and Shane.

"This is not who we are," Quinn pointed out. "For Pete's sake, a couple of hours ago, we just had a damn festival about unity and peace. Now there's rioting outside the police station?"

"We are united." Gertrude stood and primly adjusted her pearls. "United with the townsfolk against that damn Hunter."

The crowd cheered.

"We who?" Freya asked. "The town council? Because all I see

sitting next to you is Shane. Two members of the council does not equate to 'we.' I'm a member of the council, and I'm not in agreement with any of your fuckery."

Shane stood, clearing his throat. "About that… Quinn, it's highly irregular for you to call a meeting without alerting the entire council to take part in such proceedings."

"Exactly." Gertrude nodded like a bobblehead. "Others law specifically states that any resident who commits a crime must stand before the council for judgment."

"Nova is not a resident," Isabella pointed out.

"She's a Hunter!" Josie shouted. "Who murdered one of our own, Henry."

"Did you people even read my group text to the town?" Quinn demanded. "I laid out the facts. Sam killed Henry."

"Then why was her pendant found in his hand?" Gertrude countered.

The crowd clapped and nodded in agreement.

Bonnie stood, glaring daggers at Gertrude. "Sam set Nova up for the fall, and we're going to prove it."

Gertrude sniffed. "Of course you'd say that. She's your kin."

"Why would Sam set up Nova?" Shane countered. "He doesn't even know the Hunter."

I'd had enough of this posturing bullshit. "Sam doesn't need a reason," I barked. "If you're going to ask that fool-ass question, why don't you ask why he killed Dean and his kin?"

Chester the Weasel shouted, "I think the sheriff needs to excuse himself from these proceedings, given the fact that according to rumors, he has an eye for that Hunter."

"Shut up." Piper slapped him across the back of his head.

"Ouch!" Chester complained, rubbing his head. "I have a right to speak my mind."

"You have the right to shut the hell up," Bonnie replied.

"Or I'll shut you up," June added.

"First," I started, "she's not a Hunter. Second, me having an eye for Nova doesn't have shit to do with anything." I tightened my fists. "I'm fair across the board. I put her in jail just like I'd do with anyone else."

Josie stood. "So you admit to being sweet on the Hunter."

"Nova is mine," I said simply.

Josie's mouth opened, then shut, as if she couldn't believe what she heard.

Some of the attendees gasped with wide eyes as if my announcement were sacrilegious and I needed to be doused with holy water before getting staked through the heart.

"Well, if that's the case, I agree with Chester," Gertrude chimed in. "You need to remove yourself from these proceedings."

"I agree," Shane added.

Isabella eyed Shane. "Well, that's a surprise," she commented sarcastically.

"Let's be perfectly clear," Quinn boomed out. "No one in this damn room or town has the authority to say who stays or who goes in the Ridge except me." He eyed Gertrude and Shane. "I own this fucking town, and you're living here because my family and I granted you permission. My consent can be revoked at any time."

A smattering of the crowd clapped and whistled.

Quinn continued. "I own all the land in this town except for what my family bestowed upon a select few residents as a gift and what we've sold outright. Gertrude and Shane are not on that property-owner list."

I grinned when I saw the thunderous expressions on Gertrude's and Shane's faces.

"There are also stipulations in all my property contracts which state I have the right to take back any land sold or given if I fucking feel like it." Quinn eyed Gertrude and Shane. "Now I tried to play nice with you two because back in the day, your kin were close with mine. But I've had enough of your shit. This power battle that you two are trying to wage with me is futile. You own nothing in the Ridge. So you either get your shit together and play nice with the others, or get the fuck out of town."

Some of the audience whooped, whistled, and clapped.

Dean's mate, Agnes, stood. "Alpha, if I may, I'd like to say something."

Quinn nodded.

"Sam killed my mate and some of his kin," Agnes said. "And he would have killed me too if I hadn't run like Dean told me to. Dean gave up his life for me." Her voice broke, but she continued. "Y'all didn't see the madness in Sam's eyes. I did. He's feral, and he must be put down like the rabid wolf he is. Given what I saw that night he attacked us, I believe Sam killed Henry. Sam's a stone-cold killer. And you prejudiced motherfuckers are turning a blind eye to the truth. Nova did not kill Henry."

After Agnes's speech, I could feel and see that the majority of the audience wasn't as convinced of Nova's guilt.

"But evidence is evidence, and that Hunter is guilty," Josie claimed, staring directly at me with a smirk.

"Well, I'm going to find Sam and bring his ass to justice," I vowed.

Shane waved a hand in dismissal. "Good luck with that."

The crowd cackled and whispered among themselves.

I wasn't going to waste my time trying to convince them that I'd do what I'd just promised. I was military through and through, and I'd never failed a mission, especially not with so much on the line—my mate's life.

"Well then, Protector," Gertrude said, strutting out to stand before the audience. "According to Others law, you have forty-eight hours to do so." She turned, giving Quinn and me a look that radiated superiority. "After that, justice will be served to your Hunter."

Some erupted with clapping, hooting, and cheering.

The door to the hall banged open. Heads swiveled to the location of the commotion. A tall muscular man with waist-length matted hair and a bushy, unkempt beard stood on the threshold, wearing dingy pants, an animal pelt for his shirt, and no shoes.

"Who's that?" someone shouted.

"He smells familiar," another person said.

Quinn and I leaped off the stage to head off trouble from the mysterious man as he lumbered into the hall to a wave of gasps, loud whispers, and stares.

"I've got information for the alpha and the sheriff," the man said in a gravelly voice.

Quinn tilted his head as if recognizing the man. "Clancy?"

"Yes," he acknowledged.

My eyes narrowed. Clancy was Quinn's childhood friend and former military like us. Clancy had it all until he caught the feral sickness. Now he was on the Shifter Council's most wanted list.

# CHAPTER 22
## RHETT

After the town hall meeting, I gathered supplies into several backpacks, stowing them in my cruiser. We decided to leave Mack, Emmett, and Brody back at the station to keep watch.

Quinn, Clancy, Jasper, and I piled into my cruiser. And once I pulled away, Quinn said, "Clancy, I saw the video footage of you assaulting your victims. Why'd you do it?"

There was a beat of silence, and for a moment, I thought Clancy wasn't going to answer. Then he suddenly said, "That night I was running through the forest." He cleared his throat. "The feral sickness had me in its grip something fierce then, and one thing led to another. Somehow, I found myself in the human world. I was going to head back to the Ridge when I saw two shifters attacking a hybrid female. Something snapped inside me, and I attacked her assailants, and I don't regret it."

"What?" Quinn barked. "Shifters? A hybrid? That's not the Shifter Council's story. They said both men and the female were human. That your attack was unprovoked."

Clancy snorted. "Unprovoked? That's bullshit. Before they attacked the female, I heard the disgusting things they planned to do to her. And these men were her peers. Trackers like her."

"They worked for the Shifter Council?" I asked. "How do you know this?"

"Because I didn't immediately leave the scene after the attack," Clancy replied. "I camouflaged myself in the forest, far enough away not to be seen, but close enough to see and hear everything. I needed to make sure the female would be taken care of. Eventually, the female awoke, and some guy showed up. According to his conversation with the female, he was a Tracker too. Quinn, what the Shifter Council told you about that night was a lie, and the video they showed you had to have been altered."

Quinn sighed heavily. "Well, this puts everything in a different perspective."

"Yep," Jasper chimed in. "Quinn, we can't turn him in to the Shifter Council."

"Turn me in?" Clancy asked. "I was defending her."

"That's not what the Council believes," Quinn said. "You're now on their most wanted list. And I'm under a lot of scrutiny from the Council. They blame me for your attack."

"I didn't mean for that to happen," Clancy said.

"I told them that you weren't in the Ridge," Quinn said. "And that I'd turn you in if you ever showed back up. Clearly, now that I know the real story, I have no intention of doing that. But you should know that their Trackers are looking for you in the human world."

"I'm former Special Ops like you," Clancy said. "They won't find me unless I want to be found."

"Good," Quinn replied. "Because I'm not telling them where you're at."

"But what about all those townsfolk at the town hall?" Clancy asked. "They saw me."

"But they don't know you're a fugitive," I replied. "Quinn only told the pack and a few trusted friends."

"Yep." Quinn nodded. "I already had enough trouble with

the feral sickness problem in the Ridge. I didn't want to add fuel to the fire by telling residents about what you did."

Finally we made it to one of the many spots that we considered the edge of the forest.

"Stop here," Clancy ordered.

I parked, and we all hopped out. Opening the trunk, I handed out backpacks filled with supplies to Quinn and Jasper, then tugged my own pack onto my back.

Clancy pointed to the left of the forest. "Straight through there. You should find him easily with that Tracker"—he looked at Jasper—"you have there." He glared at the three of us. "Clear Sam from the edge. He's getting too close to my territory."

Now it made sense. Clancy came to the town hall to snitch about Sam's whereabouts because he wanted to ensure Sam didn't encroach on the piece of the edge that he now called home.

Without another word, Clancy lumbered off in the other direction.

"Wait," Quinn called out.

Clancy stopped but didn't turn around to face us.

Quinn continued. "Freya's found a solution for unmated males. She's cast a mating spell that called all fated mates of the unmated males to the Ridge. One of them that might show up could be yours."

"It's too late for me!" Clancy shouted. "I'm too far gone."

"Freya thinks that not only can fated mates stop unmated males from going feral but cure feral shifters like you of your feral sickness."

"I already know who she is," Clancy responded. "And she deserves a hell of a lot better than me. It's for the best that I stay away from her." Then he strode into the forest.

The three of us stared at his retreating back.

"I ain't trying to be insensitive, but I'm one lucky bastard," I said with clenched fingers. "If Nova hadn't come along when she did, in a year or sooner, I probably would have suffered the same fate as Clancy."

Along with most unmated males in the Ridge, all the men in our pack—except mated Quinn—had been spending more and more time in our animal form. Days would go by without us shifting back to our human. Our animals were going insane without our fated mates. It was a fucked-up and sad situation. And since I'd relocated to the Ridge, I'd heard of several perfectly good men going feral—or, as some old-timers called it, getting the feral sickness—and then wandering off into the vast land called the outer edges of the Ridge, never to be seen again.

Quinn nodded. "I would have for sure if I hadn't been blessed with the love of my life, Imani."

"Well, Mack, Emmett, Brody, and I haven't found our mates," Jasper barked. "So we might be taking that same walk of shame like Clancy into the outer edge."

Quinn's expression turned grim. "Not if I can help it."

I clapped Jasper's back in reassurance and solidarity. "We're a pack. We'll fight the feral sickness tooth and nail."

Jasper's lips curled up into a grin. "Well, I don't know about you two, but I'm finished talking about our feelings." He made air quotes. "Can we move the fuck on?"

Quinn and I chuckled. Jasper didn't wallow in self-pity for too long, and that was what we loved about him.

"Yep," Quinn and I said in unison before the three of us marched into the forest in search of Sam.

# CHAPTER 23
## NOVA

I jumped up from a surprisingly sound sleep when I heard a loud commotion outside my cell. Rubbing my eyes, I glanced at my phone. It was eight in the morning. My lips curled up at the "I love you" text from Bonnie.

My eyes widened when Imani appeared with Nyx and two other women—one with a blond buzz cut, the other with reddish-brown hair with white streaks who was rocking an all-leather outfit.

"Your girls are here," Imani called out. "And we brought you much-needed sustenance." She placed the gigantic basket she was lugging with two hands on the floor before walking right into my open cell.

"Are you going somewhere?" I gestured to the hard-case trunks with wheels each of them had dragged into the station.

"It's a surprise," Imani explained, plopping down next to me before giving me a quick side hug. "We would have gotten here sooner, but between me cooking up this mouthwatering feast and us having to push our way through the crowd of idiots still outside the station, time slipped away."

I appreciated the company but had to ask, "Are you guys even supposed to be here?"

"We"—Imani gestured to all of them—"have the right to be here with our friend."

"Exactly," Nyx agreed. "If they want to stand outside acting like jackasses, let them have at it." They all left their trunks behind before strolling inside the cell.

"I was this close"—Blond Buzz Cut held up two fingers—"to casting my 'shut the fuck up' spell on those morons."

Nyx sat on the other side of me, resting her head on my shoulder. "You know, this cell is a lot bigger than it looks from the outside," she marveled.

"That's Rose," Imani gestured to the beautiful, lanky woman with a pouf of reddish-brown hair with pristine white streaks.

I extended my hand, but instead, she pulled me up into a big hug. "I'm a hugger." When we broke apart, Rose gushed, "I'm so happy to meet you finally. Granted, it's not under the best circumstances." She gave the cell a disdainful stare.

"That's for sure," I replied.

"My turn," said the gorgeous woman with high cheekbones and the blond buzz cut. She hugged me, then stepped back. "I'm Izzy."

I smiled. "You're the town's healer."

She nodded. "Yep. I do my best."

"They're part of our take-no-shit crew," Imani divulged.

"Yes, ma'am." Izzy saluted. "I'm a proud card-carrying member."

"Ditto," Rose chirped.

Nyx extended the small bag clutched in her hand. "Bonnie packed some toiletries in case you want to freshen up."

I accepted the bag like precious cargo. "Thank you."

Nyx continued. "Bo, June, Freya, and Piper would be here, but they've been running around town since last night, paying in-person visits to all their connections in the Ridge."

Imani nodded. "They've been busting their asses to rally as many supporters as they can for you, just in case Quinn and Rhett miss the forty-eight-hour deadline."

I arched a brow. "What deadline?"

"Gertrude started the proverbial timer during the town hall meeting last night." Imani's expression turned thunderous. "They have forty-eight hours to find Sam and bring him in for justice."

"And if they don't?" I asked.

"Shit will hit the fan," Nyx answered. "And the rioters outside will more than likely try to come in here and drag you out to stand before the town council for sentencing."

I finger-combed my thick hair. "Well, that ain't good."

"I wouldn't worry about it," Imani said. "Quinn and Rhett have a solid lead on Sam's whereabouts."

My heart raced with fear, just thinking about the possibility of Rhett being in danger. "Are you sure I'm worth all this trouble?"

"Hell yes!" they all responded.

"No more talking about this shit," Imani demanded. "Time to feast like the queens we all are."

"I need to brush my teeth," I stated. "Which way to the bathroom?"

Imani pointed to the right.

It didn't take me long to arrive at the good-sized bathroom. After getting the morning stink off my breath by brushing my teeth, I scrubbed my face clean with the facial scrub Bonnie provided. Drying my face with paper towels, I brushed and detangled my big thick cloud of hair. When I took a quick look at my reflection in the mirror, the dark-skinned woman staring back looked refreshed and relaxed. But on the inside, I was a whirling sea of angst.

*What if Rhett doesn't find Sam?*

*Will the council punish me for a crime I didn't commit?*

*And what will their punishment be?*

*Death?*

*Mauling by animals?*

*Stripping me naked and parading me through the streets while the council shouts, "Shame! Shame!" as residents pelt shit and rotten food at me?*

I shuddered at the horrific possibilities.

*Your mate will never allow any of that to happen,* my inner animal remarked.

And I agreed with her.

I had faith in Rhett.

Somehow, he'd find Sam. I felt it in my bones.

Stepping out of the bathroom, I strode back to my cell of shame and nearly cried with joy and happiness when I saw the beautiful ambiance.

"This is pretty," I rejoiced.

They had arranged a picnic outside the cell. Pink-hued blankets were on the floor, and a small low wooden table with a flowing white table runner in the center had been set up.

"All for you," Izzy said with a smile. "Have a seat." She gestured to the pink and white pillows scattered on the blanket.

Sitting down cross-legged, I blinked back the happy tears. No one had ever gone to so much trouble and care for me.

"Coffee is in the carafe," Imani said. "I made bacon-cheese popovers, baked chicken-and-waffle sandwiches, breakfast tacos, and a fresh fruit bowl."

I stared at the mouthwatering spread on the low table. "Thank you so much, Imani."

She winked at me. "You're family now."

I smiled, touched by the genuine friendship and family that she offered me.

Imani, Nyx, Izzy, and I packed our plates with food.

"Sorry, Rose. I didn't bring enough vegetarian options," Imani lamented.

Rose loaded her plate with fruit. "No worries, darling. I'm just happy to be here in the company of new and old friends."

We all sat on pillows, tucking into our food.

Taking a sip of coffee, I moaned when I recognized the tastes of brown sugar, milk chocolate, honey, and a hint of a bright fruit flavor. "Is this Kona coffee?" I asked Imani.

Imani grinned. "Yes. It was made with a hundred Kona beans from Hawaii's most celebrated craft roaster."

My eyes widened. "Well, ain't you fancy." I adored Kona coffee for its smoothness but didn't drink it often because it was quite pricey, especially the single-origin options.

"Small town don't mean small budget," Nyx quipped with a wink.

"Let's enjoy our meal," Rose ordered while sipping coffee. "Isn't this picnic so much fun?"

"I'm here for Nova and the food," Izzy said around a mouthful of taco.

Nyx jabbed Izzy in the side. "We have to do this again."

I laughed. "Hopefully next time it will be outside the station."

"I would stream music from the app on my cell," Nyx said, "but those fuckers outside would probably hear it and have a fit."

Imani speared a piece of pineapple. "Knowing them, they'd rather hear the sounds of loud wailing and gnashing of teeth."

"Sadistic assholes," Izzy retorted. "I want to sage the hell out of them, ridding them of all that negative energy seeping from their pores."

Picking up another popover, I took a bite of the cheesy, bacon goodness. "I didn't realize how ugly people could get, but last night was horrible. The rage and hate that I felt and smelled wafting from the crowd were so thick, I could practically taste them."

Izzy stared at me with wide eyes. "If you smelled that riotous sludge, that means your animal is awake."

"She's been awake since the owl-shifter attack," I divulged.

"And the lucky man is?" Rose cooed.

"Rhett," I answered. "And yes, our eyes turned amber last night."

Rose slapped a hand over her heart. "Ooh, my goodness. Shifter jackpot. Rhett is a good man. When the unmated females find out he's off the single market, they'll turn green with envy."

"I think they already know," Izzy said. "That's why there're more women outside foaming at the mouth."

"Straight-up jealousy," Nyx contributed.

Rose shook her head. "It's so sad when women don't support one another."

"True that," Imani agreed.

"Their eyes turned amber in the presence of each other, so the mating match is official now," Rose said. "Those jealous hags protesting outside is just sour grapes."

"I'm just happy it's official," Nyx admitted. "You're staying in the Ridge, right?" she asked with her fork midway to her mouth.

"Well…" I paused just to tease out my response.

They all leaned forward, staring at me expectantly.

"Yes," I said simply.

They all sagged with relief.

Imani slapped my shoulder. "Girl, my heart was racing a mile a minute, waiting for your answer."

Rose frowned. "But why wouldn't Nova stay? She's found her mate. That's a shifter's dream come true."

"Uh, do you know how much shit I've been through since arriving here?" I asked Rose. "Rhett wanted to toss me out on day one."

"Her pendant got stolen by Sam," Imani said over a mouthful of food.

"Josie attacked her. Owl-shifter warrior-style," Nyx chimed in.

"And now Sam's framed her for murder," Izzy finished.

Rose shrugged. "Still don't see the problem."

I gave her my *Are you crazy?* stare.

"Okay." Rose held up her hand. "I'll admit that your introduction to our world was not ideal. But you found your mate."

She sighed wistfully. "I've been waiting eons for mine. I just hit forty, and my mother has pretty much given up on the idea of planning my mating ceremony. Now she's moved on to torturing me with a daily text, giving me the lowdown on which one of her friends' daughters has found their mate. That shit is depressing."

"Age ain't nothing but a number," I added. "I'm forty, and it doesn't mean it's the end of my world. In fact, midlife rocks!"

"Exactly," Nyx replied, giving me a high five. "All of us in this room are forty and fabulous."

"I second that," Izzy chimed in.

"The truth of the matter is, you're never too old to find love," Imani added, then patted Rose's arm. "Your mate will find you."

"I'm keeping the hope alive," Rose sighed. "Because when that day comes, you best believe I'll warrior-princess tackle my mate, making him mine." She chuckled. "Either way, I'd never let a bunch of crazy people"—Rose pointed in the direction of outside—"keep me from my happily-ever-after."

"I agree with Rose," Imani interjected. "The Ridge didn't roll out the red carpet for me. And remember, I literally had to fight for my man in a duel with a skanky bitch." Her eyes narrowed. "And I'd do it all again, given the happy life I now have with Quinn. That man loves me as unconditionally as I love him, and that's all that matters." She grabbed my hand. "What I'm saying is that you have to decide what you want. You're either all in or all out."

My life had been happy—but lonely—before coming here.

But now I had friends and a pack, a loving, supportive grandmother, and a chance of unconditional love with Rhett.

*I'm done going it alone.*

*I deserve love, happiness, and the opportunity to build an amazing life with Rhett by my side.*

*And I'm not going to allow anyone to steal my joy.*

"I never thought I'd find a good enough reason to settle down. All my life, I've been the happy-to-be-unattached girl because I didn't think anyone could be trusted and I thought that I was better off alone. But I feel differently now despite all the drama I've experienced since coming to the Ridge. Rhett is mine. And I'm his. So I'll fight for us because he's worth it," I affirmed. "And so am I."

"Aww," Rose said with misty eyes. "Group hug," she demanded while getting up to stand.

"Is she serious?" I squeaked, my eyes darting around.

"Yep," Imani confirmed. "Hugging is her jam. I learned to just go with the flow," she finished, hopping to her feet.

Izzy stood, grumbling something about deer-shifters and hug-fetish.

I sat cross-legged, chewing on a grape.

They all gave me a *What are you waiting for?* stare.

"Can I just sit this one out?" I begged.

"Oh hell no," Izzy held out her hand to me. "If I'm doing it, you are too."

"Yup," Nyx agreed. "Now get your ass up and join in our group hug."

"Well… okay." My lips curled up as both Nyx and Izzy helped me to stand.

As we all hugged it out, the embrace filled me with the most satisfying feelings of acceptance, happiness, belonging, and love.

When we broke apart, Rose pumped her hand in the air and squealed, "You all are the best."

I couldn't help but laugh at how charged up Rose was from our group hug. I guessed deer-shifters did need hugs.

Izzy plopped back onto her pillow. "I'm letting y'all know right now if any of you let it leak that I participated in a group hug, I'm going to cunt punt every one of you, witch-gangsta-style."

We all burst out laughing.

Despite the craziness that I'd experienced in the Ridge, I could get used to being around people who cared about me with no hidden agenda. I could tell that Imani, Nyx, Rose, and Izzy genuinely loved one another and had embraced me into their family.

I had to admit since arriving in the Ridge, I felt happier.

I'd found my family—my pack.

I looked forward to settling down in the Ridge with friends, family, and Rhett. I knew life in the Ridge wouldn't be easy, but life was never a piece of cake for me.

*I'm going to fight for my happily-ever-after because I deserve joy and love.*

# CHAPTER 24
# RHETT

Hours walking through the thickness of the forest and there was still no trace or scent of Sam.

I pulled a bottle of water out of my backpack and guzzled it.

"It's been hours," Jasper grumbled. "Are you sure Clancy's not working with Sam to throw us off his track?"

Quinn shook his head. "I trust him. He's a childhood friend and former military. His word is his bond. We just need to go deeper into the forest. I think that's why we failed to find him on our previous hunts. We didn't go deep enough."

"Agreed," I replied.

We continued to trek into the woods.

Jasper stilled. "You smell that?" He tapped his nose.

Quinn scanned the area. "Smell what?"

"Sam," Jasper answered.

"I don't smell anything," I muttered.

Jasper grinned. "That's why I'm the best Tracker that ever was or ever will be," he boasted. "Follow me." Jasper took off at top speed, with us close on his heels.

About a half hour later, I picked up Sam's scent.

"In the cave," Jasper whispered, pointing to the big stone cave entrance covered with lianas.

Quietly, we crept into the dark cave. Using our sharp shifter eyesight and senses, we avoided Sam's half-assed attempt to booby-trap his lair. It didn't take us long to find him snoring in the corner, his belly bulging from the half-eaten carcass of a moose tucked beside him like a lover.

I almost gagged from the cloying scent of damp earth, blood, and body odor that hung thickly in the air.

Quinn signaled for us to take our positions around Sam.

"Wakey, wakey, motherfucker," Quinn called out.

Sam's eyes snapped open, and he jumped into a crouching, doglike position. "You think you got me, but you don't." His eyes were crazed and bloodshot. Glaring at me, he threatened, "Protector, you're the first one that will die."

He leaped at me, half shifted into his wolf form, but I was ready. With one punch, I knocked him against the cave wall. Sam bounced against it, then rolled to the ground. He shifted back into his human form. Then he stumbled to his feet, dazed. The three of us pounded his ass, knocking him completely out.

Opening my backpack, I pulled out the handcuffs and shackles that were infused with Freya's magic. While wearing the cuffs and shackles, Sam's ability to shift would be suppressed and his strength would be significantly diminished. In essence, the cuffs and shackles would enable us to keep him under control.

Quinn yanked Sam's arms behind his back while I handcuffed his hands and shackled his ankles. It took the three of us to hoist his body out of the cave and through the forest.

Halfway into our trek, Sam awoke and tried to wrestle his way out of our clutches but failed. Then he tried to bite Quinn, who cuffed him behind his head. "Do that again, and I'm knocking you out."

"Is this how you treat a king?" Sam blustered.

"When we meet one, we'll let you know," I barked.

"It takes three of you bastards to take on the king," Sam snarled as we continued hoisting him—Quinn on one side, and

Jasper and me on the other—through the forest. "Why don't you take these cuffs off me and fight me like a shifter, one-on-one."

"Like you did with Henry?" I snapped.

"The horse-shifter was a means to an end," Sam boasted.

"What do you mean by that?" Jasper asked.

"I needed the town to believe that the Hunter did it. No one would ever be looking for me. Like I said, a pawn in a big game of chess, and I'm the king." Sam cackled. "King. King. King."

"Please," I begged. "Let me knock him the fuck out."

"Drop him," Quinn ordered. When we did, he reached into his backpack, pulling out a roll of duct tape. "I have something even better." When Quinn finished taping up Sam's mouth, we picked him up and continued on our way.

"I'm telling you now if I ever turn feral, just put me out of my damn misery," Jasper asked.

When we finally arrived at my cruiser, we shoved Sam in the back, sandwiched between Quinn and Jasper. Then I took off.

"Come on, Rhett." Jasper sniffed loudly. "Stop fucking around. Roll down all the windows. He smells like shit, blood, piss, and ass."

I agreed. Sam smelled and looked like he hadn't taken a bath in weeks, and his hair was a matted mess. Dirt and grime were so thick on his body that you could barely see his true skin color beneath. And his clothes had streaks of gore—that smelled like a potent combination of both his victims and animal blood.

The whole ride back to town, we had to put up with Sam mumbling shit beneath the tape on his mouth.

When we arrived back at the station, the mob was larger and divided into two groups. One led by Gertrude and Shane, the other by Piper, June, Freya, Bonnie, Imani, Nyx, Isabella, Izzy, and Rose, with Emmett, Mack, and Brody in the middle of the two groups, keeping them apart.

After I parked my cruiser, Quinn dragged Sam out. When Jasper and I got out, Quinn handed Sam to me, and I ripped off the tape on his mouth. Sam darted forward, attempting to bite me. I dipped back in time to avoid his teeth.

"That's what you get when you mess with the king." Sam cackled.

"I meant it. Do that one more time, and I'll knock you out," I promised.

Quinn glared at the mob. "Get back. Sam's not right in the head."

The crowd looked stunned at Sam's disheveled appearance as Mack, Emmett, and Brody herded the mob back. We dragged Sam toward the station with Quinn leading the way and Jasper and me behind.

"Oh my God, look at Sam!" Gertrude shouted. "He's plumb crazy."

It seemed as if Sam took offense to her comment and snapped his teeth at her like a wild, drooling animal. Gertrude squealed and leaped back.

She clutched her pearls. "Why, I never."

Sam's laugh was maniacal. "Oh, shut it, you dried-up piece of trash."

"His eyes are red." Shane pointed out. "And he's foaming at the mouth. I ain't never seen nothing like this."

"He's got the feral sickness!" Weasel shouted.

Piper stared at Sam with lips pursed in disbelief. "I didn't think Sam could get any crazier. I was wrong."

Sam wiggled his body like he was trying to escape even with the firm grip Jasper and I had on him.

"Hold still, you hear?" I ordered.

"If you take these handcuffs off me," Sam exploded, "I'll rip you to shreds like I did to Dean, his kin, and Henry."

Sam's confession silenced the crowd. Their expressions were stunned. Now the Ridge had no excuse to keep Nova in jail. Her innocence was clear.

Sam continued. "I'm the king. Bow to the king. You hear me?"

Bonnie yelled out, "All I hear is blah, blah, blah, I'm a crazy man."

The horde nodded in agreement.

"You all heard Sam's confession," Quinn shouted to the audience. "Sam killed Dean, his kin, and Henry. And according to Others law, justice must be served swiftly to Sam."

There was a sea of nodding heads before they started chanting, "Justice. Justice. Justice."

"Bow to the king," Sam kept repeating while Jasper and I dragged his ass into the station. We continued to the back to throw him into a cell.

Nova stood there in her open cell with wide eyes.

"Half-breeds like you shouldn't be allowed to live," Sam shouted at Nova. "I should have killed you when I had the chance, but I am the king, and you were the pawn in my game."

"Apparently you lost," Nova said coolly. "Checkmate."

We threw him in the adjacent cell, locking it before Nova stepped out of hers and into my arms.

I kissed her quickly before ushering her to the front of the station.

"Since I'm free to go, what's going to happen now?" Nova asked me.

"Don't worry yourself about him," I replied. "Black Forest justice will be served. Bonnie will take you home, and I'll be over later to claim my woman."

"I'm your woman." She grinned. "I love the sound of that."

After I escorted her out of the station, Bonnie, June, Piper, Imani, Nyx, Isabella, Izzy, Rose, and the rest of her supporters surrounded Nova.

I glared at the crowd. "Y'all got anything to say to Nova?"

"I knew it," the weasel said. "I knew she couldn't have done no shit like killing Henry."

Imani rolled her eyes. "Weasel, pick a damn side and stick with it."

"Exactly," Piper agreed. "You told everybody that Nova was guilty."

Weasel shook his head. "Not me."

With face flushed, Blanche said, "We're so sorry. We should have believed in your innocence, Nova."

Ambrose, the owner of the only hardware store in town, stepped forward. "Yeah, we're sorry, Nova."

Ivy, the town's dentist, proclaimed, "We knew you didn't do it."

"Welcome to the Black Forest Ridge family," a group of them said in unison.

With no smile, Nova studied the crowd and said, "Let this be a new start."

I reached over and took her hand, squeezing it softly.

She continued. "All I ask is that when someone new comes to this town, take the time to get to know the person before being judgmental. And last, but not least, please welcome them with open arms." At the end of her statement, the audience clapped and whistled.

Bonnie whispered something in Nova's ear before raising her arms and yelling, "Quiet down!" The crowd silenced. "I also have an announcement." Bonnie jammed her hands on her hips. "It's now official. My granddaughter is the newest family member of the Ridge." Nova nodded in agreement. "And we're damn lucky to have her serve as the town's midwife."

That announcement caused another round of whistling and clapping. But of course not everyone was happy with the breaking news—Gertrude, Shane, and Josie each had thunderous expressions before storming away.

Turning Nova to face me, I cupped her cheek. "I'll be seeing you later," I promised.

"And I'll be waiting," she whispered.

I handed her over to Bonnie, who ushered Nova away and into her vehicle before driving off.

I watched the crowd disperse before stepping back into the

station to join my pack. We were about to serve justice to Sam the Ridge way, and that called for preparation.

~

An hour later, we arrived in separate vehicles to the outer edge of the forest. Quinn and Mack helped me get Sam out of the back of my cruiser before Emmett, Brody, and Jasper joined us.

Dragging Sam away from the vehicle, we made our way into the forest. The moonlight was bright as we silently trekked deeper into the forest.

It didn't take us long to make it to our destination—a ceremonial circle at the center of the forest. According to Quinn, his forefathers created the circle eons ago. It was a sacred place designated for justice to be served to shifters who wrongly spilled the blood of the innocent.

They each took a spot around the circle while I placed Sam in the center, taking the handcuffs and shackles off him. Sam swung, cutting me on my cheek.

"Motherfucker," I yelled, shoving him to the ground. "You wanted a one-on-one fight. Well, now you've got one." I stripped off my shirt and boots.

Sam shouted, "Bring it." After he undressed, he beckoned me with a finger. "Come dance with the king."

I was a powder keg ready to explode when I faced off with Sam. My canines lengthened past my lips as we brawled back and forth and Sam foamed at the mouth.

I unloaded on Sam, dropping him multiple times. I was meticulous and calculating with my strikes, hitting him with body shot after body shot. Sam's eyes turned frantic, and he shifted into his wolf. Wasting no time, my body shook and I transformed, my clothes shredding like confetti.

My jaguar darted forward, catching him by the throat with canines sinking into his flesh. Sam's wolf bucked and thrashed, trying to loosen my grip, but to no avail. I dragged him to the ground, applying pressure. His bones made a crunching sound. His wolf choked and gasped until his body went limp.

Releasing him, I shifted back into my human form. "The king is dead," I said.

Each member of my pack said in unison, "Justice is served."

# CHAPTER 25
# RHETT

After burying Sam, we headed back to the station. I hopped out of my cruiser with no shirt on and blood and guts on my chest. And thank goodness the crowd had disappeared from in front of the station.

"You off to get your woman?" Jasper asked.

"Yup," I replied.

They all clapped me on the back before going their separate ways.

Once I got inside, Sally held her nose. "Ew, you stink to holy hell, Sheriff."

Ignoring her comment, I asked, "Did you take care of that errand I requested?"

She smiled. "Yes." She headed over to her desk, pulling out a small velvet box. Coming back over, she handed it to me. "It looks like new. It's been sanitized and polished by the jeweler."

"Thank you, Sally," I said before heading out and back into my vehicle.

It didn't take me long to arrive at Bonnie's house. I practically raced up the steps, and the door opened before I had the chance to knock. Nova stood before me with her thick hair framing her heart-shaped face. My mouth watered with the desire to nibble, suck, and kiss every inch of her full lips.

My nostrils flared when the scent of her arousal reached me. My breath caught in my throat as savage need raced through me. *Mine!*

Nova looked me up and down with wide eyes. "What happened?"

"Justice was served," I replied, pulling her against me. She moaned when my lips trailed hot kisses across her soft skin, her jaw, and all the way down to the hollow of her throat.

Nova wrapped her arms around my neck, clinging to me. "Well, that was hot."

I lowered my head, whispering against her lips, "You ain't seen anything yet. Wait until I get you home."

A smile twitched across her lips. "Promises. Promises."

"But first, I have something for you." Stepping back, I reached into my front pocket, pulling out the velvet box, handing it to her.

Nova pulled it open. Inside was her pendant, on the new gold chain I'd purchased. Nova smiled, and my heart skipped a beat. This woman was beyond beautiful, and she was mine.

"Rhett… Thank you." She wrapped her arms around my waist and squeezed.

I couldn't believe that Luna, the goddess, had blessed me with such a beautiful—inside and out—woman. Nova was strong, caring, and intelligent, and for the rest of my days, I'd thank the universe for bringing her into my life.

"Anything for you." I reached out, grazing the side of her cheek with the back of my hand. "Turn around. Let me put it on you."

Nova did as instructed, holding up her hair while I fastened the necklace around her neck.

She turned back around. "Thank you," she whispered before leaning up and pressing her soft lips against mine.

I cradled the back of her head, and our kiss was slow, hot,

and delicious. Drawing her bottom lip into my mouth, I gently sucked until she moaned throatily.

My cock twitched, just imagining my tongue lapping and worshipping her body all night like the goddess she was.

Ready to make my dreams a reality, I broke off our kiss. "Let's go home." Weaving my fingers through hers, I ushered her down the stairs.

"Wait," Nova laughed. "You didn't even let me shut the door."

"I've got it," Bonnie answered with lips split into a shit-eating grin while standing on the threshold. "Happy mating, you two."

Nova waved at her before getting into my cruiser. Shutting her door, I ran over to my side, sliding behind the wheel.

Nova turned to stare at me. "Can you roll down the windows?"

"Why?" I asked.

She wrinkled her nose. "Have you smelled yourself?"

"I do smell pretty ornery."

She laughed. "Very."

I did as requested, and crisp, cool air filled the vehicle. With one hand on the wheel, the other on her thigh, I peeled away with excitement and longing strumming through my veins.

I couldn't wait to strip her naked, exploring every inch of her.

*I can't wait to claim and mate my woman.*

*Finally,* my inner jaguar grumbled.

# CHAPTER 26
## NOVA

"Wake up, darling. We're here." Rhett's voice was low and sensuous.

My eyes popped open to find him staring at me. "Sorry. I fell asleep." I was totally tired after an exhausting day.

When I'd arrived at Bonnie's home after leaving the station, I was a bundle of chaotic energy, counting down the time until I'd see Rhett again. I took a shower, had a light meal with Bonnie, then waited for Rhett to come back from serving his justice—whatever that meant. Frankly, I didn't want to know the details, but I had the sense that I wouldn't be seeing Sam ever again.

With languid movements, I stretched. He traced a finger across my cheek.

"What?" I wiped my eyes. "Did I snore?"

"No." He took my hand and turned it over so he could kiss my palm, the sensation making a beeline for my pussy. "You just look so sexy when you're sleeping."

He gently placed another kiss on my palm before licking it. His touch stabbed through me, and heat pooled between my legs.

I smiled impishly. "You do know that you have a 100 percent chance of me fucking you, right?"

He laughed huskily. "Yep. Time to get you inside." He threw open his door and came over to open mine.

I clutched his hand, hopping out, and was stunned into silence by the sight of an absolutely breathtaking tree house, secluded by dense jungle.

"It's amazing," I whispered, admiring the massive tree house nestled on top of stilts in a canopy of flora.

"I'm happy you like it." Releasing my hand, he pressed his palm to my lower back, ushering me over to the tree house's grand entrance.

"What's not to like? You get to fall asleep in the trees and wake up to birds singing around you," I said.

We walked up the spiral staircase that was crafted around a giant tree. At the top, the house was unlike anything I'd ever seen. An outdoor deck area extended off the main entrance.

When he pushed open the door, I stepped in and gasped. There was no roughing it in this tree house. The common room had a spiral staircase, full kitchen, dishwasher, stove, and padded benches.

We both took off our shoes, and I walked over to the two living trees growing through the tree house's interior. "Did you build this yourself?"

"Yes, with the help of my pack. Jasper helped me design it. He makes a fortune designing and building luxury tree houses."

"Amazing." I strode over to the sliding glass door, peering at the waterfall.

He walked up behind me, pressing his chest against my back. "No. You're amazing." He kissed my neck, and my body was instantly ablaze with lust.

I moaned with want. "That feels so good."

"Nova, I want to claim you."

Turning around, I stared up at him. "Then what's stopping you?"

"Since you've come to this town, you've been through a lot. I don't want to rush you, so if you need more time…"

I pressed my fingers against his lips. "Let's get one thing straight. You're not rushing me into shit. I want you. You're mine, and I'm yours. So let's get to the claiming, okay?"

He grinned. "Straight to the point. That's my mate."

He grabbed my hand and directed me up the spiral staircase and into his bedroom. Once inside, he slowly peeled off my clothes and then picked me up. He carried me to his bathroom, setting me on the vanity, and turned on the steamy shower. He took off his jeans as the heat billowed around us.

His skin was golden tan and tight over the bulging muscles beneath. He was, without a doubt, the sexiest man I'd ever seen, and he was all mine.

Stepping closer, he lifted my chin with a flick of his finger before leaning into my body and kissing me hard and deep. He sucked my tongue into his mouth. A fist in my hair angled my head back, granting him deeper access. My tongue slid around the tip of his and then rubbed under it. His growl vibrated through me, and my pussy throbbed with need.

Breaking away from our kiss, he lifted me up, taking me into the massive shower stall with him. Once inside, he sat on the shower seat, tugging me onto his lap—my chest against his—allowing the water to cascade over both of us. Blood melted off his body, mingling with the water that went down the drain.

Rhett moaned, as if enjoying the hot water beating against his sore muscles.

Kissing him hard on his lips, I crooned, "Let me take care of you, baby." I made my way to my feet, putting a dollop of aromatic, woody-scented body wash onto a washcloth before lathering it all over his body, then gently sloughing away the remaining blood.

Dropping the washcloth to the floor, I grabbed the shampoo and lathered his hair, raking my fingernails against his scalp. He wrapped his arms around me, his mouth going to my nipple, taking turns, sucking each one into his hot, greedy mouth.

"My turn," he muttered. He stood up and lathered up the

washcloth. He paid special attention to my breasts and between my thighs. Water rained over my hair, transforming my thick strands into a cloud of tighter ringlets.

Turning off the water, he pulled me out of the shower, quickly drying the both of us before lifting me over his shoulder in a firefighter's carry.

I squealed, "Don't get cocky, Sheriff."

"You haven't seen the meaning of cocky, baby." He brought me inside his bedroom, dropping me onto the bed.

He straddled me, one knee on each side of my waist. I stared up at him in anticipation. His firm lips curved a little into a smile.

He stroked my hair, his eyes never leaving mine as he picked up my hands, lifting them toward the metal slats of the head-board. "Grab the poles." Eagerly, I did as directed, wrapping my fingers around the cold metal as excitement bubbled up inside me.

He moved to lie beside me, cupping my cheek in one huge hand, forcing me to meet his sensual gaze. "Do you trust me to take care of you?"

I nodded as my nipples throbbed and begged for his tongue's attention. I lay there with my hands over my head, gripping the poles for dear life.

"Rhett, I need…"

"I know what you need." He brushed a tender kiss across my lips, then nuzzled my temple. "Don't move," he ordered with a low, sexy voice before getting to his feet and walking over to the sliding glass door, opening it.

As he came back over to the bed, I dropped my eyes to his thick, long, jutting erection. *How the hell is he going to get that anaconda into me?* Not that I was going to let his big cock intimidate me. I was determined to ensure every inch got in.

He joined me on the bed, caressing my cheek before his tongue took full possession of my mouth, darting in and out, flicking and sucking.

Giving my lips a lick, he murmured, "You're so beautiful," before he slid down my body. Pressing his mouth against my stomach, he nibbled and kissed until all I wanted to do was burst into flames. I released my grip on the metal poles. Rhett stilled, his eyes focused on me, and he ordered, "Hands back on the poles, mate."

With shaky fingers, I clutched the poles again. There was something so hot about being controlled in bed by my sexy, caring mate, whom I trusted explicitly to take care of my needs with a firm but gentle touch.

Spreading my legs wide, he knelt between them, looking at my pussy hungrily. "Damn. What a beautiful pussy." I felt exposed and vulnerable before his scorching gaze.

Cupping my pussy, he locked his eyes with mine. "This pussy is mine to do with as I please." He slid his fingers between my wet folds.

"Yes. Yours." I arched up, wiggling closer, as he slipped one finger, then another inside me.

His callused thumb circled and played with my clit. "Tell me what you want."

My mind went blank. "I… Uh…"

He stroked my folds, and I shivered, on the verge of exploding. From his heated, focused stare, I knew he had no intention of pushing me over the edge until I said what he needed to hear.

"Please," I whispered. "Please lick me."

"My pleasure."

He slid onto his belly before he curled his huge hands around my thighs, spreading me even wider. I moaned when he thrust his tongue into my center. That one abrasive lick sent me spiraling over the edge, and I screamed, "Rhett!" like a prayer.

He pulled his head back, watching me as his fingers continued to stretch me. "Scream louder, darling."

With a death grip on the poles, I writhed and panted as my hips bucked wildly. He thrust harder with his fingers. I screamed louder when his finger found my clit again, mercilessly playing with it. I screamed and came again.

Rhett leaned over the side of the bed. I watched him grabbing condoms from his nightstand before sheathing his cock.

He hovered above me, his weight on his knees between my thighs, before directing his cock into position, smoothly slipping inside my waiting pussy inch by inch, giving me time to adjust to his wide girth.

He looked at me with burning possession on his face as I struggled to breathe while his cock stretched me like no other.

He gave me a slow smile. "You are mine," he grunted, fully seated, with his balls bumping against my ass. Hovering above me, he kissed my lips, then jaw, and eyelids. And I lay there, basking in his tenderness. My stomach tightened with pleasure when he pulled his cock out of me, then sank back inside, hitting my G-spot with precision.

Instinctively, I wrapped my legs around his waist as he continued to hit my G-spot, making my breasts jiggle.

My hips gyrated in sync with his deep thrusts. The deeper he pumped, the more I craved him. I writhed beneath him, meeting him thrust for thrust while trembling and moaning low and deep.

"We have all night, mate." He stilled my hips so I felt every inch of his pulsing cock. "No rushing."

I nodded, wanting to savor our first time.

He growled in my ear, "Let go of the poles."

I slid my hands over his wide, muscled back. I dug my nails into his flesh like a wild, wanton woman as he continued pumping, hard and methodical.

I felt like I was going insane from the roaring heat building inside my body and pussy. My breathing became fast and shallow, with periods of whimpers and moans intermixed.

Rhett was consuming me. Owning me like no man had ever dared to.

"Harder." I grabbed his head, pulling him closer, biting his lower lip.

He growled, letting himself go, moving faster, pushing me into another orgasm. Arching, I screamed as my pussy clenched around his thick cock. Then I collapsed—spent but greedy for more of my man.

His face was harsh as he pulled from my body, flipping me onto my belly. He drew me up onto my knees, and I moaned when he kissed my neck, shoulders, then rained hot kisses along my spine.

His growl was animalistic as he nudged me forward, onto my hands. The air crackled around us as his strong hands seized my waist, and he thrust his cock into me smoothly. I cried out with pleasure as one hand gripped my hair while the other was wrapped around my waist. His body rocked into me. Our bodies, slick with sweat, were in perfect synchrony, with a strange magnetic energy wrapping around us.

"Make me yours completely," I whispered, clutching the bedsheets.

He reared back and pushed forward. Every inch of him was sheathed in me. My body shook, my legs quivered, and my core pulsed, racing toward blissful release.

"Do you accept me as your mate?" he demanded roughly, thrusting faster.

"Yes," I moaned.

"Nova, you're mine. My mate. And what I claim, I keep, cherish, love, and protect."

His thrusts grew stronger as his body slapped against me. My fingers clenched the sheets as I rocked back into his body. My body was burning for a sweet release. A strangled shout escaped his lips before he bit the spot between my neck and shoulder.

"Mate," he growled. "Mine."

I came so hard that I screamed his name at the top of my

lungs. My inner muscles contracted, milking him. And he roared as both of us crested, surrendering to our orgasm.

He kissed me on my shoulder before carefully pulling out of me. After dragging me up farther onto the bed, he said, "Let me take care of the condom." Leaving the bed, he entered the bathroom, but it didn't take long before he was back.

"Spread your legs," he ordered while holding a washcloth. He wiped the soft, warm material over my pussy, cleaning me before placing it on the nightstand. Getting onto the bed, he clutched me against his body.

He kissed me first soft, then hard, and I knew with every fiber in my body that Rhett would love me fiercely and cherish me until his last breath. And it was the same for me. This man was a keeper. I sighed, contented, as we held on to each other, lips melding over and over.

Breaking off our kiss, I said, "So I guess you're stuck with me, Sheriff."

He nuzzled my neck. "I wouldn't have it any other way, mate," he quipped, nibbling on my skin until he found the mark he'd left on my shoulder and gently licked it. A shiver of lust and want shot through my body.

"Time for round two," he growled. "On your knees… now."

# CHAPTER 27
## NOVA

Hours later, I woke up feeling an unbearable warmth that threatened to consume me. Glancing over, I saw Rhett sprawled on his stomach, snoring. Evidently, he was pleasantly exhausted from our multiple rounds of lovemaking.

Kicking the sheet off my body, I lay there sweating. The cool night breeze that flowed inside from the open sliding glass door did nothing to abate the heat crawling all over my naked body like ants.

Easing off the bed, I tiptoed onto the balcony and stood by the railing, lifting my hair away from my neck, hoping to relieve the hot flash that raced through my body. The night air didn't help. The heat was intensifying, causing me to sweat like I'd just run through the Serengeti.

My superheightened hearing heard the thump of Rhett's bare feet against the floor.

Rhett's voice was husky and filled with sleep when he asked, "You okay?"

My pussy pulsed from a growing state of arousal.

Turning to face him, I said, "No," while wiping the beads of sweat from my forehead. "I think I might be premenopausal because I'm having a beast of a hot flash."

Rhett strode over, staring at me like I'd grown two heads. "I don't think it's a hot flash." He pressed his nose against my neck and sniffed loudly. "Your scent has changed." He wrapped his arms around me, pulling me closer.

"Changed to what?"

He had an amused expression on his face. "You're going into mating heat."

"What the hell do you mean by mating heat?" I croaked.

"It's when a mated female becomes highly sexually receptive to her mate."

I remembered Imani and Nyx telling me about "the heat," but it all seemed too real now.

"And how long is this mating heat going to last?" I demanded.

"Days. How many depends on your body," he explained.

"Days?" I squeaked even as a sharp need to fuck Rhett stabbed my pussy. "There is no way in hell I'd be able to make it through days of straight fucking." Rhett fucked like a stallion and was hung like one too.

"How do you know if you don't try?" He grinned.

"Stop being a smartass." I shoved him playfully. "We've already been fucking nonstop. My pussy needs at least a day to recover."

He waggled his brows. "You'd be surprised by the things your body can do, given proper motivation."

"Nope. Not happening. I need more sleep, and then we can get this mating heat party started."

"That's not how this works, Nova. You can't schedule the heat like a meeting. The mating heat starts and stops when it wants."

I arched a brow. "You know what I just heard? Blah, blah, blah… mating heat bad."

He chuckled. "Seriously, Nova, there's no fighting the heat. You'll be in a constant state of arousal that only I will be able to satisfy."

"Sleep first." I gave him a quick kiss. "I'm the master of my body, and it does what I want, when I want."

"Is that right?" He arched a brow.

"Yup. I'll have you know—" My words stopped short when his delicious scent crashed over me like a tsunami, causing my pussy to pulse as if it was protesting the fact that his cock wasn't already inside me, pounding away.

His lips curled up. "Know what, mate?"

"I… uh…" I gritted my teeth when another wave of heat caused my legs to buckle. Rhett caught me with ease, righting me before stepping back.

His gaze burned me. "Are you ready to submit to your mating heat?" His cock was hard and stretched taut, almost past his navel. The thick, round crown glistened with a small drop of moisture. His balls were tight with arousal.

"Nope."

"Okay, two can play this game," he replied.

My eyes narrowed as he did the unthinkable. He began stroking his hard cock tauntingly.

*Dammit! What a tease.*

It was straight-up torture as I watched the way he touched himself. Nothing screamed confidence more than a man not afraid of his tantalizingly sensual side.

My breath became more ragged. Warmth pooled between my thighs. I was so close to the edge that I wasn't above begging for his dick. And from the smoldering calculation in his blue eyes, Rhett knew it.

His stroke became more sensual, slower and methodical.

*Shit. He's trying to drive me insane.*

My cunt tingled, and my nipples puckered as I craved the taste of him.

I blew out a breath. "Fine." I threw my arms up in defeat. "I concede to my mating heat."

He stopped stroking his cock. "See how easy that was?"

"Oh, shut it, and bring your magnificent cock over here."

He stepped forward, and I slid to my knees before touching his hardness, stroking him gently, massaging the smooth, hot column of flesh between my fingers.

"Damn," he whispered. "That feels so good."

I feathered my tongue over him, swirling the salty precome from the tip of his crown, savoring the earthy taste of him. Cupping his balls, I rolled my fingers over his tight sac. My other hand firmly gripping him, I explored the peaked ridge just under the head of his shaft with my tongue.

I embraced his length with both hands before greedily sliding my lips over the head of his arousal. Rhett's hands threaded through my thick tresses as though savoring the feel of it. The low groans coming from him spurred me on.

He tightened his hand, jerking my hair. He grew bigger in my mouth as I bobbed my head up and down over his wide shaft. The more I tasted, the more I hungered.

With every flick of my tongue, the hard grip of his fingers against my head seemed to turn me on even more. I fed him into my throat, taking it all. His hard shaft was thick and broad, like him. My lips stretched around his man flesh.

He spread his legs wider. "That's it."

I hummed as he started a slow slide in and out between my lips.

A fog of desire clouded my vision.

All I could think of was bringing him pleasure.

*Mate. Mine.*

His groan deepened, becoming more of a growl, charging the erotic tension even more.

"More tongue," he hissed.

His demand sent me spiraling to the edge of a lust-induced frenzy. My body quivered with a fire I'd never felt before.

I stroked every bump and ridge of his flesh with my tongue. Moving up and down on him, I sucked him harder. I was thrilled when he moved his hands to my head again, positioning me over his cock.

"Wider." He tightened his fists even more in my hair. "Open your mouth wider."

I did, and he shoved his staff until he was lodged against the back of my throat. He was huge, the size of my wrist, but I didn't back away or struggle. Holding still, I relaxed my throat to keep from gagging. I slid my tongue along his length as I breathed through my nose and swallowed around him.

"Fuck. Do that again." His voice was hoarse and thick with arousal.

Heady with power, I swallowed around him. The sound of his harsh breath filled the air. It drove me on as he thrust into me with a slow rhythm that was rough and primal. His tangled fingers in my hair held my head still for his deep thrusts.

Heat licked over my skin as my lips danced over him. My hips swayed in tandem.

"You are mine," he whispered.

Heat pooled between my legs, loving what he'd said.

All too soon, a guttural groan erupted from his carnal mouth. "Swallow it all," he commanded a second before he shot into the sweet depths of my mouth.

I continued to suck, swallow, and lick him with gentle strokes until he gradually softened in my mouth.

After inching from between my lips with a heartfelt sigh, in one smooth motion, he helped me stand. My legs were trembling under me, and he picked me up effortlessly, cradling me against him like I was precious. Pressing my head into the hollow of his shoulder, he carried me into the bedroom, placing me gently on the bed.

He lifted my chin with a flick of his finger. "Nova, there's no shame in being in heat. It is a part of who we are as shifters, and to deny it is to deny not only you but me as your fated mate."

"I know." I nodded. "You're right. It's just that there's so much about this new world that is so foreign to me."

"Mating heat is new to me too, but we will learn together." He kissed me hard and deep before breaking off our kiss. "Now let me satisfy my woman. My mate. Facedown and present your beautiful ass to me."

Pivoting, I pressed my chest against the bed. "Like this?" I wiggled my ass playfully.

The cool air glided across the backs of my thighs. He ran a hand over the curve of my ass before parting my cheeks.

"You're so damn sexy," he praised. "Spread your knees wider."

Doing as instructed, I watched as he got a condom from the nightstand and sheathed his cock. Positioning himself behind me, he curled a hand in my hair, snapping my head back.

"You are mine," he whispered into my ear.

Releasing my hair, he pressed me facedown onto the bed and buried himself so far inside me that my whole body quaked from the sheer force.

"Oh fuck!" I cried out as he stretched me ruthlessly.

His engorged flesh sank deeper between my sensitive folds, and his balls slapped against my womanhood, sending tiny shocks through my body. My hips bucked, and my pussy burned from the width of his big thick manhood.

My body tensed from the burning fullness in my cunt. I took a deep breath, forcing my rebellious muscles to loosen.

He increased his speed from a sensuous slide to a hard, forceful pumping. "Fuck!" he cursed.

He was driving me crazy with lust, and each stroke brought me closer and closer to the edge.

"Rhett," I groaned as he continued to fuck me like a man possessed.

The pressure tightened inside me before I came brutally hard. I gasped and moaned as my interior muscles convulsed around him.

He squeezed my hips with his fingers. Again and again, he pulled out and plunged back inside me like a man on a mission.

He tensed, and every muscle rippled before he uttered a guttural groan as his smooth pumping became jerky and harsh.

He roared. His entire body shook as he came and came, his cock twitching inside me. He slumped over me, catching his weight on his hands.

He nuzzled my neck and then licked over my mating bite and growled, "Mine."

# CHAPTER 28
## NOVA

Hand in hand, Rhett and I strode through the forest, traipsing over the mossy green ground.

"This scenery is so beautiful," I mused aloud.

"That it is," Rhett agreed. "Just a few more minutes before we reach my favorite spot."

My nose twitched at the smell of damp moss intermingled with the sweet scent of flowers. Sunlight filtered through the canopy, casting an otherworldly glow over the ground and large trees.

"We're close," he said.

I could hear the gurgling of water before we arrived at a large patch of earth overgrown with deep green moss and an absolutely breathtaking waterfall.

"It's spectacular," I whispered.

Rhett smiled. "I wanted your first time shifting to be somewhere you'd remember forever."

"Thank you." I squeezed his hand.

After my days of being in heat subsided, Rhett and I had spent quality time together just getting to know each other on a deeper level. During our time together, I had no words to describe how amazing my mate was. He was intelligent, nurturing, loving, protective, and funny.

Holding hands, we silently stared at the rainbows floating above the different parts of the waterfalls.

"This is a truly magnificent display of nature," I told him.

"Yes, it's the power of the waterfalls that leaves me speechless every time." He released my hand, turning me to face him. "Are you ready?"

My heart thumped hard in my chest. "No."

He tugged me against him, running his palm along my spine. "You can do this. I'll shift first, okay?"

I nodded.

He released me, kicking off his sneakers and shedding his clothes. I followed by doing the same.

"The key to shifting is picturing your inner beast in your mind," he instructed.

My eyes widened. "What? But I don't know what she looks like." Panic started to rise.

He grasped my chin, tipping my face up. "Nova." I gazed up at his tanned face. "Close your eyes. Take a deep breath."

I did as directed.

He continued. "Call her forward but not aloud. Just in your mind."

I blew out a breath before calling out tentatively, *Hello?*

There was no response.

I tried again. *Are you there?*

*I'm always here,* my inner animal answered.

Relief flooded my body. *Can you show me what you look like?* I coaxed her.

I gasped when I caught a glimpse of a sleek, dark-brown majestic cat.

"I'm a black jaguar," I said aloud to Rhett.

"Beautiful," he remarked. "The black jaguar is a rare color. So now that you know what type of jaguar you are, it's time to shift." He reached up to run his fingers over my hair. "Call the image of your inner animal to your mind to start your shift. When you're ready to shift back to your human form, call the image of your human form to mind. Got it?"

I nodded.

"I'll shift first," he said before stepping back.

I watched with fascination as his bones rearranged under his skin, expanding and stretching as he crouched on the ground. His skin transformed to tan-colored fur, covered by spots that transitioned to darker rosettes. His feet and hands spread and thickened. A few snaps of bones later, a monstrous tan jaguar stood in Rhett's place. His jaguar yawned, displaying long, dangerous-looking canines.

A little frisson of fear engulfed me as the jaguar watched me.

*Calm down, Nova. This is Rhett. I'm safe.*

I took a deep, calming breath, dismissing my fear before crouching to stroke my fingers across his massive head. His fur was so soft and silky. I ran my fingers over his cold nose, then over his ears. He pushed farther against me, tilting his head into my hand.

I kissed the top of his head. "Rhett, you're beautiful."

He butted me with his head and roared as if ordering me to hurry up and shift.

"Okay," I grumbled. "I'm shifting." Getting to my feet, I closed my eyes and took several cleansing breaths. Bringing the image of my jaguar to the forefront of my mind, I waited.

Nothing happened, and I started to panic.

*Release me,* my inner animal begged.

*I'm trying,* I hissed.

My body grew hot as sharp pain rushed through me.

Somewhere in the distance, I heard a roar, followed by another, then I realized the roars were mine.

Hot, scorching pain whipped across my skin. My bones felt like they were breaking and rearranging. My muscles were stretching and rippling.

*Open your eyes,* Rhett's voice said in my head.

I did as directed and looked down.

*Holy shit! I have four furry feet.*

*Beautiful,* Rhett purred in my head. *Let's run, mate.*

*Catch me if you can,* I taunted him before taking off in a run.

# CHAPTER 29
## NOVA

**EIGHT MONTHS LATER... ON A FULL MOON**

Rhett kissed my hand. "You look beautiful." His eyes roamed over the floor-length moss-green ceremonial cloak that shrouded my body from neck to toe.

My lips curled up into a smile. "Thank you." I eyed him, taking in the similarly colored cloak that he wore. "You don't look bad yourself."

We'd both been waiting for this moment—our mating ceremony—for months. Not wanting to rush me into our ceremony, Rhett and I spent time getting to know each other more deeply as we settled into our relationship as fated mates. And our relationship blossomed. I'd also spent time getting to know my grandmother and my new pack and friends between starting renovations on the new spot in Main Square that I'd picked for my clinic.

"You ready?" Rhett asked.

"Absolutely."

Rhett raised my fingers to his lips, kissing them softly. "Well, let's go, mate."

Our cloaks swished around our ankles as we strode hand in hand across the thick green grass in the front yard of our tree house.

I smiled when I saw my friends and family—Bonnie, Piper, June, Imani, Nyx, Rose, Izzy, and the Bane pack—dressed to the nines as they gathered for our intimate mating ceremony. My girls were all wearing white T-shirts with the slogan GLITTER IS ALWAYS AN OPTION paired with moss-green leather skirts.

Rhett led me to the spot where Freya, dressed in a skintight, floor-length dress, waited.

Freya raised her arms skyward while looking up at the bright, full moon. "Luna. Goddess of the moon," she began loudly, her voice carrying across the clearing. "We're here tonight to ask for your blessing in the joining of Rhett and his female, Nova."

Lowering her arms, she eyed Rhett. "Rhett Ward. Who is this female you ask to mate?"

He squeezed my hand lightly. "Nova King."

"Will anyone challenge Rhett Ward's right to mate this female?" Freya asked.

No one did.

"Nova King. Who is this male you ask to mate?" Freya asked.

"Rhett Ward," I answered.

"Will anyone challenge Nova King's right to mate this male?"

No one spoke.

Freya nodded. "Rhett Ward, will you take this female you have claimed to be your fated mate forever?"

"Yes. I do."

She asked the same question of me about Rhett. "Yes. I do," I responded.

Freya raised her hands to the sky. In amazement, I watched as her fingers slowly began to glow with a mystical bright white light that took on the same color as the moon.

"By the light that shines from my fingers," Freya said, "Luna approves of this mating of our town Protector to this female.

Take your mate, Rhett Ward." She gave each of us a kiss on the cheek before saying, "Before your family and pack, we declare you officially mated."

Freya peered at the members of our small intimate gathering. "May our unmated males find their fated mates. And may the coupling between Rhett and Nova be strong, happy, and loving."

Clapping and howls erupted into the night.

Bonnie had tears streaming down her cheeks when she grabbed me in a tight embrace. "I love you, Nova."

"And I love you, Grandma," I said, hugging her for dear life before stepping back.

Quinn, Emmett, Brody, Mack, and Jasper each took turns hugging me, then clapped Rhett on the back.

Piper, June, Freya, Imani, Nyx, Izzy, and Rose each hugged me.

Imani, Nyx, Rose, and Izzy grinned at me.

"We have a tradition," Nyx said.

Imani nodded. "I hope you love glitter."

"Congratulations!" Imani, Nyx, Izzy, and Rose screamed in unison while throwing copious amounts of pink and green glitter on me.

I laughed. "Glitter is for winners."

Rhett grabbed my hand. "Time to go into the forest and complete our private joining."

Hand in hand, we strode away from our friends and family into the forest behind our tree house.

It didn't take us long to get to our favorite spot by the waterfall. The place where I'd shifted into my animal for the first time.

"You are the love of my life," Rhett said while opening the two-piece metal closure attached to the front of my cloak, then pushing the material off my shoulders. The garment slid to the grass, and I stood before him, naked.

"As you are mine," I replied, undoing the closure on his cloak, pushing it off his shoulders. He stood before me naked, with his cock jutting away from his body.

"On your knees, Nova."

I did as instructed before Rhett crouched down behind me, nudging my knees apart. I trembled when his fingers danced along my spine, then over my ass.

"Do you take me as your mate, Nova?"

"Yes." I moaned when his cock brushed against the wet and ready opening of my pussy.

"I take you as my mate, Nova King. I take you as my other half, the only female in my bed," he said clearly.

"And I take you as my mate, Rhett Ward. I take you as my other half, the only male in my bed."

Rhett pushed his thick length into my body.

I dug my fingernails into the grass beneath us.

Rhett sank his incisors into my shoulder as his cock moved hard and fast inside me.

"Rhett," I cried out as my orgasm washed over me. He bit down harder as his thrusts grew faster. He growled, his cock growing larger inside me. My stomach tightened when my orgasm tore through me. Rhett roared as his seed shot into me over and over again. He released his grip on my shoulder, licking at my bite mark before slowly rolling us over until I was on my back with him between my legs.

He leaned down, whispering against my lips, "You are mine." His nostrils flared as he inched his hard cock into me again.

Wrapping my legs around his waist, I drove my hips up to meet him as he slammed into me. My muscles clamped around his massive fullness as he took me.

*This man is mine.*

*And I'm his.*

Pressing his forehead against mine, he moved hard and fast. Squeezing my thighs tight around his hips, I clung to him for dear life, riding the wave of lust coiling through me. He brought his hands up to my breasts, gently cupping them, his thumbs sliding over the aching peaks. My fingers gripped his ass, my nails digging deep.

"All of you. Mine," I growled on the edge of an orgasm.

"I need to ride you," I demanded.

Pulling from inside me, he sat on the ground as I climbed onto him with us face-to-face, chest-to-chest. Seated on his erection, I rode him vigorously, my breasts bobbing up and down. My stomach tightened as I approached my orgasm. I nibbled my way down his throat. My gums throbbed and incisors lengthened. Settling in the juncture of his neck and shoulder, I scraped my teeth over the spot before biting down, breaking the skin.

Rhett roared.

I climaxed hard.

Licking over the area, I eyed him. "Mine," I growled.

He licked my bite mark before slowly lowering us to the ground, rolling us over onto our sides. Pressing my back against his chest, I relaxed into his embrace while he was still hard and buried deep inside me.

"So we're officially mated, huh?" I whispered.

"Yes, my beautiful mate." Rhett gently pulled out of me, rolling me to lie on top of him. "I love you."

"And I love you," I whispered, staring down at him.

"Nova King, will you marry me?"

"Yes." Tears of joy filled my eyes as I peppered him with kisses. "Yes, Rhett Ward, Protector of the Ridge and my heart. I'll marry you."

"Thank you for coming into my life and completing me," he whispered before kissing me tenderly.

Tears pricked my eyes. This man had no damn idea what he did to me.

It was still hard for me to believe the life I now had. Every morning, I woke up by his side, and every night, I went to bed in his arms. And every day, he showed me with actions and words just how much he loved and adored me.

Rhett was not only the love of my life, he was the Protector of my heart.

He rolled me over and stood, extending a hand to help me to my feet. "Come, my fated mate. Now we shift and run under the moonlight that Luna has provided for us."

We both called to our inner beasts and shifted into our jaguars. Side by side, we stood. One tan jaguar and one black jaguar.

*Run with me, Nova,* he ordered, speaking into my mind.

*Yes, my mate and Protector,* I replied before taking off into the night with my mate and Protector by my side.

# EPILOGUE

## MACK

**TWENTY-THREE YEARS AGO...**

When Dad parked along the deserted dirt road, I silently mouthed to my middle brother, Buster, *What the hell is going on?*

I'd arrived home from my second job and hadn't even stepped into our small trailer home when Dad had ordered me to get in his SUV because "We had family business to take care of."

What family business was a mystery to me because I was the only member of the family who had a job, bringing in a paycheck. Everyone else in my family—Glen, Buster, and Dad—spent their days drinking BF Home Brew, watching television, or hanging out at the local shifters biker bar.

Buster shrugged, but I knew he was lying because his ears were now beet red—his tell that he wasn't being truthful.

I peered around in search of landmarks or anything that could tell me where we were. There was nothing in the landscape besides grassland that expanded to the left and right of the road like the sea.

Nothing about being on an unfamiliar, deserted stretch of

land in the middle of the night felt right. But I knew better than to pepper Dad with a bunch of questions—it would only piss him off and earn me a brutal ass-kicking.

Dad got out of the vehicle. We dutifully followed.

"Let me hear it!" Dad shouted while glaring at Glen and Buster, ignoring me as usual.

"How many times do we have to go over your plan, Dad?" Buster whined.

*What plan?*

Dad's expression darkened. "As many times as I fucking want you to."

"We're not stupid," Glen grouched.

"I beg to differ," Dad snapped. "You three are so dumb that you can throw yourselves on the ground and miss."

Glen snorted but replied, "When we get onto the Rossi pride territory, we kill the alphas first, then separate the lionesses from their cubs."

"Then we kill the cubs," Buster interjected robotically.

My shoulders stiffened. *Fuck my life.*

*We're taking over the Rossi pride?*

All the lion-shifters in Tennessee knew about the Rossi brothers—Nick and Guy. They were alpha lion-shifters who made their money by running Home Brew and illegally selling it to humans.

"Any of their lionesses that resist our pride takeover, we kill," Glen finished.

Dad's lips curled up into a menacing grin. "Exactly. We've staked out this pride for far too long to fuck this up." His body swayed, and I knew, as usual, he was tipsy from Home Brew. "I'm tired of those pussy-ass Rossi brothers controlling everything around here. Why should those greedy fuckers have it all? Money, territory, and control over all the illegal Home Brew distribution."

Glen and Buster nodded in agreement. I stared at the three, shocked to the core. The Rossi brothers were known to be ruthless fighters, and attacking their pride was a suicide mission. And if Dad and my brothers didn't succeed tonight, we'd have a target on our backs for the rest of our lives. But most importantly, attacking a pride was morally wrong.

Dad continued. "I want everything they got."

Anger coursed through my veins. We'd never moved in on another pride.

"Dad," I croaked. "We shouldn't do this."

"You'll do this, or I'll kill you." He leaped forward, backhanding me so hard that I flew onto the dirt road with a thud. As I got to my feet, anger boiled in the pit of my stomach, but I lowered my eyes in mock deference.

*Fuck this. I'm not killing anyone.*

Dad yelled, "Eyes on me, boy!"

I raised my gaze to meet his, making sure my expression remained neutral.

Dad pointed a beefy finger in my face. "This is my fault. I've been too fucking soft on you."

I barely bit back a scoff. Forcing me to fight Buster and Glen for the right to eat first was far from being too fucking soft on me.

"But no more," Dad snarled. "It's time to be a man. Pull your damn weight in this family."

I was twenty-four—the scrawniest and youngest of three—and the only person in the family who worked two jobs, bringing in a steady paycheck. Dad, Glen, and Buster sat around in our trailer drinking while plotting get-rich-quick schemes. Tonight's plan to take over the Rossi's pride was just another one of Dad's harebrained plans. But this time, there was a 100 percent chance of all of us getting killed.

"Now get ready to claim that pride," Dad ordered.

I nodded even as disgust bubbled inside my gut. Dad could force me to come along, but I had no plans to take part in this attack.

We all undressed, shifted into our animal—a lion—then

slowly moved across the grasslands under the moonlight. We passed a small grove of scrubby trees with still no sight of the Rossi pride, but I kept my guard up. If I made it out alive tonight, I was done with my family for good. And even though breaking ties with my kin would make me a nomad, I didn't give a fuck.

When we finally spotted the large ranch-style house and circled around the back, I couldn't believe what I was seeing… It was some sort of freaky, orgy party. Fire torches were peppered around the area, illuminating the partiers. Loud music was blaring. All the women, and the two men, were nude. A few women were dancing lewdly while rubbing against one another. Some of the females were stumbling around while holding large glasses. And each man was sitting on a lawn chair with a woman kneeling between his knees while he got his cock sucked.

*This is the big bad Rossi pride?*

My thoughts were broken when I saw Dad, Buster, and Glen barreling toward the raucous party. I stood frozen, watching as the attack unfolded.

The Rossi brothers—Nick and Guy—shoved away the females who were sucking their dicks. But when Nick and Guy got to their feet, I noticed that they swayed unsteadily. *Fuck. They're drunk.* That meant Dad, Buster, and Glen had a greater chance of taking down the brothers.

Dad, Glen, and Buster tag teamed the Rossi brothers, who were putting up a good fight. But my kin were winning this brawl, and none of them noticed—yet—that I wasn't taking part in the fray.

*Fuck this. I'm not joining this fight…* despite the consequences.

The battle between my kin and the Rossi brothers was over in a matter of minutes. What was left of the brothers lay on the ground, bloody and lifeless. Dad, Buster, and Glen then set their eyes on the females, who were huddled together except for two who had shifted into their lioness form and blocked the back door to the ranch. For whatever reason, they did not want my kin to get inside. Then it occurred to me why—their cubs were probably inside.

The two lionesses roared and swiped their paws, warning off my kin. Dad, Buster, and Glen roared right back. The two lionesses were no match for my family, who was determined to get inside and kill the cubs.

*I have to do something.*

The cubs were innocent and weak.

*I have to help.*

I had to do what was right, no matter the cost.

Decision made, I ran over to the two lionesses guarding the door.

Dad roared, his eyes locked on mine.

He wanted me to get the fuck out of the way.

I roared back, telling him I wouldn't.

Buster and Glen just stared at me, stunned.

Dad shifted back into his human form. "Buster. Glen. Guard the other lionesses." They loped away to do as instructed. I remained steadfast by the two lionesses' sides.

"Mack. Shift," Dad ordered.

I hesitated but needed to communicate with him. I had to try to de-escalate this situation before he killed the cubs.

I shifted but remained vigilant.

"What the fuck are you doing?" Dad demanded.

"Enough!" I yelled. "I was brought here against my will because you, Glen, and Buster wanted to take over this fucking pride. This is wrong. I want no part of this."

Dad sneered. "You've always been weak."

I flinched as if he'd physically slapped me. "If being weak means defending the innocent, then yes, I'm weak. I'm not going to let you kill their cubs."

Dad laughed. "Come on, son. You're no match for me or your brothers."

I straightened my back. "We'll see." Yes, I was scrawny for a lion-shifter, but I was faster than my kin.

Dad sighed tiredly. "Glen, get your ass over here." Glen loped over. "Take these stupid bitches down."

The two lionesses leaped onto Glen as a unit, but they were no match for him. Dad had a huge grin on his face as he watched the three fight. Dad remained in human form, as did I.

I was torn between helping the lionesses fight Glen and keeping guard on the door to ensure Dad didn't get to the cubs.

One of the fighting lionesses fell to the ground in a heap before shifting into her human form. The female's body was battered, bloody, and bruised, but she glanced over to Dad and said, "We'll do whatever you want. Just don't kill our cubs."

Dad's lips twisted cruelly as his fingers transformed to claws. "Are you the alpha female of the pride?"

Unsteadily, she got to her feet. "Yes."

Dad lashed out with his claws, striking the woman. The woman screamed while clutching her now-bloody neck.

"Mom!" a female screamed in the distance.

Dad and I glanced over in the direction of the woman's voice and spotted a female lying on the ground within the grasslands.

My breath caught in my throat when the woman's alluring scent of sweet apple intermixed with creamy vanilla drifted over to me.

My inner beast roared before saying, *Hybrid. Mine. Mate.*

*Shut it,* I reprimanded. *She's not ours.*

Dad sniffed loudly. "She's a hybrid." He turned to glare at the alpha female, who was bleeding profusely. "What's a hybrid doing here?"

"I. Don't. Know," she gasped out, but I smelled her lie, and so did Dad.

"Liar," Dad snapped. "She called you mom." He called over his shoulder, "Buster, get over there and kill the hybrid."

My heart raced with fear at the thought of the hybrid being killed. *I have to protect her. I have to stop my kin.*

"No." I stepped forward. "I'll kill her."

Dad grinned. "Finally, you've grown a set of balls."

"No!" the alpha female wailed before sprinting toward the hybrid. "Run, Ro," she called out, prompting the hybrid to get to her feet and run off.

"Get them, Mack," Dad ordered.

I didn't bother shifting and sped after the two. Halfway into my run, I found the alpha female bleeding out on the ground.

"You are a brave and honorable female," I said. "But you will not survive your injuries." Even if she shifted from animal to human and back again, her injuries were too severe to heal.

Resignation gleamed in her eyes. "Please save my daughter."

*Her daughter was hybrid?*

She continued. "Spare her life." Blood trickled from her mouth. "Please…"

"I'll try," I said before taking off in a run across the grasslands in pursuit of the hybrid, whom I could see slicing through the night. But she wasn't fast enough to evade me. Adrenaline surged through me as I sped faster.

As if sensing my pursuit, the hybrid kicked into high gear, her arms pumping at her sides. But she made a critical mistake when she turned, glancing over her shoulder at me. She tripped over her feet, and I pounced, grabbing the backpack she carried on her back.

I yanked her body against mine, and we tumbled to the ground. I landed on my back with her chest pressed against mine.

Growing up, I'd heard shifters talk trash about the existence of hybrids—children created from a mating between a shifter and human—as if they were the equivalent of the boogeyman. Most considered hybrids abominations. I'd reserved my opinion on the subject since, until tonight, I'd never met a hybrid before.

"No!" she yelled while trying in vain to tug out her arms that were pinned to her sides by my arms, which were wrapped around her body like a python. "Let me go."

"Quiet," I hissed.

"Please," she begged.

"I'm trying to save your life."

When she glared down at me defiantly, her beauty took my breath away. Thick black hair framed her heart-shaped mahogany face, and her clean, fresh, sweet scent captivated me.

"I saw what your pride did to mine. You're a monster."

*Monster?* My jaw tightened.

"Well, this monster is the only man who can save you from my kin."

The hybrid squirmed. "Let go of me, asshole."

"Calm the fuck down. I can't save you until you stop fighting me."

"Why?" she asked.

"Why what?" I replied.

"Why are you saving me?"

*Because my stupid animal thinks that you're mine.*

"I am not like my kin," I answered, which was true. "I do not kill for sport. I won't kill you." Which was also the truth. "I won't kill you. I'm going to release my hold, but do not run. We've wasted enough time as it is. And if I'm not back soon, my family will come looking for me and you. And I don't want that."

Releasing her, I gently rolled her off me before getting to my feet. I extended my hand to her, but she hesitated before accepting it. And when her hand touched mine, an electric shock stung my palm.

"Did you feel that?" she asked with wide eyes.

I pulled her up to her feet. "Feel what?" I lied.

She shook her head. "Nothing."

"Hold out your arm," I demanded while extending the claws on my right hand.

She backed up. "I thought you said you wouldn't kill me?"

"I won't. I need your blood as proof of the kill."

She bit her plump bottom lip, peering up at me.

I sighed heavily. "The clock is ticking, hybrid."

"Ro," she offered. "My mom calls me Ro."

I started to tell her my name but stopped. *Why waste my time? I'll never see her again after today.*

"Give me your arm, Ro."

She hesitated before holding out her left arm. I swiped a claw against her bare mahogany-hued skin, executing a long, shallow slash. The female's piercing scream was like a knife to the heart, but this had to be done. Her wail would give my kin the satisfaction of hearing her pain, and they would assume I was killing her as Dad ordered.

Blood dripped down her arm and onto the earth. Rubbing my hand against the wound, I coated my palm liberally before rubbing my hand against my bare chest. I collected more of her blood, making sure to get the fluid on both my hands and face.

Stepping back, I said, "Run."

"Thank you," she whispered before hugging me.

Every muscle in my body tightened with shock. I'd never been touched by anyone in such a gentle way. But before I could respond, she pulled back and unhooked a braided black leather bracelet with small silver beads from her wrist, handing it to me. "Here."

I just stared at her, dumbfounded.

"I saved up for months to buy it," she explained. "It's my gift to you for going against your kinfolk to save my life."

Without another word, the hybrid ran off through the night.

***Shifters of Black Forest Ridge* isn't over yet, not by a long shot. Get ready for Mack's story by grabbing *SHIFTERS OF BLACK FOREST RIDGE: MACK* right now.**

# ABOUT THE AUTHOR

USA TODAY BESTSELLING AUTHOR SEDONA VENEZ lives in New York City with her former military hubby—hooah—and their fur babies. She loves writing sizzling, sexy intricate stories about strong but broken characters who push limits, overcome their fears and risk it all for love.

*Sedona loves to connect with readers!*
www.sedonavenez.com

www.ingramcontent.com/pod-product-compliance
Lightning Source LLC
Chambersburg PA
CBHW070341200726
48294CB00003B/742